MURDERS AT
MOON DANCE

MURDERS AT
MOON DANCE

A. B. Guthrie, Jr.

Introduction to the Bison Book Edition
by William Kittredge

University of Nebraska Press
Lincoln and London

First Bison Book printing: 1993
Most recent printing indicated by the last digit below:
10   9   8   7   6   5   4   3   2   1

Library of Congress Cataloging-in-Publication Data
Guthrie, A. B. (Alfred Bertram), 1901–
Murders at Moon Dance / A. B. Guthrie, Jr.; introduction to the Bison
edition by William Kittredge.
p.   cm.
ISBN 0-8032-2150-9 (cl).—ISBN 0-8032-7039-9 (pa)
I. Title
PS3513.U855M84   1993
813'.52—dc20
92-38605
CIP

Reprinted by arrangement with Carol Guthrie

In the front matter of this Bison Book edition, the page numbering has
been changed from arabic to roman numeral in order to accommodate
a new introduction. Although Chapter One begins on arabic p. 7, no
material from the original edition has been omitted.

∞

TO
J. T. G.

INTRODUCTION

by William Kittredge

On a bright gray afternoon in October 1991, Annick Smith and I were lucky enough to spend a couple of hours with Bud Guthrie at his place called The Barn, west of Choteau and south of the Teton River. There were eight or so of us on the glassed-in sun-porch: Bud and his wife Carol, a step-daughter, a son-in-law, a daughter-in-law, a grandchild, a dog.

The first snow of winter had come sweeping over the Rockies a night or so before. The Montana mountains were vividly distinct against the white sky. Bud was articulate, his eyes bright with good humor and a no doubt abiding sense that these were last times. He told us jokes.

The next day, a few miles up the road toward the Rockies' Front, there was a gathering in celebration of Guthrie which was hosted by the Nature Conservancy in their headquarters at the Pine Butte Swamp. It was a mix of literary people like James and Lois Welch, Ripley Hugo, Mary Clearman Blew, Richard Ford, and locals like Alice Gleeson, most of whom had known Bud for decades.

In the afternoon, after a day of literary talks and happy pontificating, local people began to arrive, and then Bud arrived, with his family. The best part of what followed, for me, was listening and watching while his neighbors, each by each, stood and told some little story about Bud. Alice Gleeson, close to weeping and almost Bud's age, told a story from long ago, when Bud asked her to pick up some groceries for him and some cronies while she was in town. His list, she said, read, "Bread and bourbon."

In the winter Bud was gone. But he was carrying on right out to the edge, telling us, by the look in his eye and the sound of his ruined voice, by the direct way he was staring down the devil, things he always told us: *love what you love, fiercely as you can, and never lose heart.* Play your cards.

Montana was a far-away land where giants walked, at least in my imagination, when I moved to Missoula in 1969. One of the giants was Bud Guthrie, the old man of the mountains as I imagined him, and king of the prairies, the storyteller and true talker.

The summer I was sixteen, 1948, down in our landlocked valley in the high deserts on the Oregon/Nevada border, I was old enough to do a man's work in the haying. I spent ten hours every day driving a home-built power-buck (Buick chassis, transmission reversed, engine in the rear), bucking hay across the stubblefield meadows to a beaver-slide stacking crew.

After dinner in the cookhouse I would shower and put on a fresh tee-shirt and sit on our screened-in veranda, lights from other ranches showing in the distance, and lay hands on the reward of my day, another couple of hours with *The Big Sky,* reading slowly, maybe fifteen pages at a sitting, making it last, loving it for reasons I didn't at all understand.

It was maybe the first time I was really captured by a book. My role models in that ranchland world saw reading as a mostly useless activity, like whittling. In school I had learned some quickly forgotten Latin and geometry and some James Whitcomb Riley. My senior year in high school we memorized and recited long swatches of *Macbeth* and *Henry V* and it seemed like language from some other planet. Things you might learn from reading, according to our priorities, were of little consequence next to the urgencies of getting the work done.

Most immediately Guthrie was telling me about attending to the natural world, paying attention to intricacies I had never suspected. For that summer I knew more about natural life along the Missouri River watershed than I knew about the way things grew together in the hayfields where I worked every day, in the valley where I had always lived. I was beginning to sense the dimensions of my ignorance, and I was a little shamed, feeling as if I had lived my life wearing blinders. But I excused myself; I was young.

Guthrie was telling me a story about powerful people in a great untouched place, a paradise, and what they made of it and did to themselves in the working out. He was telling me about a place like the valley where we lived, and about the consequences of overweaning ambition. In his storyteller's way he was telling me about men like my father and grandfather, who shook at least the little fragment of the world I knew, and made it go their way. He was telling me about my future.

Guthrie was helping me see that my people and their stories were part of history in the country where I lived. He was leading me to the idea that the place where I lived *had* a history, which connected to larger stories, like the one about conquest and settlement in the American West, introducing me to the idea that actions generate long strings of consequence that reverberate through generations and over great distances; he was leading me to the concept of responsibility for your own actions and for the place where you live.

Not that I, at sixteen, out on that porch, got these concepts to the exact forefront of my mind. It took decades for Guthrie's messages to settle into my head in an articulated way. Some of them are still settling. All we need to do, to understand Guthrie's ongoing importance, is look around and see our society still struggling with the ideas he began articulating so long ago.

In 1964, on our ranch in southeastern Oregon, I was driven to try writing. Part of the impulse came from my admiration for Guthrie. I had it in mind to talk about people and places I revered, just as Guthrie wrote about Montana. It was a naive impulse—I didn't have any clear understanding of the stories I wanted to tell, I just wanted to say we were important in our outback. I wanted to make southeastern Oregon live forever in people's imaginations.

Since then I've learned that's not what writers do, they don't freeze things. They tell stories that help readers come to understand the way things are working out. When stories are useful they help us see for ourselves. But I didn't know such things. I was a long way from any literary society, floundering along, sending out stories, getting them rejected, and desperate for help.

One place I found that help was in Guthrie's autobiographical book, *The Blue Hen's Chick*, which I got from the Lake County Public Library. In Chapter Seventeen, Bud tells of getting seriously down to the writing of *The Big Sky* while on a Nieman Fellowship at Harvard in 1944. He learned, he says, to quit "hamming" and *show* the readers the story, not tell them about it. He learned to find "identity with my characters—which meant I lost my own for the time. I was at Harvard but wasn't. I was in the young mountains trapping prime beaver."

It was the sort of instruction I needed, and I knew it. Chapter Eighteen is a primer of fiction writing as Bud understood the art. I copied its maxims in my notebooks with underlining, and stars and such. I was learning practical rules.

And I was exposed to more complex considerations in Chapter Twelve of *A Blue Hen's Chick*. There Guthrie talks about the writing of his first book, *Murders at Moon Dance,* and its publication.

In 1936, when his mother was dying of cancer at the age of 63, Guthrie says, "I tried to drug myself with gun-and-gallop and whodunit books. I could write, I told myself finally, as well as these writers; and there must be money, which I needed, in such stuff.

"Within a month I was bored with what I'd set down and bored more by the whole prospect—the contrived and implausible plot, the knights and knaves, and love too pure. . . ."

But, after his mother died, he returned to it. "I went back to Kentucky and finished my damned manuscript." The book was published by E. P. Dutton and Company in 1943. "I can't say it's the worst book ever written, but I've long considered it a contender. . . . When I see it displayed on paperback racks, where somehow it survives, I turn away.

"Two or three inadequate things can be said about it if not for it. I needed the $400. . . . a writer must write a first book; he can't begin later on. . . . I like to think the example may encourage young writers to push on despite their first efforts."

He was talking about the inadvisability of betraying what you understand to be your true attitudes. The message, loud and clear, reaffirmed my feelings—Work with all the passion you have and your reward will be the work. Anything more is pure gravy. Those are things I learned in childhood, on the ranch, and heard reaffirmed in Guthrie, things I believed, and still believe.

The Nez Perce, I've heard, believed that the first telling of a lie was permissible, even the second, but the third was deadly. Enough inauthenticity and you will have eaten yourself alive. You won't be anybody.

"Saturday night in Moon Dance arrives as the goal of the week. It is the release from discipline and reward for the drudgery and rebellion at routine." In his best days Guthrie would never have subjected us to the abstractions in these topic sentences.

But he gets down to business. "Little knots of men gather at corners to talk of livestock and weather and politics. A perfumed vapor fogs the barber shops, a compound of talc and tonic and steaming leakage from the public baths." He gives us things to experience, to see and smell, he takes us there. We begin to care for his people, we begin to enjoy ourselves and think well of the storyteller, for showing us this richness, and allowing us to make sense of it for ourselves.

It is in the intimate neighborhood of this passion for communality that I find what I most admire in Guthrie. He told us, all his life, that we must take care of one another, and the world we love, where we love each other. He was telling us right in this beginning.

In *Murders at Moon Dance*, as is usual in genre Westerns, the trouble starts with greed (individuals who are not acting in the best interests of the community), and the solution is found in violence (killing).

There lies the enormous social problem which festers at the core of Westerns (and our society): the Western teaches us to use violence to solve our problems, be they personal or those of civic disorder. But, as we know, the impulse to violence (and revenge) will eventually destroy both the self and the communality it seeks to preserve. If you don't believe me, ask Shane as he rides away into the Tetons, taking the guilt for killing with him so society won't have to live with it (Guthrie wrote the screenplay and by then he understood very well).

When people are threatened, however good they may be, they are capable of terrible things. In *Murders at Moon Dance* Guthrie graphically demonstrates the dangers inherent in the use of vigilante violence (again, revenge) to restore civil order, anticipating Walter van Tilburg Clark's antimythological story, *The Ox-Bow Incident*.

A young woman is kidnapped. Outside the town of Moon Dance there is a place called Breedtown, where another kind of people live, in their own communality, some of them outlaws and all of them outside the community (most of them of mixed blood, Native American and whatever). Citizens around Moon Dance think someone from Breedtown must be responsible for the kidnapping. Fear, fueled by xenophobic righteousness (fear of strangers—in this case, as so often in the Western—racism), drives anger.

One of the Moon Dance elders, an old judge, says, "We can't have a pigsticking at Breedtown. There's women and kids there, and some good-enough breeds, too." But they do have a "pigsticking."

"They began streaming to other cabins, whooping as they ran. They jammed before entrances. . . . they broke through doors. They fell to with pistol barrel, boot, and first . . . button-eyed children squalled through the broken doorways. . . . Squaws stumbled out. . . . After them came the flung bodies of their men who hit the ground and lay still or moved little and looked on wordlessly, out of bloody faces, while the avengers surged from shack to shack. Above the cries of the victims the voices of the invaders rose in a roar that rang back from the hills."

A lynching is narrowly prevented.

"String him up."

"Get a rope."

"Kill the Injun."

A good man stops the mob for an instant, and "fire blossomed in the gathering dark. . . . It shot from log to log and from wall to roof and flung banners in the sky. The crackle of wood became a blowing roar. The raiders howled in exultation. . . ."

Then it's over.

"The departing invaders . . . sat their horses silently. . . . Their exhultation was gone now, and their violence, too. Red in the glow of the flames, their faces were slack and lifeless."

But in this story Guthrie, unlike Walter van Tilburg Clark, who was writing at almost the same time, doesn't really follow through to illuminate the consequences. That would have to wait, as we know, until *The Big Sky*.

In *Murders at Moon Dance*, Guthrie was writing a traditional Western, and his answer to the problem of communal violence was the traditional answer. A good man, a lawman and a gunfighter, kills the bad man, who was not only an outlaw but an outsider who belongs in that other place, Breedtown. The book, in this sense, could not be more racist. It's one thing to say Guthrie was portraying a deeply racist society, and he was. But it's another when the book portrays evil as the product not only of outlaws but of racial outsiders.

Our good man does the killing, he weeds the garden, does the dirty work, and absorbs the horror of killing into his soul. Society is off the hook.

Listen to this talk, from the old judge. "What did the western man do? Do? Why, he fought them Indians, and he chased the outlaws out of the country or buried them in Boot Hill. He saw a job had to be done, and he done it. Direct action, that's what he was, and no one waiting around for some bolder, stronger, saltier man to come along and tend his knittin' for him. He was the man, that genu-ine western man, who made things safe for women and children. Yes, and for weaklin's too. He was the man that settled the country."

A young woman says, "Sometimes he seems so sad."

"A man's got to answer," the judge says, "if the case calls for a man."

At the end, the killing done, the gunfighter says he's going to put up his guns for good. The young woman, who loves him, says, "Until the case calls for a man."

A man who will solve our problems with violence.

Having co-written nine genre Westerns myself (under the name Owen Rountree, with Steven M. Krauzer), I have to think Bud Guthrie was too hard on himself when he completely disclaimed *Murders at Moon Dance.*

I got a lot from writing Westerns. I learned something about managing the workings of extended narrative, and more about the genre Western. I came to see it as story about about conquest, and to despise it once the imperialist, sexist, racist implications came clear. But I don't regret having published the books.

Steve and I thought we were opening up the Western a little bit, with humor, paradox, and parody, and because one of our heroes was a Latino woman who wouldn't stand for patriarchal postur-ing. We had good intentions, and our books didn't do the world grave damage. Obsessive purity is almost always a mistake, we know. We learn, and move on. That's what Bud Guthrie did.

Murders at Moondance, if it had been written by a writer of less accomplishment, probably wouldn't interest many beyond hardcore Western fans. But it's Guthrie, at the beginning. It gives us a chance to examine his first attempts at artistry, and his efforts to begin making sense of the ways our determination to stand up for justice and communality work to foster violence.

The example of his life, and his later books, are gifts to us all in our own struggle with the same huge problems. *The Big Sky* is a brilliantly articulated story about the way the impulse to violence worked out (and continues to work out) in the American West. In my innocence, when I was sixteen, I saw it as a story about the end of a heroic era, the inevitable and quite natural running down of things, as in death, and it broke my heart.

Now I am sixty years old, and I understand it as a story about men who brought the end down on themselves. They wanted absolute possession of all that they loved, and in the process of possessing they killed the beloved. Violence is so often the fool's answer.

You can say they didn't know any better, and it's true, but it doesn't change anything. Boone Caudill is not tragic, he is a damned fool who ends up empty-hearted and empty-handed. And it was his own fault. *The Big Sky* is a cautionary tale: Don't Kill The Things You Love. It is a useful story about us, our society, right now.

The beloved, Guthrie told us, is not a thing to own, it is to be cherished. In order to cherish whatever you love, give it freedom, let it be what it is. This is the message at the heart of his later environmentalism. In *Murders at Moon Dance* we see him beginning to figure out ways to tell that story.

MURDERS AT
MOON DANCE

CHAPTER ONE

Marty McLean stepped out of the kitchen into the entry, closed the door slowly after him and drew his tattered gray-and-red mackinaw from the hook on which it hung. He put it on absently, adjusted an old Stetson over his grizzled hair, and turned to go out.

As he did so, the kitchen door swung open and Kate stood there looking at him.

"What will we do then, Martin, if we don't sell to Seldom Wright?" she asked with a weary and insistent anxiety. Her breath made little puffs of vapor in the chill of the entry-way.

He looked at her and down at the splintered floor. His hand fumbled in the pocket of his faded overalls and drew out a worn plug of tobacco. He blew on it before he gnawed off a chew.

"Now, Mommie," he remonstrated, hunching his sagging shoulders inside the mackinaw, "don't you worry."

"We already know what they're going to say at the bank."

He was out of the doorway by now, and she came to the threshold, holding him with her eyes. Around her mouth and on her brow, the skin was white, as if from long fatigue, but her cheeks and the tip of her nose had been reddled by the cook-stove. Looking at him, she wiped her damp forearms with her apron.

"Maybe not," he argued hopelessly, and spat on the damp earth.

He scuffed the ground with the heel of his broken

boot and, breathing deep, turned his head away from her
and gazed down at the old barn and its shabby company
of hen house, corral, machine shed and root cellar, and
beyond it over miles of prime grazing land, bleak and
barren though it was now, to the naked blue spine of the
Rocky Mountains. In a clump of willow west of the
corral, a half dozen crows were quarreling.

"It'd be better to sell and have a few hundred dollars
than to have the place taken from us," she persisted.

His voice suddenly was harsh.

"Sell it?" he inquired sharply. "Sell it! I come here
fifty years ago. I grew up with the country. This outfit's me. I'm it. I'd just as leave go die."

His withered hand shook as he tugged at his hat, and
her face went stiff with compassion.

"They can't sell a man out in a day," he said.
"Sump'n'll turn up."

She kept silent, as if there were no place now for
speech, and he started to go but stopped impulsively,
blew out his cud, wiped his stained lips with the back of
his hand, and trudged back to her. "Good-bye, Mommie,"
he said, and held out for her kiss a cheek hispid as a
cactus.

She sighed and leaned a little against him, as if in
despair, and he reached up and touched her clumsily on
the shoulder. Neither looking at the other, they stood
thus for a moment.

As he turned again to leave, his mouth spread
crookedly. "Maybe I'll run on to the Early Day Mine,"
he said for a joke.

"I don't see why you want to pack that gun any more,"
she digressed.

"You never did see. I got good reason to carry it, the
way things are."

He walked on toward the barn, moving with the stiff-kneed gait of age, but before he got there she called doggedly, "Adlam's and the Family Liquor Store can't do you any good."

"Not a drop," he promised with signal of the hand.

A yearling calf nosed his coat as he swung the barn door back. He stopped to scratch around its horns. "Always a pest, ain't you?" he asked, adding as the calf's long tongue rasped his hand, "No, I ain't got nothing for you."

Inside, he spoke to the old blaze-faced horse that was munching hay in a stall and, patting it on the rump, moved up to its head and slipped a bridle on. He led the animal, then, over near the peg from which his saddle hung, smoothed a blanket on its back and, grunting from the effort, swung the hull up. "Naw," he said as the patient beast turned to eye him reproachfully as he fumbled with the latigo, "we won't pull 'er up too tight, old Blaze. Snug is enough, but don't you go gettin' snorty."

He was at an age and condition of life in which a man gets into a saddle by a climb-and-pull and, having forked it, settles himself before giving the word to his mount. Even then, he seemed somehow loath to start. He looked about him again, and his eyes came to rest on the house, from the chimney of which a wisp of smoke was blowing. Kate had gone inside.

"Sure is hell," he mumbled aloud, "especially on her."

Indignation and false jocularity had gone from his face now, leaving it spiritless and bleak and old. "All a man can do is try, even if my tryin' to date ain't been much. All right, Blaze, make tracks! I won't take on anything, either, except maybe one to warm me up."

A white and tan shepherd dog that had followed him

from the house circled round in front of him and barked in expectant inquiry.

McLean shook his head. "You get on back to the house, Tip," he said. "This here's business."

Crestfallen, as if it had been betrayed by an old friend, the dog turned and limped back up the path, its eyes full of reproach as it regarded McLean over a shoulder.

As the horse settled into stride, McLean drew on a pair of worn gloves and hunched himself deeper in his mackinaw, for the wind at his back was still raw with winter. Against it, the sun, climbing toward the zenith through drifting clouds, seemed distant and feeble. The atmosphere was clear, however, so clear that far off to the right in the sharp outlines of the foothills could be glimpsed the decaying roof of the abandoned house that men called Indian Pete's Palace.

The trail to town was stiff as dough with wet and cold, and broken here and there as the ground had heaved with frost. After the fork at the Smoky Water crossing, it was worse, for a heavier traffic had channeled it with wagon tracks and pitted it with hoof prints. Here McLean pulled his horse to the side of the road, letting it set its own pace in the viscous sod.

It was afternoon when he reached Moon Dance, and he went directly to the Stockmen's Bank after leaving his mount at McCabe's livery stable.

Hugh Jerome, the president, himself greeted him and took him back behind the cages to a small private office in the rear. A former rancher, the banker still bore some of the marks of the outdoor man, though the office had grayed his face and added a paunch to his sturdy frame.

"Well, Marty?" he asked.

"Well?" answered McLean.

Jerome reached into the drawer of his desk, took out a

bottle, uncorked it and offered it to his visitor. For a
little, McLean looked at the flask wistfully. "A man gets
kind of pinched, ridin' on a rough day," he explained
then, and extended his hand. When he had drunk, he
returned the bottle and waited for his host to drink.

Then he said, "Well, you know how it is, Hugh."

Jerome regarded him gravely, his lips pursed. "Do
you know how it is with us, Marty?"

"I can come out, if I have a little time. I ought to be
able to take a big bite out of that loan this year, after
shippin'."

"You ought to, maybe, providing your stock isn't all
run off."

"Well, of course, I been losin' a little, I guess, just
like everybody else," McLean answered defensively. "But
hell, Hugh, that'll stop! Rustlers can't get by very long
these days."

"Maybe no, maybe yes."

"And I got some nice stuff comin' on. One more year
and I'll really cut 'er."

"It's been ten years."

McLean got up, stiffly and abruptly. "I ain't askin' no
favors, of you nor no man, Hugh."

Involuntarily, the banker reached out as if to steady
his visitor, but the old man looked at him with such
stubborn pride that he let his hand fall on his desk.

"I wish it was my money, and not the bank's, Marty,"
he said quietly, gazing at the hand. His sigh was barely
audible.

"I'll be sayin' so long."

"Wait a minute."

The banker picked up a letter opener handled with
deer horn and fingered it absently.

"You ought to sell to Seldom Wright."

"I ain't sellin'."

"He'll buy the place, and for less, when it's put up."

"It takes a little time for all that."

"O. K., Marty. Have another drink?"

"No more." There was a bitter, constricted tone of confession in McLean's voice now. "If it hadn't of been for that, I guess I wouldn't of come to this."

"Oh hell, Marty!" Jerome objected, getting impatiently to his feet. "Everyone's hard hit these days, teetotalers and all."

"Anyway, I'll be goin'."

"I'm sorry, Marty."

When his visitor had gone, Jerome cursed aloud. "Damn such a business! Damn it to eternal hell!" In sudden violence, he hurled the letter opener at the opposite wall, where the point imbedded itself in the paneling and gave to the heavy haft a quiver like the old man's hand at the word that his note would not be renewed.

Outside, McLean gazed up the main street of Moon Dance toward Adlam's Saloon and the Family Liquor Store, but when he moved it was to cross the street and enter a restaurant. "Cup o' coffee'll do just as good," he told himself as his laggard feet took him there.

As he entered and closed the door after him, a whining Scandinavian voice rose in greeting.

"Hi, Ma-arty. Here iss he, little Tana, da t'ird part-ner in da gold mine, yah."

The speaker, a roughly garbed wisp of a man, was seated at a table in the rear of the room. Near him, a girl stood uncertainly.

Abruptly as he had spoken, the man checked himself, as if fearful that the place contained more than the three of them.

"Shu!" he cautioned as McLean walked toward him. "I tal you in a minute."

He reached into the bulging pocket of a sheepskin coat that he had draped over the back of his chair and from it abstracted a bottle half full. His hand was unsteady as it brought the flask to the table, and his eyes, taking stock of its contents, came to focus slowly.

"Vay round 'em, Shep!" he exulted. "We have a swallow. Little Tana, vun more glass, please. It iss goot, Ma-arty, vot happens now. Yah, you goot to me, da sheepherder, too. We drink. Skoal!"

He had poured three thick fingers into each of their glasses, and McLean, watching the whisky splash out, reached over in sudden decision, picked up his tumbler and gulped its contents. Then, slowly, he let himself down into a chair.

"Hello, lass," he said to the girl. "The drink went good, Sven. I needed one."

"Yah," agreed the herder, setting his glass down. The smell of sheep emanated from him in an identifying effluvium. His pinched face, on which a mustache sprouted forlornly like a lone bush on a fallow acre, would have been desolate except for the eyes. Small, red-rimmed, slate blue like shallow water, they had an intensity and vigor that contrasted with the sterility of his countenance, as the gaze of a mad man sometimes contrasts with his vacancy of feature.

"Ve rich!" he rasped, leaning jerkily across the table toward McLean. "You goot to me, little Tana goot to me, and my dream iss goot to me, too, you petcha. Of a gold mine ve iss da part-ners. I find it. You haf it, too. Now da world pe goot to us, py gollies."

McLean looked questioningly at the girl, but she only

shook her head guardedly and started to move away, puzzlement written on her young face.

The herder brought himself unsteadily around. "No, Tana," he said, reaching out a hand brown as a saddle. "You hear, too. Ve part-ners."

Carefully he divided what remained in the flask, lifted his glass, yelled "Vay round 'em!" and irrigated his sorry growth of mustache with the liquor.

A brown sheep dog, marked with white, squeezed itself out from under the table, eyed its master questioningly and dropped to the floor in limp relaxation at the herder's "Down, Shep. I vas yust fooling, old poy."

The girl had sat down, a little timidly, and looked anxiously from the herder to McLean.

"We'll be goin' in a minute, lass," McLean assured her with an understanding inclination of the head toward the other man.

The herder had brought another bottle from his coat. With slow determination he loosened and drew the cork, mumbling gently to the bottle meanwhile as if to persuade it to yield its riches. He had reached that point of drunkenness in which a man's whole aim seems quick oblivion. He poured two tremendous drinks. McLean lifted his glass and eyed it speculatively, after the manner of a drinking man whose first thirst has been appeased.

"I tal you now," said the herder, but first he arose precariously, tiptoed over to the counter with great stealth and peeked behind it. Returning, he crouched to look under each table, though he could have seen from where he sat that nothing was under them.

"Py gollies!" he whispered. "I haf a dream and it is goot. I find da Early Day Mine."

He ended his declaration in wobbling triumph, and studied his hearers for reaction.

McLean said, "Oh, hell, Svenson!" and added, " 'Scuse me, Tana."

"Hal and tamnation!" ejaculated Svenson. "Vunce more a drink, yah?" McLean nodded, and the swaying herder spilled more whisky into their glasses.

McLean began to feel good. The liquor, warm and cozy in his middle, was reaching out, even to that cold dread that pinched his entrails.

There was a pattering of metal on the oil-clothed table. Svenson held, up-ended, a small leather poke on which he had loosened the draw string.

"Hal, now, iss it, Ma-arty?" he asked.

Incredulously, McLean picked up a bit of the metal and stared at it, fascinated, as he rolled it between finger and thumb.

His voice was almost a whisper. "Good Lord Almighty, Sven!"

The herder grasped the edge of the table for support and leaned across it until he was almost nose to nose with McLean. His tongue labored with his words. "Me, Sven Svenson, da crazy sheep herder, I find it. How crazy vas I now, Ma-arty? Yah, all da rest iss crazy peoples. Me and you and Tana, ve yust smart. I find da Early Day, I tal you. I go vere I learn in my sleep, Ma-arty, and dere she iss, rich, you hear? Rich."

McLean drew back from the insistent face and looked wonderingly at the fleck of metal in his fingers, until suddenly a flood of exultation, quickened and fortified by the whisky he had drunk, swept over him. His hand shook.

"Can you find it again?"

Svenson had passed over the dividing line between alcoholic excitement and alcoholic paralysis. Through a fog, his eye sighted the bottle and his slow hand poured a drink. As if from a blow, his thin form shuddered at the hot clutch of the whisky.

"Show us!" urged McLean, and drew a paper napkin from its holder and thrust it before the herder. "Get a pencil, Tana."

When she had returned with it, the rancher put it in the herder's limp fingers. "Make a map!" he asked.

Svenson's gaze was dull. "Yah, sure," he said through loose lips. "Who iss crazy now?"

With great effort he put pencil to paper and drew a long, staggering line. He brought the point back, then, and made a slow X midway on the sheet. What he might have done next, they never knew, for the pencil flattened out of his nerveless grasp and his head came down in weary collapse. "Vait, yust a minute," he mumbled.

The girl spoke now, for almost the first time since McLean had entered.

"You must take him somewhere," she urged. "He needs a bed, and people will be coming in to eat before long."

McLean folded the paper on which the herder had scrawled and tucked it in a pocket. He took two pieces of the metal, then, and put them with the paper.

"You take the rest of the dust, lass, and maybe you'd better not be showin' it around."

"Sven's always imagining something, especially when he's been drinking," she answered.

"He didn't imagine them gold nuggets."

McLean got up, careful now to move with sober control. The girl looked at his shrunken body and declared quickly, "He's too much for one man, Mr. McLean. You wait here. I'll get someone."

Before he could object, she was on her way, moving with the quick, light ease of girlhood.

Jubilation put a quaver into McLean's old voice. "Kate," he said as if he were not talking to himself, "we ain't going to have to sell, by grab. My pardner here's found the Early Day." Suddenly he reached over, grasped the bottle that Svenson had left uncorked, and took a quick, stout pull. In uneasy haste he put the flask back.

When Tana returned, she brought with her two young huskies from the street, and, as if they already had received their instructions, they took the limp body of the herder between them and started out. "Clarence Lamb always lets him sleep in the jail," the girl said in final explanation, "so you won't have any trouble. Tell the constable I'm keeping his money."

The sheep dog got up lazily and trailed after its unconscious master.

McLean went out, too, leaving with Tana a parting request for silence. "We don't know about this yet," he argued, "and until we do and get a claim staked out, we better not say anything."

Outdoors, he breathed deep and looked about him expansively. The early dusk of late winter had begun to settle on the town, now that the sun had fallen below the hills. Up the street, he saw a man turn into Adlam's Saloon. " 'Nother little one wouldn't hurt me," he told himself. "Man's got a right to celebrate, comin' into a mine like I have." Happily, then, with the whisky in him singing of incredible but indubitable good fortune, he walked to the saloon.

The place was rank with the stink of stale spirits, wet cigar butts and tobacco smoke, but of the patrons who had fouled it only two remained. In the rear of the place, the gaming tables stood empty in a thickening gloom. One of the two customers, a whiskered oldster, leaned

with an elbow on the bar. The other, a dark, thick
wedge of a man, sat tilted against the far wall, immobile
except for a pair of eyes that caught a glitter from the
lamplight as the bartender, mounted on a chair, touched
match to wick.

"Nice place to have a saloon, Jake," McLean jibed,
"if they was any customers around."

Puffing, the bartender lowered his fat bulk from the
chair. "Water always was a good drink," he answered,
"though some thinks different."

"Me for one, anyhow right now," McLean volunteered.

The whiskered man turned around and extended his
hand. "Hi, Marty," he said. "I'm buyin'."

McLean took the hand stiffly. "H'ar'yu, Seldom?"

"Bring a bottle over to a table, Jake," Seldom Wright
asked the barkeep.

The latter scrutinized McLean through his heavy lids.
"Sure you need more, Marty?" he inquired with friendly
hesitancy.

"He don't have to make an affidavit to get a drink,
does he?" Wright asked good naturedly.

"Jake's all right," volunteered McLean. "I ain't going
to take but a small one or two, Jake. I only had a drop."

They walked over to a table and sat down, and Jake
brought a bottle and glasses.

"How," toasted McLean after Wright had poured
drinks.

Wright approached his subject circuitously. "Hit's
hell, the way the market is and all, ain't hit?"

McLean nodded. The whisky had made him look a
little owlish.

"Guess you been losin' a few head, too?" Before he

spoke, Wright had glanced toward the dark man in the tilted chair, and he asked the question in a mutter.

McLean's mild, unwinking eyes rested on the third man.

"Who's he?" he asked.

"Him? Robideau," Wright answered. Then, louder, he went on, "You know I'm willin' to buy, Marty."

"I ain't willin' to sell."

A friendly insistence came into Wright's manner. "Look, Marty," he said, squinting for emphasis, "they're going to take the place, I'm tellin' you and you ought to know. You won't get a dime then. This way, you'll have something."

Saying nothing, McLean drained his glass and, setting it down, poured a short one.

"You owe hit to Kate," Wright persisted, his beard bobbing with his earnestness. "Hit ain't as if I would be a-wantin' the place, particular, though it don't go bad with mine, but more that I'm a-wantin' to see you save something."

There was a stubborn resentment in McLean's, "I'll get along, Wright."

"How?"

McLean took his short one and got up.

"Save your wind!" he ordered. "I ain't losin' the place." His voice rose hoarsely. "Me and my partners have located the Early Day."

At the magic of that name, the dark man's tilted chair came to the floor with a light thump.

Wright rose from his chair. His eyes studied the other man. "You've had a mite too much, Marty," he said.

At that moment, the doors of the saloon swung open and two men came in, talking.

More owlish than ever, McLean bobbed his head emphatically. He pounded the table. "I'll pay off! I'll pay off in raw gold!"

His words stilled the voices of the newcomers. The dark man in the rear of the place came forward, silent and alert. Jake, the barkeep, stopped his work, his face reflecting curiosity and unbelief.

McLean looked around him. The impression he had created flushed him, as applause exhilarates a public speaker. With exaggerated deliberation, he moved over to the bar, reached into his pocket and got out the paper and bits of metal.

"This here's the map," he declared, waving the folded paper, "and you don't get to see it, but these ought to talk loud enough for you." On the bar he dropped the metal pieces.

They crowded in on him, straining for a look.

"You seen enough, I guess," he said, picking up the specimens as other hands reached out for them. "First thing, you'll be wantin' to see the map, 'fore I can get the claim recorded. But there's just three of us in on it, see? Me and crazy Sven and the lass down the street."

He turned around to face the bar. "Drinks on me, Jake."

Jake's voice was low, but still it penetrated McLean's alcoholic glory: "Marty, you old damn fool! You damn fool!"

McLean turned about, a dawning apprehension in his look.

They hemmed him in, Wright and the dark wedge of a man and the two newcomers.

"Hello, Miles," he greeted. "Didn't see you."

"Maybe because you had a lot to say," one of the two newcomers responded. He was big, rawboned and florid.

Grinning, he slid in beside McLean at the bar to face the other three.

"You don't need to be breathin' down his neck, Robideau, just because he's got himself a gold mine," he said to the dark man. His right hand hung loosely near his holstered side.

The others glanced uneasily at Robideau, but he neither moved nor spoke. From him, however, there extended a suggestion of a deadly physical force that awaited its own time.

The challenge ignored, Miles Larion turned to Seldom Wright, and his big mouth curled.

"It's just gonna kill you, ain't it, Wright, if you don't get to steal Marty's spread?"

The older man's eyes flashed. With dignity, he drew himself up, measured the other for a long instant, spat on the floor in contemptuous judgment, and turned and walked to the seat at the table he had left.

"It's my turn now," jocularly observed the man with whom Larion had entered. He was as tall as Larion himself and almost as hefty, but his long face was not good-natured even when he smiled as he did now.

"Just keep your pants on, Cox," Larion advised. "Marty, as a friend I tell you, you ought to get the hell on home."

In dumb obedience, McLean made for the door. Though he swayed a little as he walked, he was soberer now than he had been. The whisky was letting him down from the first high tide of exhilaration, and he was aware that he had talked too much.

"Don't stop!" Larion advised as he went out the door.

Before he had crossed the street on his way to the livery stable, however, McLean had convinced himself that a man would be foolhardy to attempt such a ride on such a night without equipment for emergencies, particularly when he had to pass the Family Liquor Store anyway. And though he hardly admitted it, doubts had begun to gnaw at him concerning the good fortune about which he had been so certain in his first intoxication. He wanted more whisky to bring back that happy assurance. And so it was that when he finally set out, he had one more drink inside him and a pint in the pocket of his mackinaw.

Half the pint was gone, too, when they found the old man the next morning, shot through the head near the Smoky Water crossing.

CHAPTER TWO

THE MAN rode slowly now, letting his mount make its own pace. As it plodded along, low-headed with fatigue, he gazed to the front and to right and left with the long, slow gaze of one who looks upon remembered scenes. To his left, the mountains lifted, purple under the declining sun. To his right, the country fell away, by rolls and pitches, to the crooked bed of the Crazy Cree, and beyond the river and its edging of naked trees it flowed on in humps and hollows until at the horizon it appeared to lip up like the rim of a saucer. Ahead of him, a ranch house, with its outbuildings and corral, came into view at the edge of a windbreak of willows, and he pulled his horse up to look at it.

Low and sprawling, it rested mellow in the sun, suggesting in the generosity of its embrace and the easy informality of its composition an old and enduring cordiality.

"It hasn't changed," the man said as his eyes took in the scene. He breathed deep. "It hasn't changed, and maybe the people haven't."

He touched his horse lightly with his spurs, and after it had fallen into stride kept flicking it lightly on the rump with the end of his reins in a gesture compounded of impatience and restraint.

The wind had died and the afternoon had turned off warm, for April, and as he approached the ranch house he unbuttoned the leather jacket he wore and, looping the reins around the horn of his saddle, grasped the jacket in either hand and fanned his flannel-shirted middle.

"Warm here, almost, as in the southwest," he remarked aloud, in the manner of a man accustomed to his own company.

There was a blur of movement between the poles of the corral, and he rode toward it and brought his horse to a halt and sat watching the man and broncho inside the enclosure. Blindfolded and saddled, the horse was snubbed short to a post, and the man was slapping it on ham and flank with an old slicker. The animal's fore hooves pushed into the ground as it strained against the snub.

"Whoa, Boy! Whoa, now!" the man said, low-voiced, to the swish of the raincoat. "This don't hurt you. Whoa, now!"

Under its shaggy coat of bay, the muscles of the beast ran in ripples of fright. At each touch of the slicker, it sounded a long, trembling snort of panic.

Watchful of the animal's heels, the man circled its rear and came up on its other side to continue the lesson. As he did so, he caught sight of the rider outside and muttered a reluctant "Howya."

"Hoddy."

As if his visitor were worthy of no further notice, the man turned his attention to the horse. Gingerly he grasped the horn of the saddle and shook it. The beast's back arched in a hump that raised the rear of the saddle clear of its spine.

"Going to top him off?"

The man stepped back and regarded his interrogator searchingly, as if he had been guilty of an impertinence, letting his eyes rest on his accoutrements, from the new hat that could be seen above the poles of the corral to the new boots that could be seen between them.

The other sat impassive, returning his scrutiny.

The bronc-breaker spat in the dust and rubbed the

spittle with the worn toe of his boot. "Not for two-three days, unless you'd like to try him out now."

The words were as much challenge as suggestion, but they brought only a negative, "Guess not."

The man on the ground hitched his faded overalls higher on his lean waist and spat again. His face showed the lines of years and weather. Under the brim of his old hat, gray streaked the rust of his hair.

"Didn't guess you would," he said exploratorily, looking up from under his brows.

The rider sat his mount silently.

"Give me fifteen year, and I'd fork a cyclone, 'specially if I had all that fancy riggin'."

The speaker looked up expectantly, but there was nothing in the quiet face of his caller to indicate that his words had excited any reaction.

He kicked at the ground again, thoughtfully, during a long minute of silence, and when he spoke, his voice was pointed with understanding.

"You can nearly allus tell a man by the outfit he wears, Sonny."

There was no hint of change in the visitor's expression, except perhaps that it reflected a composure even greater than before, but in slow deliberation he swung off his horse, walked to the gate, drew the bar, and went in.

Despite his boots and spurs, he moved with a sort of soft ease, like an Indian, and the other, who had let a smile pull at the corner of his mouth, squinted in abrupt uncertainty and put his caller to a fresh and closer scrutiny.

There was no belligerence in that face, no anger and no fright. There was nothing in it, indeed, except a kind of assured and thoughtful calm, which might have been the mark of innocence—or of control. For the rest, the man appeared to be somewhere in his twenties, and beyond a doubt he wore on his lean and supple frame an outfit too new and too costly for a cowpuncher.

Reassured, the older man relented. "I was just testin' you out, Kid. You don't want to fork this jug-head. He's sure-enough mean."

"You set the act up," said the other, without heat.

"I was just seein' how much you'd take."

"I took enough, Uncle."

"Don't call me 'Uncle'."

"Same goes for 'Sonny'."

They stood face to face, appraising each other, and the elder of them, looking now into the other's eyes, found some reason to revise his opinion.

"You ain't exactly fresh-dropped, at that," he said uncertainly.

"O. K., Pardner," he added then, baring his tobacco-stained teeth with a grin. "You stand back. I got to fan this bronc a little more, so's he won't turn inside out when I do get on him. I'm a little old for a twister."

But the other moved up to the horse and expertly began adjusting the cinch.

"You can yank the blinder off when I get up," he said, and took the rope from the snubbing post.

"Naw, now. You called my bluff. Let it go!" insisted the challenger. "I warned you," he trailed off then, helpless before this unpretentious resolution.

"Thanks," the visitor answered, and slid into the saddle. "Let him go!"

The cow hand announced, "It's your funeral," and with that he flicked off the blindfold and ran stiffly to the side of the corral and climbed up.

For a paralyzed moment, the broncho stood humped, his eyes gleaming white at the corners, and then with a squeal he dropped his head and the whole of him seemed to explode. His first jump was a preparatory up-and-down pitch, ending in a stiff-legged, jolting return to earth, but he was in the air again almost as he landed and with his back bent like a bow and head and feet held together in a space no bigger than a hoop he rose high on the oblique and landed and came up the other way, like a ball thrown against the sides of a trough. But still his burden bestrode him, and without a split-second's break, the broncho changed tactics. He pitched now and wheeled in mid-air, like a ballet dancer on a turn, and, landing, came off the ground as if it were rubber and flung himself about again.

On the top pole of the corral, the watcher was talking to himself. "Dang me!" he half whispered as his eyes followed horse and man around the corral. "And I thought he was a dood! He's a chip ridin' a wave."

Abruptly he raised himself half out of his squat, lost his balance and fumbled backward for a hand-hold on the pole, but as he fumbled he was shouting, "Watch it! Watch it!" And his eyes never came off the scene before him.

For the broncho was trying the most desperate and dangerous trick of the outlaw. He was throwing himself, seeking to crush his rider under him, but throwing himself not backward, as bad horses do, but forward, as not one animal in a thousand will.

Again without a halt in the sequence of violence, he had let his forelegs buckle as his hooves hit the ground. His back legs flexed and straightened, and the heavy rear of him flew up and over in a somersault.

"Dang me again!" said the man on the corral, breathing deep, for as the tail of the beast came up, the rider had kicked clear of the stirrups. His hands felt behind him for the cantle and he shoved himself off barely ahead of the descending heels.

He landed lightly, on both feet and one hand, and swung around and vaulted back into the saddle as the shaken bronc got up, snorting with shock.

But there wasn't much buck in the horse now, and the man atop the corral squirmed into an easier position and took time to spit. "That's one on Rusty," he acknowledged to himself, wiping his mouth with his hand.

A voice sounded behind him. "Who's your friend?"

He looked around and down at the burly figure of the rancher who stood there. Then he swung a boot over the pole of the corral and descended.

"No friend of mine," he answered, "but he sure can peel a bronc."

The rancher moved around toward the gate, for the horse was ridden out and the rider had dismounted and, still with that soft ease, was coming out of the corral.

"By Joe, Pardner, you put up a nice ride," said the rancher, extending his hand. "My name's Buck."

The other grasped the proffered hand and for an instant studied the heavy, open features of his new acquaintance. Then, slowly, his mouth twisted into a grin. It was the first time since his arrival that his face had indicated anything but a quiet reflectiveness, and the smile, perhaps by reason of its rarity, made him seem younger and somehow almost diffident.

"Good to see you again, Bally," he answered.

The rancher's eyes widened and suddenly a look of recognition and welcome flooded his face. He shouted a delighted curse. "Damn your bones, West Cawinne," he exclaimed, pumping the other's arm. "Thought I wouldn't know you, didn't you? How come I found you toppin' my bronc?"

The man called Cawinne made a little motion toward the third member of the company. "He kind of seemed to want me to."

The rancher turned. "You mean Rusty did? Rusty Jones here?"

"Yeah," Jones admitted sheepishly. "I guess I did kind of haze him into it."

Buck laughed jovially and clapped Cawinne on the shoulder. "By Joe, Rusty," he said, "you ought to know better. This here's West Cawinne, son of old John Cawinne, and he grew up on a horse over at the old Bar-G-Bar. Rusty's my foreman, West. Shake hands."

He went on, "Martha'll sure be tickled, West. You come back to Powder County to stay? Don't tell me different."

"Yep, to stay."

"That's good," said the rancher. "Been ten-twelve year since you left, ain't it? Well, we sure are glad to see you."

He halted suddenly, as if before a fresh and secret thought, and put Cawinne to an inquiring reconsideration. "Yeah," he said slowly while his eyes searched the other's face, "we're awful glad to see you." There was a speculative deliberation in the words that seemed to require a sequel, but as his visitor's steady gaze bore on him he switched to a question: "How come you to come on a horse? You haven't rode a thousand miles, of course."

"No," came the answer. "At Cottonwood I was tired of wheels, and I hired the horse at a stable there. The man said he was coming to Moon Dance and would pick him up tomorrow."

"Uh-huh," said Buck. On his rough-chiseled, open

countenance there was a look almost of guile. "Seen anyone you know?" he asked, watching the younger man out of the tail of his eye.

"You're first. I came right here."

"Good. Glad you did. Let's go up to the house. Martha'll want to see you. Then I got to go to town. I was comin' out to saddle up when I saw you on that bronc. Rusty'll take care of your horse."

They went to the back door of the house, and Buck opened it and shouted, "Hey, Martha! Guess what the dogs brung home."

Mrs. Buck turned away from the kitchen stove and stood looking as Buck ushered Cawinne in before him.

The younger man's lips twisted again in that slow, unpretentious grin, and he stood there silent, waiting for her recognition, while he turned his big hat in his hands.

The mouth in Mrs. Buck's plump face dropped open and her generous bosom heaved in a gasp of astonishment.

"If it ain't little West Cawinne, only not little any more!" she exclaimed. She extended her square hand and shook hands like a man, and then, as if the gesture were inadequate for the occasion, she reconsidered momentarily and kissed him resoundingly.

"It's just like my own boy comin' home," she explained as a flush stained the lean cheeks of the visitor. "Come in and set, West! Come in! Bally, whyn't you tell a person, 'stead of surprising 'em half to death? Had anything to eat, West? I can get a snack in a minute."

"I'll wait, Mrs. Buck," he answered. "It's good to be back."

"I'll set with you for just a minute, even if I got to hurry," said Buck, and they all went into the big living room and sat down.

"How's Judge LaFrance?" asked Cawinne after he had made and lighted a cigarette.

"Jus' fine," replied Buck, "except he's deefer'n ever."

"Still making harness?"

"Makin' harness and construin' the law."

"And Marty McLean and Mother McLean?"

"Why, West—" began Mrs. Buck, but her husband shot her a swift glance and at the same time broke into her answer.

"Heah," he rumbled vaguely, drowning out her faltering voice, "Marty McLean, too, and Mrs. McLean."

"Marty still hitting the bottle?"

"No, West," the rancher answered, "Marty don't hit it any more," and then he quickly switched the conversation to the subject of his guest. "We were about to think you'd never leave that sand-and-cactus country. You never wrote anybody."

"I always planned to come back."

"We heard about you once in a while, though," said Buck meaningfully.

"Wasn't much to hear," the other responded unencouragingly.

"I don't know about that," persisted Buck.

"It's all behind."

"Well, maybe, West. Still and all, a thing like that kind of follows a man, even if he moves a thousand miles and more."

"It's all behind," repeated Cawinne, his voice edged with insistence. "I'm going to ranch. I'm starting up on the Bar-G-Bar." His face was grave but somehow inexpressive, almost as if he wore his composure as a mask. "What about the old place?" he inquired.

"Just about like when you left it, except for a little wear and tear. I been goin' over there now and then."

Buck rose abruptly. "I sure must leave now," he announced. "West, you're stayin' here tonight, of course, and every night you want to, far as that goes. I'll be late gettin' home, Martha, but I'll be back sometime. I'll get supper at Moon Dance."

Silently, she got up and followed him through the dining room to the back door in the kitchen, and when they were there she demanded in a whisper, "You remember what I said now, Bally Buck!"

"Oh, sure, sure," he agreed, his voice muted to a murmuring rumble. "I'll remember."

"You're not going out with them if they go?"

He hedged a little. "I don't think they'll be goin', Honey, anyway not tonight."

"They'll want you out in the lead if they do."

"I been thinkin' about another plan."

"I know," she said, understanding him at once, "but you aren't going to get him tied up in this business?"

"Honey, you wouldn't know the answer to a prayer if one hit you smack in the face."

"This boy's a lamb."

"I ain't so sure there's not some wolf in him."

"Don't do it, Bally. You don't know what you might be gettin' him into."

"Somebody's got to do it. Me, or him, or somebody."

Her silence seemed to dispute him, and he continued earnestly, still in that heavy murmur: "What I do will be what I think's best for everybody." Uncertainly, he worried his heavy jaw with the knuckles of his fist. "Only thing—I wish I did know more about this boy, about what he's really done down south. He looks kind of innocent-like, sure enough. Now don't you let out anything about old Marty McLean."

"Why?"

Buck was vexed with the delay. "Just because I don't want you to," he whispered vehemently. "Maybe it 'ud be all right to tell him, and maybe it 'ud work out better if we told him later. Maybe we got to shock him into it, for instance."

"I would hate it," she protested.

"There's things I'd hate worse. Now don't keep me here arguin'! I got to see Judge LaFrance before the meetin', and I'm late as it is."

With that, Bally Buck put a little peck of a kiss on his wife's full cheek, pulled open the door and started down the path toward the barn. Mrs. Buck stood in the doorway and watched with troubled eyes until he disappeared inside the stable.

CHAPTER THREE

W EST CAWINNE shook his head.
        "I'm going to run cows," he said.
It was the next day after his arrival at Bally Buck's Circle-I, and he and three other men were in the back of Judge LaFrance's harness shop at Moon Dance.

The three received his answer silently, until finally the ancient justice himself gestured with his trumpet and spoke in the toneless voice of the deaf.

"That ain't all, West," he said. "It ain't just a matter of a few head of stock being rustled and a few roughs hurrahin' the town."

His red-rimmed old eyes under their frosting of brow were fastened on the other's face.

"Marty McLean was found dead on the road at the Smoky Water ford. Dry-gulched!"

"The hell!" said Cawinne with a slow intake of breath. "When?"

He stood leaning against Judge LaFrance's work-bench, with his back to the dusty window through which filtered the light of mid-afternoon. Shadowed against that background, his face had the look about it of youth that had seasoned early. It was lean and strong and narrowed at the lids as if for laughter, but the eyes that looked out of it were unsmiling and deliberate.

Seldom Wright, perched on a stool near a pot-bellied stove that rested on a box of earth, answered through the stained gray jungle of his beard.

"A week ago, come Friday," he answered. "To be exact,"—his gaze shifted to the dingy calendar on the end wall—"Friday, April the twenty-first."

A patch of white hair, like a goat's tassel, grew from the point of his chin and split the darker shag of jowl and neck.

The younger man bent his head.

"Marty McLean," he said slowly, in regret but not surprise, as if the uncertainty of life had been written deep in his experience. "Why would anyone kill old Marty?"

"It's considerable of a story, West," Bally Buck answered, "and we'll take you over it later, but Marty thought he'd run onto the secret of the Early Day Mine. He got full of whisky at Adlam's and announced he had, and it seems someone took him serious. Anyway, he was shot that night."

Cawinne's lips were tight in his impassive face, and something about him suggested that the committee was getting somewhere now. Buck went on with added vigor.

"He was shot from behind, we tell you, West. Bullet tore half his face off. Couple of nuggets and a map of the mine were gone when they found him."

Cawinne asked, "Where's Mother McLean?"

"Left yesterday, bound back to Missouri," Buck answered. "Wright, here, was mighty anxious to get the ranch, and she was just as anxious to sell and get out."

"I paid a fair price, too," Wright interjected defensively, and spat a smear against the belly of the stove.

"I ain't sayin' you didn't," Buck replied. "Same time, the market's down, and you didn't get a bad buy."

Wright grunted, "A man 'ud be a plumb fool to do that."

They were silent again, waiting for Cawinne to speak. He lounged against the Judge's workbench, hands fiddling with a pocketknife. In the company of the other

three he appeared over-dressed. The dark trousers that
fell outside his cowman's boots showed a crease. The
boots themselves were smooth and black with little use.
Against the collar of his gray flannel shirt a black four-
in-hand pressed. The broad, light-gray hat that tilted
slightly on his head obviously was expensive and had
seen no great service. A leather jacket, buttoned at the
bottom, emphasized his taper from shoulder to waist.

"Did McLean find the mine himself, or what he
thought was the mine?" he asked at last. His tone seemed
almost indifferent, as if he spoke only because they expected him to.

"Naw," said Buck. "A crazy sheep herder named
Svenson is the one that thinks he found it. He let Marty
in on it because Marty let him graze a little bunch of
sheep on his range when the rest of us was for runnin'
him out."

Cawinne studied the knife in his hand and presently,
looking up, answered the question in their manner.

"It's no go," he said. "Win or lose, a gunfighter still
loses."

"Sure, Kid, I know," Buck answered. "Same time—"
He finished with an inquiring outward gesture of his
thick hands.

"Why don't some of the young bucks around here do
it? Why don't you yourself, Bally? You're not so old."
He added significantly, "Or so slow, either."

Buck held his right hand out and scrutinized it as if
it had grown alien in disregarded years.

"Five years ago," he muttered, "I'd of done it. Two
years ago I would of. And by Joe I would right now if
I could oil up that hand. Ever hear of arthritis?"

"West," the Judge broke in, taking his trumpet from
his ear, "we don't have any young men any more. The

sons of cattlemen are hopping counters and peddling gas and pecking typewriters in the cities." The vast tragedy of change came into his hoarse voice. "There's no youth in the cattle business these days. Just us old duffers. No young men any more." His words trailed off sadly.

"I guess Miles Larion is still around," suggested Cawinne.

Wright snorted. A gust of words fanned the yellowed hair about his mouth. "Now wouldn't that be a hell of a note! Miles Larion!"

"He's my friend," said Cawinne, and his voice was still slow, but Wright looked at him quickly, turned his thin hams on his stool, uncrossed his legs, spat again, brought his gnarled hand across his mouth, and replied with a sort of grudging courtesy, "No offense."

"Sometimes," volunteered Buck in explanation and what might have been reproof, "two men can't seem to hit it off, partic'ly if both's a little ringy."

With half a smile Cawinne suggested, "What about Horace Fladd?"

"He's still around," acknowledged Buck, grinning too, "and he's just as good a blacksmith as when you left, and just as crazy to get fancy with a six-gun, but he don't shoot no better than ever."

Judge LaFrance's booming tones filled the room.

"We're drawin' to a deuce, sure enough, West," he insisted, his chin thrust out in trembling emphasis of his old-man's earnestness.

"I guess you have some idea about the guilty party," Cawinne observed.

Wright jerked up stiffly on his stool.

"A good idea, we got," he answered hotly. "A damn good idea. Hit's Robideau, the half-breed, and his pack."

At mention of the name, a silence fell on them all.

Judge LaFrance was hunched forward in his chair, his eyes on the floor. Buck had tilted his chair against the wall, and his gaze went from face to face in some inward inquiry. Wright sat defiant on his stool. Cawinne leaned against the bench, and after a long minute his eyes went from the knife in his hand to Bally Buck's watchful face.

"Robideau came from down your way," the rancher remarked. "Maybe you've heard of him?"

"Some," acknowledged Cawinne cryptically.

"Well, he's here all right. He's holed up at Breedtown on the south fork of the Crazy Cree."

"And he's behind all the stealing and the rough stuff and the killing," Wright added fiercely.

Buck put in mildly, "Last night Seldom had the boys all set to go out and get him. The Judge talked 'em out of that."

"And so fixed me to get a bullet between the shoulders at any time," Wright charged.

He got off his stool after he had spoken and stood facing the three of them. The afternoon sun had slipped below the rear eave of the shop and through the window it cast a beam that caught his face and made the white of his beard glisten. Standing there, silent and poised, with his ragged whiskers shining and the flush of conviction reddening cheek-bone and brow, he looked like some ancient patriarch. Out of the beard his voice came harsh and compelling.

"I said last night and I'm a-tellin' you again, this whole business is shyin' away from what we ought to do ourselves, 'specially if we want hit done right." His voice rose, clear and sharp now, in a natural rude oratory. "What we up agin? Stock stolen for nigh onto a year! Rough stuff! Gun-slingers hungerin' to put daylight through a man! Robideau and the rest, all cold as snakes

and just as pizen! And a good old man done to death!
A kind old feller that never hurt ary soul! Shot, robbed
and left to rot because an Injun wants a mine!

"And what do we do?" he asked accusingly, sweeping
them with his eyes. "We say, 'Wait! We'll get somebody to tend to this for us. We just don't feel quite like
a-doin' it ourself!' "

He was panting with vehemence, and he stopped and
swallowed, and when he spoke again it was as if Cawinne
were an exhibit rather than an individual.

"So," he charged, looking at Buck and LaFrance,
"because you two say so, we decide on this young feller
here to tend to our knittin' for us. This young feller,"
he repeated, and his eyes went over Cawinne, from new
hat to holsterless thighs to new boots. "I ain't sayin'
anything agin him, you understand, but he don't look
like a man-hunter to me. And 'specially he don't look
like a man-hunter when the man's Robideau."

Judge LaFrance took his deaf-man's horn from his ear
and struggled to his feet and studied Wright over small-
framed glasses set low on the bridge of his nose. In his
wasting figure that trembled a little with its years was
something still of the appearance of independence and
command.

"Seldom," he barked in the full and inflexible voice of
one who cannot hear himself, "you spoke your piece last
night, and we decided against you. No one's asking what
you think about West Cawinne. Your job, as a member
of this committee, is to try to sign him up. Now supposin'
we attend to that job!"

"Besides," Buck chimed in, "there wasn't anybody at
the meeting that seemed to want to trade lead with Robideau."

Wright retorted, "Like I said, when you're a-huntin'

polecats you shoot before they have a chance to mess you up."

"Well, are you runnin' with the herd, or aren't you?" asked Buck bluntly.

"Yeah, I'm runnin' with you, 'til I get a bullet in the back. You know I've spoke my mind free and full, and word'll get out about hit. Word'll get to Robideau, and he don't figure to let an enemy run loose. Hit ain't that I give so much of a damn about my hide. Hit's old and nigh worthless. I'm just a-tellin' you others that you'll have to keep a nice, tight tongue in your head to be safe. Me, I believe in meetin' trouble when hit comes."

Muttering in his beard, Wright resumed his perch on the stool.

Cawinne's steady gaze followed him as he hunched himself back on his seat. "Robideau got out of Arizona with one mob on his tail, Wright," he said quietly. "I wouldn't think he'd invite another by gunning you."

Wright grunted unbelievingly, "Hit didn't keep him from killin' McLean."

Cawinne studied the wall against which Buck had tilted his chair. At length he asked, "Who heard old Marty say he'd found the Early Day?"

Buck's glance went to Wright, who answered, "I was one of them. And there was Miles Larion and Blackie Cox and Jack Schwartz, the barkeep, and Robideau, all listenin' in."

"I guess it's Robideau, all right, West," Buck acknowledged. "You remember the Injuns around here always believed mighty strong in the Early Day. Stories about it have come down from their great-granddads, and some of 'em, specially the breeds, have banked on findin' it some day. I don't guess anybody else would take it very

serious. No gold ever found on this side the mountains, in our time, anyway."

"Same time," the Judge amended, "that old story about
the Early Day has got a pretty strong hold, and not
among Injuns alone. You remember something about it,
West?" Though the other nodded understandingly, the
judge went on, with the oldster's concern for detail.
"Injuns used to have plenty of gold, they say, and then
a couple of beaver trappers was supposed to have run
onto the place. They got killed there when they tried to
go back to it. And then, somehow, the Injuns themselves
lost the location, 'cordin' to the story. But there's a
bunch of 'em believes in it yet, and a lot of white people
to boot. And whether they believe in it or not, Bally,"
he concluded, addressing himself particularly to the
rancher, "just the mention of gold's enough to throw
some fellers into a stampede."

There was the odor of oil and leather and tobacco
smoke in the room. Through the wide back window the
slanting beam of the sun focussed on the rough and
reddled face of Buck, who moved out of the shaft and
ran a blue bandana around the back of his neck. "Never
knew it to be so warm this early," he offered. "Bet it
means hell and high water later on."

Again they fell silent, and again it was the venerable
justice of the peace who picked up the thread of conversation. "Killing's bad," he observed with a sort of
weary melancholy, his voice for once subdued, "but
when a man gets older and begins to feel it in his bones
that we all have to end up by dying one way or another,
sometimes something not so important begins to look
more important. You know, West, us old-timers have
lived the lives of hard men, but by and large we've all

been honest. We never shot a man in the back, even the outlaw respected a man's home, and the lousiest sheep herder would leave a camp spick and span, with nothing missing except the grub he ate."

He paused, and, when he resumed, it was in the manner of a man bidding farewell to cherished things.

"Old times, old ways, they're important, too," he said, "especially when you get up close to the end and can look back over the trail you've took and the kind of country you've gone through. And when the old ways go, it ain't always to make room for progress."

Suddenly he lifted his seamed and baggy face, and his voice boomed out again: "Why, damn it to hell, West, people are beginnin' to lock their doors at night now."

When the words had sunk in, Buck picked up the subject. "That old box in front of the Moon Dance Mercantile Company where people throw the keys to the latches they buy?" he reminded Cawinne inquiringly. "Well, I guess she's seen her last key. Wright, here, can tell you one reason why. 'Twasn't but two or three days ago that his place was broke into."

Cawinne's slow gaze turned to Wright. "They didn't get nothin'," the latter said. "Wasn't much to get. They mussed the place up right smart, though."

"We ain't sayin' it would be easy, West," said Buck, returning to the argument. "Robideau's good." He paused and added, as if justice demanded it, "He's about as good as they come, I guess."

"Yes," said Cawinne to his inquiring halt.

"And there's three or four run with him that don't have to rest their pistols on a post to shoot the eye out of a jacksnipe, either, besides some others that's liable to wing you any time if the light's good and your back's turned. Like Wright argued last night, we don't know much about you as a growed man. Maybe we got no business askin' you to go up against a hand like this Robideau. Maybe you ain't up to it. But," he added as a contradiction, "we been hearin' something about you in the time you been away. A man don't last long enforcin' the law in that desert country if he's slow on the draw, and he don't take up the business if he's over partic'lar about his hide. And besides, you're old John Cawinne's boy, which means a lot to all of us savin' maybe Wright here, who moved in from Kentucky after your dad's death. Anyhow, we're speakin' for the stock association. We'll have you deputized, and we'll see that you get paid and paid good."

"You act," replied Cawinne, "like the sheriff wasn't a law-enforcement officer."

Buck had taken a fat cigar from his vest and bit off its end. Now he spat out the tip and ejaculated, "He ain't, for a fact. A pale, spineless ex-bookkeeper who's too busy down at the county seat arrestin' drunk sheep herders and doin' other dangerous and necessary business to pay any attention to a little old felony forty miles away."

"Marshal?" inquired Cawinne.

Buck swore disgustedly. "Clarence Lamb! They call him Mary's Lamb. That tell you enough?"

He paused expectantly and, when Cawinne made no reply, went ahead like a man showing a holed ace.

"Sure as you get into the cattle business you're going to have a run-in with Robideau anyway. You ain't going to sit around and watch him haze off your stock—if it is him."

A sharp question was in the eyes that bored at Cawinne.

"Besides," the rancher went on as the other kept silent, "you've heard of Robideau, and I guess he's heard of you, all right. Now he's kind of old-timey. He ain't going to want to share honors in the use of the six-gun, if we understand him right. It'll be you or him."

"A chief," Judge LaFrance emphasized, aiming at Cawinne with the trumpet he had kept glued to his ear. "A chief like in the old days of Alder Gulch and Last Chance."

Buck waggled a stubby forefinger. "West," he predicted, "I'll bet a stack against a white one that you and him tangle, regardless. The cards just fall that way."

Abruptly he stood up, as if fearful that persuasion, pushed too far, would defeat itself. Standing, he appeared not fat but short and thick through the chest, solid and assured in his middle years. His tone now was light and jovial.

"Well, whether you take it or leave it, you can see we're up against something. Reminds me of old Ezekiel Smith, who was a tailer here before your time, West."

The rancher trimmed the mangled stub of his cigar with his front teeth, spat out the trimmings, and eyed the result reminiscently.

"Them days," he related, "we didn't have no undertaker in Moon Dance, but we needed a coroner, if only to kind of make sudden death official, and so we elected Zeke.

"Zeke was quite a feller," he went on. "Right fancy dresser, he was, and mighty sober and dignified in his manner. Well, he hadn't been in office more'n a week until they found a freighter froze to death up on the bench. Been dead two-three days, and he was stiff as a poker. Just to try Zeke out, the boys decided to have an inquest, and so they put a door across a couple of sawbucks in the Moon Dance Mercantile Company, and put the froze freighter on it.

"We was all anxious to see how Zeke would do," Buck proceeded, "and so when he showed up there was quite a bunch of us there in the store. Zeke had prettied up considerable for the affair. He had put on a pair of choke-bore pants and a coat with long tails to it, but the crowd seemed to fluster him some, at that. He kind of got himself together, though, and went over to the door where the body was lyin' and studied it very sober-like. Then he went around to the other side and did the same thing, ending up by stickin' one finger out and touchin' the corpse."

Buck paused to give emphasis to his conclusion.

"He turned to us then," he resumed, "and he said, 'Boys, this man's in a damn bad fix.' "

When they had quit laughing, the rancher drew his comparison. "That's the way we are, West—in a damn bad fix. But there ain't any cause to hurry you. You can let us know tomorrow, or the next day, or the next."

They had all risen and were moving toward the door.

The old judge laid his hand on Cawinne's shoulder.

"You armed?" he asked and, when the other shook his head, insisted, "Here, take my old hog-leg, take it, I say, until you round up your own." From a shelf at the side of his bench he lifted a worn forty-five.

"Take it, West," Buck advised. "I wouldn't wonder if word's out about this proposition. That might make you it."

"There's enough in town to play, too," Wright added. "I seen Robideau down in front of the Horse and Cow Saloon an hour ago."

"No," said Cawinne, "I don't want it."

"Now, West—" Buck began, but there was something

in the younger man's face that discouraged argument, and he concluded, "All right then. I guess you know what you're up to. Put 'er back on the shelf, Judge."

The ancient justice's brow was wrinkled with worry as he stood in the door and watched the three on their way.

"I do' know," he said, shaking his venerable head. "Looks like a mighty peaceful young man, except maybe sometimes for his eyes."

He turned back into the shop, sighing.

CHAPTER FOUR

SELDOM WRIGHT took his leave of Buck and Cawinne half way down the block, excusing himself by saying he had some purchases to make.

The three halted while he said his good-bye, and after he had gone Buck suggested, "Like to set in a game for a spell? I thought I'd hunt one up."

"You go ahead," Cawinne responded, "I'll look around."

"Goin' back to the ranch tonight, ain't you? You can get another horse easy enough."

"No thanks. I sent my war-bag along by train, and I'll pick it up at the depot and go on to the hotel tonight."

"I guess I'll stay in town myself then," said the rancher. "See you tomorrow, and maybe sic the wolf on you again. But listen, we're expectin' you to spend a lot of time at the Circle-I, Martha and me both."

After the other had promised another visit, Buck swung off the board walk and clumped across the street toward Adlam's Saloon.

Cawinne went on, walking slowly, studying with a home-comer's interest the flanking of buildings along the street, the weathered landmarks and the few raw additions that went to make up the business section of this Moon Dance that he had not seen for a dozen years.

Not until he reached the end of the block was his journey interrupted. Then, though still yards in front of him, a man began yelling, "Hey, you, West! Darn your hide! Howya comin'?"

He came swinging across the intersection, a large, raw-boned man, and arrived a little breathless from haste and halloo. He thrust out his right hand, crying delightedly, "I'll be damned! You can tell the world is round because every mangy coyote that ever leaves here always comes back."

He carried a forty-five, open-holstered, at his hip.

"Shake, friend!" he commanded, while his grinning mouth slit his red face. "You're looking at prosperity, or my name isn't Miles Larion."

Impulsively, he reached into a hip pocket, abstracted a wallet and, removing the contents, riffled through a fat stack of bills. As he did so, a soiled and wrinkled slip of paper fanned out and fluttered to the walk. Larion bent quickly to pick it up and placed it at the side of the bills as he returned them to the fold.

Cawinne whistled. "All the tea in China!"

"If you live right, the pasteboards fall right," Larion moralized. Then, changing the subject, he volunteered casually, "Already, the birds are saying it's good-bye to bad men."

"Birds twitter something awful. Keep you awake, if you let them. Glad to see you, regardless."

"These birds I'm talkin' about ain't so flighty."

"Wish you'd put me in touch with one of them. Lot of things I'd like to know."

He looked at Larion quizzically.

"About Seldom Wright for one."

Larion's red face slowly flushed redder.

"He been talkin' again?" he asked with suspicious belligerence.

"Ah, no. Nothing to amount to anything," Cawinne replied guardedly.

Larion's big mouth ran out a rich curse. "I told him I'd hang his hide on the corral."

"Take it easy."

The other massaged his chin impatiently. "Listen," he said abruptly. "I got a god-awful lot still to do, so I got to be movin'. Time for one drink, though. What do you say?"

"Thanks," answered Cawinne negatively. "I'm heading for a cup of coffee."

"Well, I want to see you again, and see you soon. Hear? I was at Adlam's the night Marty McLean announced findin' the Early Day, and I got something to tell you."

He swung his big bulk around on his heel, in a manner that fitted his brusque and impetuous speech, and collided with Seldom Wright, who had been about to pass in his rear.

Knocked apart, the two eyed each other.

The blood flooded Larion's cheeks again. He said, "For a minute I was about to say excuse me."

"Manners come hard to some," Wright answered, his voice a thin rasp.

"Then again," Larion picked up, "manners can be a kind of weakness, like this one I got of not tromping on old things, even old coyotes."

A crowd, drawn from the street and the adjacent shops, had gathered with a watchful curiosity about them.

Wright's whiskers moved like a thicket in which something unseen stirs, but he controlled himself sturdily and, silent, looked the other in the eye.

Larion taunted, "Yellow belly."

More suddenly than it had gathered, the congregation

melted away. With an attempted show of unconcern, its members speedily sought cover. Two shifted behind a tree. A half-dozen rounded the protective corner of the Stockmen's Bank. More jammed into the recessed doorway of the Family Liquor Store.

Wright's shooting hand opened and closed convulsively, but his voice when he spoke was low and steady.

"I don't set up to be no gunman, Larion," he said, facing the other unyieldingly. "I know you can perforate me easy enough. But I ain't a-scared of you, Larion, and there's other ways and other times to settle trouble, if hit's bound to come."

He backed now toward the outside of the board walk that flanked the street and, as he looked around to save himself an unexpected step off its edge, the look of controlled composure on his face froze into dismay.

Cawinne, leaning in an attitude of casual but alert interest against a hitch-rack at the edge of the street, turned toward the object of the older man's stare. A decrepit Model T had pulled to a stop just behind Wright, and from its side, noosed by a length of binding twine to a bracket, writhed the yellow length of a big rattlesnake.

"Even this old boy got fooled by the weather," the unsuspecting driver called genially into the tension. "He thought it was summer, sure enough."

Stiff-legged, Wright backed from the squirming reptile, until his heel struck the front of the bank building. Wordless, he edged to the corner and disappeared from sight.

Larion spat disgustedly. "Snakes fear snakes," he announced. "I bet I pay for not ventilating him. So long. Don't forget I'll be seeing you."

The spectators began to reassemble, dividing talk between the encounter of the two men and the size of the snake.

Looking at the serpent, Cawinne was pushed aside as a spare figure in tattered coat and faded overalls crowded through.

"I swannee!" the man said, peering close. "That's what I call right smart of a rattler."

He turned and looked at Cawinne for confirmation.

Checked with wrinkles like sun-baked mud, his face had about it a monkey's look of senile inquiry. And when he spoke the resemblance to the simian was marked even more, for his lower features were extraordinarily mobile, as if they had no mooring on his skull.

"Man and boy, here and in Kentucky," he said through his loose lips, "I've seen a power of snakes, but never one like this."

With his out-thrust forefinger, he poked the scaly cylinder experimentally and laughed as the reptile managed a warning buzz, and, straining open-mouthed against the tyranny of the noose, revealed fangs set like curved ivory in the pinkish satin of its jaw.

With a sort of fearful fascination, the crowd had begun to hem them in, and Cawinne, after a final glance at man and serpent, stepped off the walk and crossed the street toward a restaurant and filling station barred with black and white stripes, which a sign proclaimed the "Motorists' Mecca." Patterned after roadside resorts on busier thoroughfares, alien to a class of people who still traveled largely by horse, it was as out of place as a Chinese pagoda in this old cow town of frame stores, hitching racks and cottonwoods straggling before the fronts of business houses.

Entering, Cawinne sat at the counter. Behind it at its lower end a girl stood with her back toward him. Across from her on stools were two men who seemed divided in interest between the girl and a bottle that sat half empty on the counter. The closer of the two was a man apparently in his early thirties. Muscularly set up, he had begun to grow stout and had the heavy, sagging look of an athlete going to seed. A smile half-mooned his swollen face. More arresting was the other, for in a country in which wind and sun combine to tarnish the complexions of the fairest, his color was as milky and transparent as vegetation in a cellar. Between their half-closed lids, his eyes, as they surveyed the newcomer, had a flickering, blue-white shimmer.

The girl came to wait on Cawinne.

She was straight and slim and young enough, almost, to be a child. Brown-haired, blue-eyed, colored at cheek and mouth with the flush of young blood, she looked at Cawinne half in inquiry, half as if in secret imploration.

"What will you have?" she asked abstractedly, as though a circumstance more urgent than service demanded her thought.

"Coffee, please," answered Cawinne.

"Come on back, Sister," the fading athlete called impatiently after she had set a cup before Cawinne. "I want sump'n else."

Fear ran liquid in the eyes she turned on Cawinne.

"Kiss I want, Tana," the man explained as she took a hesitant step toward him.

"I get dessert, don't I?" the athlete demanded, and laughed at his wit.

"Please," said the girl, halting.

"Aw, Stud," the ashen man objected. "Why'n't you leave her be?"

"You shut up!" commanded the man called Stud. "Just

because you ain't got an eye for a pretty thing is no
sign I don't." Then to the girl he announced, "Papa's
going to come and get it."

"Aw, Stud," the other said again.

The door to the kitchen swung open and there
appeared framed in the casement, like an old picture of a
dandy, a man of exquisite feature, set off by a spruce
mustache, whose gentle and expressive eyes looked reproachfully at the love-maker.

"Now, now, Mr. Manker," he called in an extraordinarily clear and resonant voice, "let us be gentlemen!"

Manker started around the end of the counter, answering contemptuously over his shoulder, "Get back to
your flapjacks, Duke. Can't you see we're busy?"

The girl had stiffened suddenly at the sound of the
dandy's voice. She composed herself with visible effort,
looked sturdily over the approaching shoulder of her
pursuer to smile a reassurance at her defender, and called
in a voice urgent with anxiety:

"It's all right, Daddy. They're just playing. You can
go back."

Cawinne said, "Sometimes, some places, it ain't healthy
to press a girl too hard."

He had moved down the counter beside Manker's
companion, and as the two jerked about to stare at him
he stirred his coffee thoughtfully, on his face an expression of grave composure.

Full face, the perpetual smile of the fattening athlete
seemed a deformity, for in his cold eyes there was no
mirth. For an instant he studied Cawinne. Then he
laughed.

"You watch the pilgrim, Whitey," he demanded of his
companion.

"Yuh," grunted the white-faced man, his objections to the other's actions apparently canceled by the intrusion of the outsider.

As Manker continued his advance on the girl, Cawinne laid down his spoon and, in a smooth and unforeseen continuation of the gesture, whipped out his fist in a line as true as a taut rope. It caught the albino on the chin, spun him half around on the stool, and dumped him, stunned, on the floor.

The force of the swing carried Cawinne off balance, and he let himself fall ahead to a crouch on the floor, out of sight of those on the other side of the counter. He took two swift, stooping steps toward the end of the stand and reached out and seized by the neck a tall brass spittoon. At almost the same moment, Manker charged from behind the counter, his right hand stabbing at the holstered revolver that slapped against his thigh.

From his crouch, Cawinne pitched the spittoon underhand. The throw was not hard, but the heavy butt of the vessel, catching Manker full in the face as he rounded the corner, knocked him back, reeling. Cawinne leaped ahead and with one wrench tore the revolver from his bewildered hand.

"Easy!" he warned then, backing away. "Easy!"

The man on the floor had struggled to his hands and knees. His hat had rolled from his head, and with his milk-blue eyes he looked up from under his tangle of white hair like a puzzled dog. "I'll take the revolver," Cawinne announced, covering him while he stooped and slid his weapon from its holster.

Manker had recovered himself now, and he stood still and speechless for a moment, studying Cawinne as if he could not believe his eyes.

Then he said with his smiling mouth, "Next time, Handsome, I won't take you for no pilgrim."

With Manker's revolver, Cawinne motioned toward the door. "Make tracks!" he ordered.

The albino had put on his hat and struggled to his feet, and Manker came forward now and put his hand on his arm, saying, "Come on, Whitey. It's his trick."

He turned after they had taken a few steps, however, and with exaggerated courtesy announced, "I am Stud Manker, Handsome, and this here is Whitey Salter. We trail with Robideau and we'll be seein' you."

"Your six-guns will be at Adlam's," said Cawinne.

The door closed behind them, and the dandy came forward like the soul of grace.

"My dear sir!" he said in his rich baritone. "My dear, dear sir! I thank you. We both thank you. A gallant deed, bravely done!"

He held out a slim hand while his eloquent eyes, under their delicately arched brows, welled with gratitude.

"It was lucky about the spittoon," said Cawinne.

The dandy apologized. "We just must keep it there. It's by what you might term popular request."

"But let me make ourselves known," he went on. "I am Tandy Deck, and this lamb, as you may have surmized, is my daughter, who is named Tana, somewhat after me."

"I am West Cawinne."

"A pleasure, a very great pleasure," acknowledged Deck, and bowed a little, as if he had made a pretty speech to a woman. "My daughter and I are the proprietors of this modest eating house and gasoline station," —the gesture that accompanied the information included only the country west of the ninety-eighth meridian—

"and we shall be happy at any time to extend to you its hospitality. It is not all that we could wish, but the wise accept what the gods bestow."

"Thank you," said Cawinne, and glanced at the girl, in whose smooth throat there still beat the throb of excitement.

She came forward impulsively and put out her hand. "We do thank you," she told him, "ever so much."

"Don't think about it."

"Perhaps all of us had better think about it," Deck contradicted, "particularly you, Mr. Cawinne, if you know the nature of the men you have just crossed." He looked toward the door apprehensively, then added in lower tones, "Really, we'd rather they did not patronize our little place. They are hard men, Mr. Cawinne. We do not like it even if friends come here to drink, but they—"

"Thanks for the warning," said Cawinne. "Now maybe I'd better take their artillery over to Adlam's."

"Please," entreated Deck, "let me attend to that for you. I can slip them in the back to Mr. Schwartz and no one will know 'twas I who brought them."

At his insistence Cawinne surrendered the revolvers and turned to go. Tandy Deck bowed his head in a gesture of leave-taking that was almost a curtsey, but the girl stood straight and unmoving, watching the departing man with eyes that were wide and full of wonder.

From the restaurant Cawinne went to the station to pick up his modest luggage, and from there he walked to the Moon Dance House, where he was shown a room on the second and top floor. He made use of the white pitcher and bowl that the management provided in lieu of running water and brushed his hair by the light of a kerosene lamp that licked fitfully against the quickly gathering dusk.

His toilet finished, he started to blow out the lamp, but stopped thoughtfully and turned to his suitcase and opened it and for a long moment stood looking at the double-holstered belt and the two black-butted forty-fives that lay on top of his gear. Slowly he picked up the belt and strapped it about him. The left-hand revolver he slid from its sheath and returned to the suitcase. He blew down the chimney of the lamp then, in an exhalation that was half sigh, and descended to the dining room.

He ate leisurely with a half dozen other diners and afterwards rolled and smoked a cigarette. Later, he visited the lobby, but there were few about, and he went out presently and walked up and down the quiet street.

Returning, he climbed the stairway to his room and went to bed.

It was early when Bally Buck awakened him, hammering on the panel.

"West! West!" the rancher's voice roared. "Wake up!"

Cawinne sprang from the bed.

"What the hell, Bally?" he cried, and flung open the door.

Buck's face was grim in the gray light of the hallway.

"Hell enough!" he shot back. "Miles Larion was killed last night."

"Killed!"

"At the Smoky Water crossing, like McLean was!"

CHAPTER FIVE

C AWINNE AND BUCK rode hard in the direction of the
Smoky Water crossing. The latter spoke a time or
two, tentatively, loud-voiced against the crackle of their
rigging and the whistle of the breeze by their ears, but
presently fell silent before the other's unresponsive
monosyllables.

It was a mild spring day in the valley of the lower
Crazy Cree. The great snow drifts that had piled up
around brush-patch and hummock had shrunk before the
unseasonable warmth and now spread their soiled tracery
on the ground like a mourning for winter. The valley
looked shaggy and drawn, as a beast looks after a hard
season, but the sun sailed clear in the shoreless sea of the
sky and the barren earth stirred with impulse. Scattering
colonies of old and paunchy gophers bounced along in
front of the riders and, pressed too hard, dived squeak-
ing into damp burrows around which the earth had been
freshly turned. Mildly alarmed, small bunches of cows
with calves by their sides quit their eager cropping of
the awakening turf to turn aside as the horsemen approached.

The canyon of the Crazy Cree was a darker gore in
the blue ruffle of the Rockies twenty miles to the west.
Five miles behind the riders lay Moon Dance, snuggled
in a bend of the river. Down from a divide they topped
presently, the Smoky Water traced its bleak and tortuous
course to the northeast.

Finally Cawinne spoke, easing his mount off a pace
that was too stiff.

"Know two fellows named Manker and Salter?"

"They're Robideau's aces."

"I got into a little tangle with them yesterday."

Buck whistled a long, low whistle, and the grim lines of his face spread to a quizzical grin.

"And you were going to stay out of all this!"

Cawinne told him about the encounter in the restaurant.

"Next time," warned Buck, "they won't low-rate you. Watch Manker, Kid. They say that Salter, in spite of that dish-water eye, is just as quick on the draw, but he's not near as tricky. He's dangerous, all right, but dumb. I been told Stud Manker was kind of sweet on little Tana Deck, but I never heard before that he got off the reservation. Damn his hide, I'll dust him myself if he don't behave. Tana's a friend of ours."

Buck ground off the end of a cigar and thrust it deep in his mouth.

"Listen!" he said like a man forcing a consideration too long suppressed. "What do we do? Go get Wright for pluggin' Larion? If we're goin' there, we cut off the trail at a fork up here a ways."

Cawinne ignored the question. "Tell me about Wright," he asked.

"Looks to me like a case of a man finally losin' his head," the rancher answered. "Seldom really ain't such a bad sort, but he's a hard-headed old coot, and pretty fiery sometimes, and so I guess he decided all of a sudden to lay for Larion, bein' as he couldn't let himself take any more off of him." The rancher shook his head regretfully. "I hate it, West, on account of Larion and Wright both."

"When did Wright come here?"

"He came from Kentucky with his brother, about the

time you left," Buck answered through teeth set deep in the cigar. "He had a little money, and knew how to make more. He's a smart trader and careful with his money, but honest enough for all that. He could buy and sell us all, I guess, though he lives mighty simple. His brother's a pretty good money-getter, too."

"They have separate places?"

"Yeah. They don't get along none too good. Seldom bought the old Brewer spread over west of here, and his brother located south of him, on the old U. T. His brand is the E-Lazy-R."

"Are they married?"

"Naw. No families, though I did hear Often was married once."

"Often?"

"That's Boone Wright. Out here they started calling him Often soon as they found out his brother's name was Seldom."

"Is that really it?"

"Honest to God! It's a funny story, too. Seems they come of a Kentucky hillbilly family. The old man had sired a whole slough of girls but couldn't get him a boy, and one day he swore, by Joe, that if ever he had a son, he'd call him Seldom Wright. When one came along, another came with him, and I guess that sort of stumped the old man, because he just named him Boone. Didn't stump us, though."

Buck chuckled, and added, "Often's got a face that kind of ranges all over his head."

"And a look like a monkey's?"

"That's the gent. Know him?"

"Think so."

"You sure have got around," Buck commented.

"Bally, how bad did Seldom Wright want Marty Mc-Lean's spread?"

"Well, he wanted it all right. Tried to buy it off Marty. And then, when Marty got killed, he made the offer again. Didn't shave his price, either, though he might have got it for less, what with things bein' the way they are and Mrs. McLean crazy to sell and get back to Missouri."

"Did he need it?"

Buck considered, while he maneuvered his cigar to the other side of his wide mouth. "Well, you know Marty's place is right next to Wright's Box-O, so it makes it pretty nice. But my guess is you're on a cold trail if you're tryin' to make out that Seldom shot Marty. It could be so, of course, but it ain't likely, in my mind, anyhow. Seldom might kill a man if he got mad enough at him, like it seems he killed Larion, but I don't believe he'd do it just to get hold of a piece of land."

"Wright and Larion, they had trouble before?"

"Some little mix-up over some calves was all, up to yesterday. But you know how Miles is, or was. Hot-headed and blunt-spoken. And Wright can rile you considerable, even when he's tryin' to be agreeable. Once those two got set against each other, they found plenty to keep 'em that way. You seen how Wright felt at our meetin' with you?"

Cawinne nodded thoughtfully.

"Well," the rancher insisted, impatient now, "let's speed up and go get Wright. I guess even he ain't likely to deny shootin' Larion."

When his companion did not reply, he added, " 'Less we do get a move on, some of the boys are liable to beat us there and have a necktie party."

Cawinne pulled up. "I hadn't thought of that," he said. "You mean Wright's unpopular enough that they might string him up?"

"He ain't any general favorite, West, though as I say he ain't been such a bad feller, in a way. But there's some wouldn't mind slippin' a noose over his head, partic'ly in an open-and-shut case. And then Moon Dance and Powder County has been workin' up to something like this, what with stock bein' rustled and old Marty killed. It ain't so much that it's Wright. Pretty near anyone would do. The boys are just itchin' for a chance to give some rein to their feelin's."

Cawinne consulted his watch.

"We got a good start," he said. "It isn't likely that anyone will beat you to him."

"Huh?"

"Look, Bally! I'm going to the crossing and see what I can pick up. The necktie party might start from there, as far as that goes. I want you to go to the Box-O and warn Seldom that a party's liable to be along."

Buck snorted, "Warn him!"

The other nodded.

"And give him a chance to skip! You mean bring him in."

"Not yet. If he's going to skip, he's skipped already. You said he was sharp."

"Even wise ones go dumb," Buck objected. "Wasn't so damn smart, for instance, for him to gun Larion in the first place, so I guess he might hang around afterwards."

Cawinne built his cigarette carefully.

"Bally," he said, "if I take the case, I take it, not anybody else. Otherwise, no go."

"You don't think he done it?"

"Don't know."

Buck studied the ground, his rough and open face seamed with rebellion. "All right," he said reluctantly, "I'm goin' to fold." He smiled a rueful little smile of speculation as his eyes searched his companion's face. "For a mild-lookin' boy, you sure got ideas of your own."

"You go on to Wright's and I'll go to the Smoky Water."

"You want me to tell Seldom to light a shuck out of there, 'less he wants a rope around his Adam's apple?"

"Yes. How far is it?"

"Couple of miles."

"And we're still about nine from the crossing?"

Buck nodded.

"You better not drag," Cawinne advised. "If a party's coming, it'll be along pretty soon, no matter where it starts from. Tell Seldom to hide out some place 'til the fever dies down."

Where the road branched to the left, Buck turned and spurred his mount. "I'll get there pronto," he promised. "See you in town if not sooner."

Cawinne rode more slowly now, and it was almost two hours before he rounded the shoulder of a low hill and came into the narrow valley of the Smoky Water. Within easy hail, a dozen horsemen had dismounted and stood in a huddle where the trail forded the stream. Reins trailing, their horses browsed on the spears of dead grass along the bank.

One of the group caught sight of the approaching rider and spoke to his fellows, and they all turned to look, silent and questioning.

"Hi," one of them responded shortly as Cawinne raised

his hand in greeting and came across the ford to them.

"Hoddy," Cawinne returned, and got off his horse. Their veiled eyes followed him in unfriendly inquiry.

What was left of Miles Larion lay just beyond them, face up in the road. Cawinne went to the body and stooped and turned the head on its stiff neck. A bullet, entering over one eye, had torn a hole as big as the palm of a hand in the young rancher's skull. Drained of the blood that had ruddied it, his face was ghastly.

A heavy man, tall, big-boned, and, by an accident of anatomy rare in the cow country, wider at the hips than the shoulders, pushed out from the others.

"Now that you've seen him, maybe you'll want to be makin' tracks," he suggested.

Cawinne looked up, his face bleak.

"No. Guess I won't."

A sullen displeasure clouded the other's face, which was long and flaccid, and loose and untidy at the mouth like an old horse's, but he did not press the point.

"Stay, then," he rejoined. "We're ridin'. Come on, men!"

"Where to?" asked Cawinne, rising.

"Who are you?"

"West Cawinne, friend of Larion here."

"Hell of a friend, askin' that question. Friend 'ud be ridin' with us."

Two or three others in the huddle of horsemen joined in the big man's hostile impatience. The others shifted on their feet, uncertain and watchful.

"Let's go!" cried the big man.

Cawinne's cool glance took in the rest, one by one. "You'll be riding soon enough," he advised.

A small man, sprung at the legs like a drawn bow, edged out of the group.

"Wouldn't have knowed you, West," he said. "Been so damn long."

Cawinne put out his hand. "John Bruce?" he asked. "How're you?"

"You comin'?" the big man challenged the crowd. He had taken a dozen steps from them in the direction of the horses.

"I'll ride with you if you hold up a minute," Cawinne told Bruce.

The latter studied him out of narrowed eyes. "I voted for you," he confided, low-voiced, "and I'm glad to see you're takin' the job." He swung around to the others.

"You know West," he declared. "Old John Cawinne's boy. Wants to look around a minute before we hightail it."

Three of the group came to Cawinne and offered their hands. The rest eyed him speculatively, but they all waited, their mettle not quite tempered to the deed the big man proposed. Bruce called to the latter, "You can wait a minute, Cox. Old Seldom ain't going to spoil."

Cawinne began to examine the ground around the body of Larion.

Bruce walked over to him to announce, "We found his gun over here in the grass, four feet or so from his hand."

"Looks like he went for it then?"

"Yeah. Guess so. I got it. It's been fired once."

"Find anything else?"

The cowpuncher shook his head.

"Who found the body?"

Bruce jerked a thumb in the direction of the big man. "Blackie Cox was here first."

"Uh-huh."

Bruce said, "I ain't trailin' with Blackie, y'understand. Not necessarily, anyhow."

Cawinne began to go through the pockets of the dead man.

Bruce walked over to the restless group. "Be just a minute. Let him satisfy hisself. Anyhow, we wouldn't want to go before the wagon comes for Larion."

Cox had mounted his horse and waited, morose and silent, for the others to join him.

Unobserved, Cawinne had transferred to his own pockets from the dead man's a folded scrap of paper that he found in an otherwise empty wallet. He beckoned to Bruce.

"Where'd Marty McLean's body lie?" he asked.

" 'Bout twenty yards beyond Larion's. Just up the trail there."

Cawinne studied. "The man that shot Marty must have cached himself in the willows by the ford and drilled him after he passed, since he was shot from behind," he speculated. "Gun that killed Larion, though, must have been fired from up the trail, about where they found McLean."

He strode up the trail, scanning the road, but turned back almost at once. "No use," he told Bruce. "Any sign that was left has been tracked out."

"Through lookin'?" asked Bruce, trailing him down to the bank of the stream above the ford.

"Guess so," answered Cawinne, casting a final glance about him as he stood among the low growth that flanked the stream, but suddenly he moved and stooped and picked something out of the grass.

Bruce regarded him inquiringly.

Cawinne held out his hand, showing a worn buckeye.

"What is it?"

"Somebody's pocket-piece. It could have slipped out of his pocket while he was hunkered down, waiting for Marty."

North over the brow of the hill a team and wagon appeared and jolted down the trail. The driver, a toothy blond, pulled up the horses, jumped down, squatted to look at the body, and asked, "Where do I take him?"

"To Todd Willis's at Moon Dance," answered Cawinne.

"Let's get him in," suggested Bruce, and four of the men came forward and helped lift the body over the tail-gate. The driver mounted the box, spread a soiled tarpaulin over his load and climbed into the seat. At his cluck, the team splashed across the stream.

"Let's ride!" yelled Cox, and started on ahead. The others ran to their horses.

The distance from the Smoky Water crossing to the Box-O is a little short of eleven miles. Ordinarily, a man will cover it in something less than three hours and something more than two, but this was no ordinary time and, with Cox showing the way, the horsemen pulled up before the modest cabin that Wright called home in almost an even hour.

On the way, they passed a gnarled cottonwood that pushed out a naked arm as if for a rope, and their impatient leader cried, "We'll bring him here, to Hangman's Tree."

Cox, who looked top-heavy on a horse even when slouched in the saddle, raised himself in his stirrups as they stopped at Wright's dwelling.

"Hullo, hullo, Wright!" he bawled. "Do you come out or do we come in and get you?"

There was no answer. The cabin looked empty. No smoke came from the chimney. The windows stared vacant and cheerless at the visitors.

Cursing, Cox leaped from his horse, strode to the door, and after trying the knob, broke in the panel with a thrust of his sharp shoulders.

"Gone!" he ejaculated, turning back toward the group after a hasty look inside. "Skipped while Cawinne kept us waitin'!"

He shook a long finger at the object of his displeasure. "By God, we'll get him yet!"

While men and horses milled about the cabin, Cawinne entered.

The place smelled of tobacco smoke, soiled clothing and stale food. Meagerly furnished and untidily kept, it was plainly the abode of a man who had not a helpmate. A bed, its grimy covers in a wad, occupied one end of the single room. A squat cook-stove was in the center, hedged about by two rough-hewn stools and an old apple box. Near the window stood a table on which lay a tin plate, a battered pail half full of water, a kettle and a small stack of eating utensils. The rough wood of the floor was littered with bits of paper, tobacco crumbs, barn-yard dirt and debris from the stove. Along the walls hung two old coats, a leather jacket, a skillet and a mixing spoon.

Cawinne took quick inventory, dismissing all he saw until his eyes fell on a half-dozen letters strewn along a shelf over the table. He started to look them over, but a voice outside called, "West! Hey, West!", and he stuffed them all into a pocket and went to the door.

Bally Buck came puffing to the entrance.

"Look!" he said, his tones suppressed. "I warned Seldom all right, and he lit out, ridin' that iron-gray horse of his. I lit out, too, not wanting to be found here, and then came back. And what did I find!"

With a gesture he commanded Cawinne to follow him and in a half-run led the way through the shifting horsemen to the barn and around it to a corral.

"There, by Joe, West!" he exclaimed, pointing.

Seldom Wright's gray horse, saddled and bridled, stood in the open corral. Around a hole that a bullet had drilled, gouts of blood, like a decoration, stained the high cantle of the saddle.

Loud and quarrelsome, Cox reined his horse around the barn. After him came the other riders.

"Tryin' to figure out a way to save Seldom?" he sneered.

"Yeah," Buck rejoined in kind. "We're right in the act of callin' back a bullet."

Contemptuously, he motioned toward the riderless steed.

CHAPTER SIX

O NTO JUDGE LAFRANCE's workbench, West Cawinne
tossed the letters he had taken from Seldom
Wright's cabin.

LaFrance and Bally Buck, bent over thoughtfully in
their chairs, followed him with upturned eyes.

"No clue there," he announced. "Few circulars and
some receipted bills."

The Judge took off his glasses and studied them as if
they might provide an answer to his wonderings. Buck
put his big hand on his knees and sighed from deep in
his thick chest.

"I got something, though," Cawinne added, and fished
in the pocket of his shirt.

To Judge LaFrance he handed the soiled slip of paper
he had found on the body of Miles Larion.

"Read it."

LaFrance hooked his spectacles back on his ears,
unfolded the note, and looking about first like a school
teacher making sure of attention, read laboriously:

"We see you at the Smoky Water. You be at Hangman's Tree tomorrow at 3, with map, or we talk.
Friends, maybe."

The Judge looked up when he had finished and demanded, "Where'd you get it?"

"Out of Miles Larion's pocket."

"Good Lord!" Buck ejaculated, and, snatching the
paper from LaFrance's palsied hand, peered at it, head
on one side like a hen sighting at a bug.

"Somebody plant it?" the judge suggested.

Cawinne shook his head slowly. "First day I hit town Larion was showing me his winnings in a game, and a piece of paper like that one fell out, and he stooped quick and put it back. The note was still on him yesterday, but the money was gone."

Buck's face was furrowed with perplexity. "You think Larion was mixed up in this!"

"There's the note."

"Was someone tryin' to blackmail him?"

"Someone was trying to blackmail somebody. Lock that note up, will you, Judge?" He arose. "I'm going to Breedtown."

The Judge regarded him strangely. "Who with?"

"Myself."

"There's such a thing as bein' brave and such a thing as bein' a fool," Buck was quick to object.

Cawinne's slow gaze rested on him.

"What'a'ya expect to find, anyway?"

The younger man shrugged, then added to the answer of that action, "Robideau, at least."

LaFrance tightened his lips, indenting the florid pucker of his face.

"Sometimes you have to run it blind," Cawinne explained. "We have two men dead, and maybe three. For clues, we have a pocket-piece and a note and a saddle with a hole in it, and the note seems to ring in one of the dead men and the hole in the saddle might remove a suspect."

"No sense in puttin' your foot in a bear trap, just the same," Judge LaFrance protested, motioning with his trumpet.

"It's probably not set, anyway," the other answered, and pulled his hat down tight on his brow. "Look, Bally," he asked. "Get two or three riders and scour the country

Wright might have been knocked off in, will you? We've got to find him. I'll look you up soon as I get back."

The rancher pursed his lips in regretful disgust. "All right," he conceded, "bein' as you ask it, but I'd just as leave go snipe-huntin'."

"Another thing. Better not let on we tipped off Wright to skip."

Buck nodded, and Cawinne turned on his heel and left the shop.

At Jerry McCabe's livery stable he spoke for a horse.

"I got one that's awful spooky," said the stable keeper, pocketing the knife with which he had been pointing a stick and raising himself reluctantly from the chair he had set outside the door. "He'll get you there and bring you back, though, if you don't let him jump out from under you."

"O. K. Bring him out."

The old hostler disappeared inside.

Cawinne waited, facing the door of the stable, until he heard a footstep behind him. He started to turn, and out of the corner of his eyes saw a grinning giant, grimy from the forge, and then a hand fell on his shoulder in a playful clap that would have staggered a steer.

"I been wantin' to see you, West," the giant said, "to see if I couldn't help. How-dee-doo."

"Hello, Horace. How's business?" Cawinne answered and extended his hand.

Horace Fladd answered, "So-so. But I don't want to see you about shoein' no horses or anything. I hear you've got mighty slick with a six-gun, and I'm pretty slick myself after all these years of practicin'."

His grin faded out as he confided with simple earnestness, "You know, West, how I always been interested in shootin'. Well, I can put a poker chip on my shootin' hand now and tip it off and draw my gun—and blowie! Sometimes I hit it 'fore it lands."

"That so?"

"Yeah," the smith continued, "and so I think maybe I can help you, West. Maybe you're goin' to need me. And when you do, me and my hog-leg will be johnny-on-the-spot."

"Maybe I will, Horace. Thanks," Cawinne conceded to his hopeful expectancy.

The stable keeper came out, leading a warp-nosed, staggy roan. "He's got plenty of bottom," he promised. "Hello there, Horace."

"Hello, Jerry."

Cawinne mounted.

"I heard," said McCabe in the whining curiosity of age, "that you're the deputy sheriff of Powder County now, but I don't see no badge."

"Weight bothers me, draggin' on my shoulder," Cawinne answered, unsmiling. "So long."

"Don't forget," cautioned Fladd, "I'm goin' to help you." His big, dirty face, upheld toward the rider, was eloquent with sincerity.

With his hand, Cawinne signaled acknowledgment.

At the touch of the spur, the horse crow-hopped for half a dozen steps and then settled into stride.

By early afternoon, horse and rider were entering the foothill country that serves as an insufficient preparation for the majestic bulk of the mountains, in whose creeping shadow Moon Dance lies by mid-afternoon.

It is in or at the base of these foothills that Powder County stockmen have their headquarters, ranging their cattle westward into the mountains and eastward for forty miles and more into the Freezeout, a lowland gashed by gullies and welted by barren hills. No trees relieve

the monotony of this vast eastern pasture. No stream
that a man cannot stride across waters its acres. During
most of the summer, the sun keeps it burned to a panther
tan, and in winter the bitter winds whip great drifts along
the bases of its low buttes. In its nakedness and in the
harsh extremes in which its coulees are cut and its hills
pitched, it appears to the watcher on the westward
heights like the relief maps seen in school rooms.

But Cawinne, turning to survey it, appeared to find
pleasure in the scene. The Freezeout, indeed, has its
gentler aspects. When the spring rains are ample, it shows
green to the farthest skyline, and even in the heat of
summer the small flats at the downward reaches of its
numberless coulees are rich with wild grasses. Cattle
multiply and grow fat on the forage native to its slopes.
In the winter, frequent chinooks—those friendly winds
that sweep over the hills from the west—shrink the snow
drifts like rain and expose the seasoned vegetation to
the questing range stock.

Midway between the Freezeout and the upland that
slopes to the foothills lies Moon Dance. Just as it was
thirty or forty years ago, the community remains a cow
town, for the Freezeout, like the mountains, presents
few opportunities to the plow. In the land-rush days, a
few tenderfeet staked out claims, but a resentful nature
turned on her heat and her cold and her drouth and her
wind, and the last reminders of their tenancy are rotting
fragments of the tar-paper shacks that fretful cattle
shouldered to the ground when their owners had gone.
North and south, the new mode has had its way. Cottonwood, the county seat, forty miles to the south, has
relinquished its reputation as the center of a vast cattle
industry and now is host to Norwegian and Danish
farmers who talk of summer-fallow and strip-farming.

Its harness and saddle shops have given way to filling stations and delicatessens. The curb-service sign has replaced the hitching post. And farther south, and eastward, too, the same transformation has taken place. But Moon Dance, by an accident of geography, remains as it was. Hitching racks line Main Street. Half-barrels of water stand before stores for the relief of thirsty animals. High-heeled boots, plain and fancy, colored shirts of flannel and silk, wide-brimmed, high-crowned hats and the other accoutrements of the ranchman, at work or on parade, get prominent display in the windows of the Moon Dance Mercantile Company. Men whose curvature of leg attests years in the saddle clump up and won the board walks, the eyes in their weather-beaten faces by habit screwed into a squint against sun and wind. The talk on the streets and in the saloons is of cattle and horses and grass and water, as it was in the beginning.

The frame stores and modest wooden homes of Moon Dance were softened and made cheerful now by the early afternoon sun, and Cawinne sat quiet and thoughtful for minutes while he contemplated the scene. When, finally, he turned his horse and touched spur to flank, he rode at a jog. Where the trail forked, to lead off to the north and Buck's Circle-I spread and south to the ranches below the Crazy Cree, he chose the latter route and clattered over the bridge that spans the river. Across it, he turned west again and two hours later came to the south fork of the Crazy Cree and urged his mount into its canyon. First, however, he unbuttoned his jacket and thrust it back at the sides and adjusted the revolvers at his hips.

For a mile the trail led high along the wall of the canyon, above the gorge through which the Crazy Cree funnels its flood before releasing it to the valley. It dipped then, as the canyon widened, and followed through a long mountain park, at the upper end of which a grove of pines struggled up a slope a hundred yards removed from the stream.

As Cawinne topped the ride, Breedtown came into sight below him, a scattering of mud-chinked cabins that had housed Indians and part-bloods and occasionally fugitives from justice for more years than the oldest inhabitant of Moon Dance could remember.

The rider pulled his steed to a stop and gazed down on the place speculatively. After a moment of deliberation, he rode boldly down into the settlement, toward a cabin that appeared somewhat more substantial than its fellows.

There was scant sign of life around the cluster of cabins. A mangy dog ran out of a ramshackle lean-to and worried noisily at his horse's heels. A button-eyed child scampered fearfully into a half-open door. A small flock of chickens, in the lee of an old corral, scratched disconsolately in the damp and fruitless earth.

Cawinne pulled up before the doorway of the cabin toward which he had been making.

"Hi!" he called.

The response was slow, as if the occupant were attempting to identify and make ready for his caller before receiving him, but the door finally opened and a man leaned against the casement and began to make a cigarette. There was the mark of sleep in his heavy-lidded eyes, and the look of sleep in his garb, for his shirt was open and his boots were off, but a sheepskin coat that hung unbuttoned and six-guns that showed at its opened sides bore evidence to some slight preparation for the reception of his guest.

"Howdy," said Cawinne.

The other grunted and blew out a thin jet of smoke while his veiled eyes scrutinized the rider. His face was swart and wide at the cheeks, like a Mongolian's, and there was something reptilian in his shielded, steady stare. His face sharpened somewhat at the jaw and came to a blunt point at his chin, which was strong and close-set under a short-cut mustache that had begun to show gray. A trifle too heavy, his body, nevertheless, held the promise of animal agility. In his attitude, too, there was a suggestion of the controlled tension of the waiting beast. In his bold way, he was a striking man, with that hint of the sinister about him that men beware and a certain type of woman finds fascinating.

"Long time I no see you, Robideau," his visitor volunteered, taking tobacco and papers from his pocket.

The breed's eyes raked him before they shifted to the ground. Again there was the slow pull on the cigarette, again the thin exhalation.

"So?" he asked.

He stood square in the doorway now, legs wide apart, hands loose at his sides.

"I'm West Cawinne, case you don't know."

Robideau gave the barest of nods, and there was nothing in his shielded eyes or in his attitude to indicate whether he had known.

Finally, he said, "Yeah?"

Cawinne lit his cigarette. "Just riding this way," he explained lightly.

"Yeah?" said the breed again. As the other kept silent, he yielded tardily to western courtesy and invited, "Light."

Cawinne got off his horse.

"Down south, they all said you were dead."

The breed grunted again, closed his coat against the chill that was freshening from up the canyon, and muttered, "Come."

Inside, Cawinne sat on a dirty tarpaulin that covered a rumpled bunk. Robideau leaned lightly against a splintered table.

In the center of the room a rusty stove, freshly fired, began to put forth a lively heat.

"Never expected to find Moon Dance so exciting," Cawinne remarked casually while his eyes studied the other's face. "Seldom Wright plugged, and all."

Robideau's gaze barely narrowed.

"Wright?" he repeated.

Cawinne inhaled deeply.

"Haven't found him yet, but from the looks of his saddle when they do they'll find him dead."

"Uh," answered Robideau, and rolled another cigarette, one-handed, with the manual dexterity characteristic of jewelers, dressmakers, and gunmen.

The heat was beating out fiercely from the stove, and sweat began to bead the face of the coated half-breed.

"When it happen?" he asked.

"Yesterday forenoon."

The hybrid pulled on his cigarette. "Myself, I wanted to get him," he admitted, and suddenly his eyes were slits and he asked in a voice as smooth as prayer, "Wouldn't be meaning anything, uh?"

Cawinne leaned forward until his holsters swung clear of the bunk.

"Just talking along," he said evenly. "Wright swore and be damned you killed Marty McLean."

Robideau brought his sleeve across his wet forehead, spat on the floor and through his close lips muttered, "Coyote!"

"I guess he would have laid the killing of Miles Larion on you, too," Cawinne observed, his eyes steady on the other man.

"We hear about that, already."

Cawinne stood up.

"Only clue I could find was this," he said, and from his pocket took the buckeye he had found on the Smoky Water. "Want to see it?" Carelessly, he tossed the buckeye to Robideau, but the latter, without so much as a twitch of his hands or a flutter of his eyes, let it fall to the floor.

"It is a trick very old, Cawinne," he said, "to get the drop on a man."

"You're off the trail, Robideau," answered the other, and with that he stooped, picked up the pocket-piece and dropped it into the breed's opened left hand.

Robideau looked up inquiringly. "It's a buckeye," Cawinne answered. "Someone's been carrying it, just for luck."

When the half-breed had handed back the token, Cawinne mopped his face with a handkerchief and complained, "You sure like it warm. I've either got to get out of here or shed this jacket."

A rivulet of sweat ran down Robideau's jaw and formed a pendulous drop on the blunt point of his chin.

"It's good for you, the heat," he said indifferently.

"It is not often that a man rides thirty miles just to tell me the news," he said, his eyes hooded and unwinking, as Cawinne made for the door.

"No," replied Cawinne easily. "This is something special in the way of favors."

Robideau eased away from the table.

"How do we say it?" he demanded softly.

"Friendly," answered Cawinne just as softly.

"Suit yourself," conceded the gunman. "To me, it is no difference."

They went outside and stood silent, watching the chickens scratch in the debris of the corral.

"Stay for supper," Robideau suggested. "We have a hen."

The crack of a revolver drowned the answer. In the corral fifty feet away a fowl began to flutter, its head shot away.

Robideau's eyes glinted as he sheathed the smoking weapon that his left hand held.

"Sorry you go," he said. "Maybe you won't come again. A man, he is hardly safe."

Cawinne's manner was casual. "I don't reckon a man would be wanting to come often, unless he had urgent business."

He went over and forked his horse, which had danced away snorting at the sound of the shot.

Robideau followed half way to the beast. "A thing, though," he promised. "Here, in Breedtown, we do not shoot in the back."

Restraining his impatient horse, Cawinne leaned over and looked the gunman in the eye. "And another thing," he said. "When I have business here, I'll be back."

CHAPTER SEVEN

IT WAS GROWING DARK as Cawinne rode away. The wind had stiffened and carried with it scattering particles of snow. A great bank of slate-gray clouds, sweeping in from the north, had overcast the sky.

Buttoning his jacket closer around his throat, he halted where the North Fork Trail swings off to the left and, after a moment of indecision during which he consulted his watch and scanned the bleak sky, turned off the route he had followed on entering the canyon. The other one led steeply down to a ford at a point half a mile from the beginning of the gorge.

The current was stout and the ford deep, and the roan lurched snorting among the boulders while the water boiled against shoulder and flank, but he was a sure-footed, sturdy beast and clambered safely to the farther shore.

The North Fork Trail climbs the divide that separates the two streams and dips down to the other branch, forming the west side of a triangle of which the confluence of the two rivers five miles below is the apex. It leads then across the fork and turns eastward, parallel to the stream, leading, farther down, along a rocky gorge like that through which the South Fork foams.

In that uncertain twilight in which familiar objects take strange forms, Cawinne reached the second ford. It was wider than the first and neither so swift nor so deep, and the roan, after a hesitant step or two, splashed confidently across.

Where the trail is easy on its approach to the gorge,

Cawinne set his mount to a good pace, while pine and aspen came out of the shadows ahead, loomed dark and distinct for an instant, and faded behind, like sentinels moving in a mist.

Two hundred yards above the gorge, Huger Gulch cuts into the canyon from the north. Before dropping to it and ascending the far slope to the gorge, the trial rises and narrows at the shoulder of the gulch, so that a man traveling there by day can look down fifty feet of ragged cliff to the stream almost directly below.

Cawinne halted when he reached that point, for from the black cavern of the gulch there came a deadened murmur like the voices of men. A cow bawled low and long.

The rider slipped from his saddle and pushed ahead of the horse to listen. Fearful of the night, the animal danced nervously on the narrow trail, its breath rattling in its nostrils.

Cawinne reached back until his hand rested on the beast's nose. "Steady, boy! Steady!" he soothed.

He leaned forward intently, listening, and at that instant the frightened horse lunged ahead. Its shoulder spun him half around, on the very edge of the drop. He clawed for a hold on the saddle, until the broader belly of the beast knocked him from the ledge. The bridle, clutched by the reins in his other hand, tore loose from the horse's head as he plunged downward. He hit once, against the broken rock, and then he was in the urgent stream.

It spun him about furiously, but he came after a while out of the crest of the current and began to swim with slow and uncertain strokes. When, finally, he reached shore, he was on the farther bank. He lay there in the shallow water, injured and spent, anchoring himself with a hold on the slender branch of a dwarfed bush that grew at the water's edge.

Cattle were breasting the current above him. They came lurching free from its powerful pull and clattered among the rocks almost within reach of his hand. A pair of horsemen, silhouetted vaguely against the night sky, followed them.

After they had reached shore, one of them asked, "What the hell's that back in the water? A bear?"

Cawinne tried to rise, but his right leg buckled under him. Fire bloomed from the bank and water jetted against his face. Automatically, his right hand moved to his empty and sodden holster. Light streaked from the shore again, and he released the bush and pushed back, ducking as the water deepened, and the hungry current renewed its grip on him. It swept him into the boiling gorge.

Seen by day, the water is green there and clear as glass, and the surface moves to the muscled current in patterned gnarls and running dimples and long, smooth swells laced with silver. Whirlpools spin at the margins of the tide, and perverted flows suck at the speeding drift. Out of the scoured stone that channels the flood, great boulders jut, and the waters fling up against them in a raging foam and fill the canyon with the deep, dismal voice of the river.

For part of the time Cawinne was above water; for more of it he was under, rolled and pulled down and wrenched, but by some lucky chance spared the direct crash against rock that would have splintered his bones. He fought for air, gulping choking lungfuls when he could get his head up, strangling when he could not, while he sped with the current in a chasm as black as a cave. He tried to slant over to the side, to beach himself in some tiny cove, but when he got there the worn stone ran rasping under his fingers like a file, and an eddy seized him and whirled him back to the racing current. He struck an upthrust rock and washed over it and shot down into the trough and came up slowly, stroking without force or direction against the drag of his boots and chaps. As the stream calmed and broadened and the thunder of the waters withdrew grumbling to the gorge, he came to a still, deep pool and floated, now inert, now fighting for air, until the stream carried him to the edge of a bank whitened with snow. He pulled himself up, inch by inch, and lay there in the shallow water, gasping, while his body rolled to and fro in the playful marginal eddies and the waves lapped about his neck.

He began to shiver, and abruptly he was sick, and he lifted himself to a sitting posture in the water and retched. He tried to rise, but his right leg still refused him, and he began crawling away from the river, dragging it.

Whipping down from the north, the wind struck at him furiously as he pulled himself from the low stream bed to the flat above it. It shelled him with a fine, keen sleet. The ground was covered already with a white half-inch of the spent shot of the storm.

He trembled violently, like one in a fantastic exaggeration of a chill. His shaking arms threatened to collapse with the weight of his chest. He halted a moment and took bearings, like a lost dog sniffing the wind, and when he went ahead he grunted, "North! North!"

His hands and face were freezing, and he stopped again and tried to rub the blood back into them. When he moved now it was in a different manner. Using his good foot and his hands, he gathered and stretched, gathered and stretched, like a measuring worm. "North!" he whispered through stiff lips to the heave of his body. "North!"

He looked up, squinting into the toothed wind, and there was a glow of light before him, like a Japanese lantern left burning after its season. He tried to call, but the wind tore the words from his mouth and left him breathless, and he began crawling again, straining at each slow forward pull like a man in a desperate last effort.

When he looked up again, the Japanese lantern had grown into a lighted prairie schooner. He cried out against the gale. A dog began to bark, and the door of the covered wagon released a yellow shaft into the swirling snow. In the doorway, a man held a rifle.

"Vat iss it, Shep?" he called as the dog came bounding. "A man dis time, or ghoosts again?"

The dog nosed the prostrate man, and the other came forward, rifle at ready.

"No ghost," muttered Cawinne.

Silent, the man scuttled back to the wagon and left his weapon and returned to lift Cawinne on his narrow shoulder and stagger, panting, to the door of the schooner with him. He laid his burden on the threshold, stepped over him and pulled him inside.

He began to mutter unintelligibly, oblivious of his visitor, like one absorbed with the variety of himself, while he dropped cow chips into a flat-topped, tin stove.

He turned from it to hunt in a litter of cans and boxes and presently abstracted a bottle half filled. He spilled a drink of it into Cawinne's willing mouth, popped the cork in the bottle resolutely, reconsidered, drew the cork again and took a stiff drink himself.

As he pulled at Cawinne's sodden clothes he said in Scandinavian singsong, "Not many herders could keep a bottle of visky."

He was an old man and shriveled, as if his juices had been forfeit to wind and sun. A wispy mustache fell across the corners of his mouth. In his eyes was the blank, blue stare of Norway.

But more remarkable than these features were the bruises that discolored and swelled his face. One side, from jaw to temple, was black and tight with congealed blood. On the other side, a wide, dark streamer ran from eye to cheek-bone and beyond. When he moved, it was stiffly, as if his muscles had been injured, too.

The top of the tin stove began to show red, and a glowing warmth spread throughout the canvas shelter.

The old man pointed to a narrow bunk that occupied the far end of the schooner and, when he had managed to get Cawinne into it, he felt carefully of the helpless leg.

"Broke?" asked Cawinne, but the other did not answer. He splashed horse liniment over a swelling knot of flesh above the knee and began to massage the leg awkwardly.

Outside, the dog barked.

"Ghoosts," the man half whispered, stopping his work to listen. The wind whined around the schooner, and the canvas shuddered to it like a loose shingle. His eyes moved to the battered Springfield he had set in a corner. He waited, intent and still, as if for a signal, while the flickering light of the lantern threw into darker relief the marks of his bruises, but the dog did not bark again, and he resumed his kneading.

Cawinne had ceased to shiver.

"Sven Svenson?" he said, studying the face that was bent over him.

There was no reply.

"Ever see anybody? On the back trail, maybe?"

"Ghoosts," the old man muttered, shaking his head.

He had finished his task. He pulled the soiled bedding about Cawinne, picked up the whisky bottle and handed it over while his regretful eye took stock of its contents.

"Drink," he directed.

When Cawinne gave back the flask, he upended it and let the remaining liquor drain into his throat. Slowly, as if the effort hurt him, he took a heavy coat from a hook then and pulled an ear-flapped old cap low over his head.

"I come back," he said. Before he left he took the old Springfield from the corner and shook his head ominously. The door flung open as he touched the latch, and a spray of snow came sifting in. "Come, Shep!" he called, and limped out.

After a while Cawinne sat up and inched stiffly on his buttocks to the side of the bunk, closer to the stove, and spread his hands toward its heat. The flickering lantern, suspended from a peg on the other side of the wagon, cast his shadow, huge and wavering, against the canvas behind him. He looked back at it, in the manner of a man entertained momentarily by an oddity, and as he looked a hole appeared in the pattern and a bullet battered through the edge of a tin plate in an open cupboard at the other end. Outside, a rifle cracked.

Cawinne fell back. As hurried steps sounded outside, he looked swiftly around, reached to the corner of the bunk and the side wall and seized a stout, knotted stick that the herder apparently used as a staff. He laid it in the bunk by his side, under his hand.

The herder thrust open the door. The eyes in his sorry, black-and-blue face swept the place expectantly and came to rest finally on Cawinne.

"Ghoosts," he said meaningfully, and went out again.

Cawinne rolled over the edge of the bunk and let himself to the floor. On the end of the staff he draped his soggy jacket and, lifting it, began moving it back and forth so that its shadow played on the wall above him.

Again there appeared the puncture in the canvas and there sounded the rifle shot.

Cawinne dropped his scarecrow and climbed back into the bunk with stiff haste.

Puffing, the herder reappeared.

"Ghoosts," he said again.

"It's all right. You got him."

The old man put his rifle in the corner and took off his wraps.

"Svenson," Cawinne said then with studied directness, "I'm hunting the man who killed Marty McLean, your old partner in the Early Day."

The herder turned on him a look wild and suspicious, but though his mouth moved, no words came from beneath the straggling mustache. He looked away, as if to escape the other's gaze, and his uneasy eye found Cawinne's wet clothes on the floor. He picked them up and spread them by the stove, which he fed again from the box of cow chips by its side. He laid his sheepskin on the floor and to it added a mackinaw and jacket that he dug from under the bunk.

"You stay vere you be," he directed. Blowing out the light, he tunneled into his bed.

"Ghoosts," he muttered once to himself, and in a few minutes was snoring.

CHAPTER EIGHT

Mrs. Buck spilled a tub of wash-water into the melting snow at the edge of the narrow board walk at the rear of the ranch house, stood erect with tub in one hand, while a cloud of vapor steamed from ground and tub and stout, wet forearms, and with the other shielded her narrowed eyes against the blinding glare of sun and snow.

A rider on a sad and shaggy mule was coming up the back pasture, and she eyed him with the honest, curious stare of one who has visitors infrequently.

The rider lifted his hand.

"Morning, Mrs. Buck," he said.

He rode at one side of the saddle, as a man does to favor an injury or to rest himself after long hours ahorse.

The tub dropped in the snow.

"Well, land sakes, West Cawinne!" Mrs. Buck ejaculated. "Get down. I been wanting to see you again, but I didn't expect you to come riding to the Circle-I on a sorry, miserable mule like that."

She extended her square and capable hand as Cawinne dismounted stiffly.

"Got rheumatism at your age?" she asked sharply.

"Naw, just bunged up a little," replied Cawinne, limping as she ushered him toward the kitchen.

"Here!" she ordered. "Tie that ornery beast to the post there. I never knew one of them that would stand, yet. Now come in and we'll have some coffee."

She belonged to that type of assured and friendly women, big-bosomed and heavy-limbed, who make successes of church suppers by insisting that the hesitant have second helpings.

"Sit down here in the kitchen, West," she directed as they entered. "No need to ask you if you're hungry. It sticks out all over you. You look real peaked, for a fact. I'll get you a bite to eat in a minute. First, though, maybe I better get your mule taken care of, and I want to send one of the men into town to tell Bally and the Judge you're here. I know Bally wasn't expecting you. He came home last night for the first time in three days, and he didn't say anything about you paying us a visit. The way they been herding with you, I bet they'd get plumb anxious not knowing where you were."

"Good idea," Cawinne replied, nodding.

She stepped outside the door and called stoutly toward the barn.

"Rusty! Oh, Rusty! Come here!"

The lean, sandy-complexioned hand came hobbling presently to the door.

"Yes, ma'am," he said, lifting his worn Stetson as he thrust his head in the entrance. He spoke through close lips, as tobacco-chewers do under the stress of polite society. One side of his jaw pouched like a hoarding gopher's from the indulgence of his habit.

"Rusty," Mrs. Buck said, "you know West Cawinne. Saddle up and go to Moon Dance and tell Bally and Judge LaFrance that West is visiting us. And, Rusty, on your way back to the barn take that sorry mule and give him a good feed of oats."

"Yes, ma'am," muttered Jones, and added solemnly, "Only he don't hardly look to be worth it."

When he had gone Mrs. Buck asked, "Coffee and ham and eggs and some wheat-cakes suit you, West? Or has your taste gone pernickety?"

"What do you think?"

"You cowboys are all alike, far as appetite goes," answered Mrs. Buck, busying herself with pot and skillet after she had thrust wood into the firebox of the big range. "Pretty much alike as far as looks go, too, except you'd be a little fancier than most if you hadn't slept in your clothes and didn't smell like a sheep."

"A man can't sleep in a herder's wagon and come out like a wild rose."

Mrs. Buck regarded him quizzically.

"If you stayed with the Mad Swede, as everyone calls Sven Svenson, you're lucky you're not holding a lily."

"I could smell 'em a time or two."

Mrs. Buck went "Humph," as she broke an egg in the skillet and then, with sudden concern, turned to him.

"You ain't shot in that bad leg?"

"Naw. I bruised it, that is all, but it's coming along all right. I'm going to turn in for a while after I eat, if you don't mind, and I'll take some liniment upstairs to burn it with."

"All right," she replied. "For a minute I thought you might be keeping something from me, and I declare it wouldn't surprise me to have you coming in, any time, all shot up."

Her eyes spoke inquietude.

"I tell you, West, I don't like this business of Bally and the Judge and the rest lining you up against that Breedtown bunch, 'specially Robideau. It ain't right, and I told Bally so."

"He'd have done it himself."

"Yes," Mrs. Buck responded, "of course he would, if he could. But I don't like it, just the same. Darn the men, anyway! Always fighting and getting crippled up and having to be nursed by women whose hearts stand still with the fear they won't make it, like mine's done more than once when Bally came in bloody and full of glory. And the waiting beforehand, wondering just how bad it's going to be, is enough to set a woman crazy."

Slightly breathless from the vehemence of her speech, Mrs. Buck pursed her lips and breathed audibly through her nose while she transferred food from stove to table.

"Anyhow," Cawinne volunteered lightly, "I'll not be putting any woman in the crazy house."

"No, and it's high time you did," Mrs. Buck retorted. She poked an admonitory finger at him.

"Hear me?"

"Yes'm," replied Cawinne meekly, starting on the third of four eggs. "I hear you."

A little wheezily, she let herself down in a chair.

"West," she said more gently, "I'm serious. It ain't right, not having Cawinnes on the Crazy Cree, and it ain't right for you to lone-wolf it. A good man don't have much trouble around here, locating a girl, what with school teachers and such."

"Yes'm."

Fresh force came into her voice. "And you," she said, pointing, "it's a lot of trouble you'd have, with the looks you got, if only you'd get rid of that kind of weighty, sad-professor expression! I declare, I hadn't noticed it before, but you and that miserable mule have sort of the same look."

Cawinne chuckled.

Like a hound on a trail, Mrs. Buck went ahead. "Now I'll tell you what, West! I've got the girl for you. I really have. She's a little mite and a sight too good for any puncher that ever lived. And besides that, she's too young to have thought about men, but she's ready to begin thinking."

"Yes'm. And what's the bride's name?"

"Her name's Tana Deck, and she works at the Motorists' Mecca. Runs it, you might say."

Cawinne was silent.

"What's more, Bally went to town in the buckboard this morning, and he said he might bring her out tonight. She comes sometimes."

Cawinne looked up from the cigarette he was making.

"I got to be going before then."

"You do not!" Mrs. Buck surveyed him with womanly shrewdness. "Tell you what! Your clothes need some fixin', if only to get rid of that sheep smell, and you just throw your things outside the door when you take your nap, and I'll see to them. I'm washing, anyway."

Cawinne regarded her doubtfully.

"Fact," she insisted. "What did you think I was doing with that tub when you rode up?"

"O. K.," conceded Cawinne. "And should I ask her tonight?"

Mrs. Buck muttered contemptuously in her throat.

When he arose, she said, "Go up to the north room, West, and don't forget about the clothes."

He went upstairs, undressed, donned one of Buck's flannel nightgowns, laid his clothes outside the door and, sitting on the edge of the white iron bed, massaged his leg with the liniment she had given him. The leg was blue and green from knee to thigh.

He awakened hours later as voices drifted up the stairway. Buck's hearty tones and the light and clearer ones of a girl came to his ears. He sat up, felt gingerly of his leg, and presently went to the door. His clothing, washed and ironed, was stacked in a neat pile just outside. He picked it up, laid it on the bed, and at the low washstand laved his face and hands, shaved with an old and lethal straight-edge razor, and combed his hair. He had difficulty in forcing his feet into his stiff, water-whitened boots, but presently he was dressed and started downstairs.

Buck and Tana Deck were seated in the heavy leather chairs that seemed to crowd even the big living room of the sprawling ranch house. Buck had worried an immense jack-pine stump into the fireplace, and it flashed light and shadow at them.

Buck took the cigar from his teeth and heaved his burly body up as Cawinne entered.

"Come in and light, West," he invited. "The Judge and me was just about to get us a posse formed when Rusty rode in and told us you were here. Old Jerry McCabe had come in 'bout fifteen minutes before to tell us the roan showed up without a rider. Here, do you two know each other? Tana, shake hands with West Cawinne. Tana Deck, West."

Cawinne took her hand and said, "We know each other."

The girl smiled.

Buck went on: "Martha tells me—but I don't believe it—that you come here with a game leg, riding a mule and smelling like a sheep. Now if that ain't some way to call on a friend!"

His eyes grew serious with inquiry as he noticed the other's limp.

"Doesn't amount to anything," Cawinne replied to his unspoken question.

The girl regarded him with an expression of grave wonderment. Against the high, dark back of the chair in the fitful light of the fire, her complexion seemed delicate as tinted china.

"How did you hurt yourself?" she inquired, asking

directly a question that Buck would have approached circuitously.

"Plain awkwardness. I let my horse bump me off the trail."

"Yes?" she encouraged with youthful curiosity, leaning forward in her chair. Her mouth was soft and had a look about it of delicate over-bloom, like a baby's, but the gentle thrust of her chin and the direct gaze of her blue eyes were the marks of a character who takes life on even terms. Even as kernels of corn, her teeth shone white when she smiled.

"Tell us about it," she urged.

In the light of this feminine assault, Buck grunted, "Might as well, West."

"I was on the ground, walking, and the horse spooked and crowded me off."

"Where?"

"On the North Fork. At Huger Gulch."

Buck, about to take the cigar from his mouth, looked up quickly, squinting.

He laid the cigar on the table then, turned to Tana, and remarked jocularly:

"Next thing, he'll be tellin' us he shot the gorge."

As his eyes moved back to the silent Cawinne, a sudden, amazed comprehension came into them. His mouth moved incredulously to one side, making a dent in his tanned cheek.

"And you got to the Mad Swede's!" he ejaculated softly, more to himself than to them.

"I never did see a fellow so afraid of ghosts," Cawinne disgressed quickly. "Every time the dog barked, he thought it was a spook. Maybe he had reason to be scared," he added, "for he looked like someone had beat him up. Bruises all over his face."

"He's always gettin' drunk, and drunks are always gettin' hurt," explained Buck indifferently.

"I know that old man," Tana volunteered. "When he comes to town he leaves half his money at the restaurant, so he won't spend it all on whisky. Then, when he runs out, he comes and begs it back, to buy more whisky with.

"And besides," she added with mock gravity, "I'm a partner in his gold mine."

"We know about that," Buck said, looking at her with a fatherly affection. "I don't know which you ought to brag on most," he went on in mock seriousness, "knowin' a sheep herder or havin' a share in a sheep herder's gold mine. You know, West, not many people have had the privilege of meetin' Sven. He just come here lately."

Mrs. Buck came hot and flushed to the open doorway to announce, "Supper's ready."

She moved over to the girl and put a stout arm about her slim shoulders.

"I declare, Honey," she said as they started into the dining room, "it's good to see you! You ought to come out real often. Way it is, we always have to send you a special invitation."

The girl looked up and smiled into the older woman's eyes. "You know how it is."

Mrs. Buck nodded understandingly and patted her on the arm. "I expect that restaurant could get along sometimes without you just the same."

As the others sat down, she bustled back into the kitchen, to emerge presently with a great roast of beef circled by browned potatoes and onions. On other trips she brought a bowl mounded with mashed rutabagas, a quart of gravy in a boat, and baking-powder biscuits which she kept augmenting from an apparently inexhaustible oven.

Mrs. Buck was the kind of hostess who feels less than satisfied unless her guests reach the full stage of surfeit. Seconded by Buck, who never suffered from a lack of appetite, she kept urging food on her two visitors.

"Until I got married," Buck observed as his wife whisked away the plate and a surviving biscuit to return with a hot supply, "I used to wonder what happens to the last biscuit on the plate. I know now, though. They give it to you the next day, and you better like it, too, by Joe!"

"Until I got to coming out here," Tana laughed, "I never could understand how customers could expect so much of a restaurant. And just think! Mrs. Buck's already fed the crew."

" 'Tisn't anything," insisted Mrs. Buck. "Tana, butter another biscuit while they're hot."

She added, "Tana here can cook every bit as good as I can, West, and she's a sight better at pastries."

"She has to be good then."

Buck, unconscious of any point in his wife's artless persuasion, broke in: "Snow was mighty hard on stock, West, but it'll make a lot of grass."

"I want that recipe for chocolate cake with the date filling," Mrs. Buck persisted. "You ought to taste that, West."

Cawinne mumbled, "I'd like to."

In the lamplight, the glow of copper shown in the soft hair that framed Tana Deck's fresh, school-girl face.

"Yes, sir," Buck continued, "we'll have pasture, you bet."

For dessert, Mrs. Buck brought in dried-apple pie and coffee hot and stout.

When they had finished, Buck pushed back from the table and nipped the end from a cigar while Cawinne rolled a cigarette.

"I hope," said the rancher, sighing heavily with satisfaction, "that the meal will buck you up some, West. You look like you needed something against your ribs. Let's go set in more comfortable chairs."

Against Mrs. Buck's protest, Tana went with her to help with the dishes, while the two men returned to the living room.

"We couldn't find hide nor hair of Seldom Wright," Buck announced after they were seated. "We combed the country good, too, south and west of his place. Don't look like he could of gone far."

"How long do you say it was from the time you warned him until the necktie party showed up?"

"Three hours, anyhow."

"He could go quite a ways in that time if he set himself to do it."

"Yeah," admitted Buck, "though you got to take off the time it took his horse to get back to the ranch."

Presently the rancher observed, "I guess maybe you're right in thinkin' that Wright wouldn't hardly of been waitin' for me to warn him if he had killed Larion."

When the other did not respond, he asked, "How about you? Got anything to report, or want to wait until the Judge can hear, too?"

"Might as well wait," replied Cawinne. "What little there is will keep."

Buck nodded. "Suits me. I'd like to turn my mind out for a spell anyhow. It's gettin' ganted up, bein' worked so hard."

"I would have bet," he remarked quizzically after an

interval of silence, "that even an oak barrel wouldn't have made it through the North Fork Gorge."

"Matter of luck."

"Matter of bein' bound with bull hide," the rancher amended.

They talked, then, of former times and of opportunities in the cattle business and of horses, good and bad. After a while, the women joined them, and later Buck yawned and stretched.

"Time for the hay, for me anyhow."

"For me, too," said Tana. "Remember, you're going to get me back to town early."

"Yeah," answered Buck. "West, I'll take the buckboard to Moon Dance in the morning, and you and Tana can go in it, providin' you're ready to leave. If you ain't, you can stick around here, and welcome, 'til the cows come home."

"I better go," the other replied. "Would you have one of the boys take the mule back to Svenson?"

"Rusty'll take him."

"I'll see you get up in time," promised Mrs. Buck. "You take this lamp, Bally, and show 'em to their rooms. I'll be up, soon as I blow out the kitchen light."

CHAPTER NINE

O N THE FRONT of Judge LaFrance's shop hung a
    scrawled sign: "Gone to Cottonwood. Back to-
night."

Bally Buck pushed his big hat to the back of his head
and dug his scalp with a horny forefinger.

"Judge was sayin' something yesterday about goin' to
the county seat," he told Cawinne. "Matter of renewin'
his bond, or something."

Cawinne pondered.

"Doesn't make much difference, anyhow," he concluded after a minute. "Thing we've got to do is find
Seldom Wright."

"Hell, West," Buck protested, "me and some others
galloped over the hills all day, lookin' for sign."

"Might be you missed him, just the same."

"Sure," assented Buck. "And forty parties huntin'
forty days could miss him in them breaks, too."

A slow smile relieved the habitual severity of the
other's expression, and a glint of friendly amusement
showed in his eyes as he looked into Buck's face. Seen
thus, by contrast with his usual mien, he seemed pos-
sessed of an uncommonly capricious and perceptive
humor.

"We have to find him, no matter what."

Buck sighed.

"O. K.," he said resignedly. "If I'd known, though,
we'd of trailed some horses in with the buckboard.
Way it is, we'll have to get a couple from the livery

stable, and I suppose you're just goin' ahead without re-placin' the hardware you lost on the North Fork?" His eyes were on the empty holsters at Cawinne's thighs.

"We'll do that first," Cawinne suggested, and they walked down the street and across it to the Powder County Hardware Store, where George I. Smith, gaunt and bony as an old horse, leaned listlessly against the counter. He grunted as they greeted him.

Buck jibed: "Been so long since George had a cus-tomer, he don't properly know how to behave, West."

"That depends," retorted Smith, unsmiling, and looked at Cawinne expectantly.

"Got a pair of Colt's forty-fives, George? Single action, seven and a half inch?"

"Old-fashioned, uh?" Smith commented, and turned back to a showcase full of arms that flanked the passage-way behind the counter.

"These do?" he asked, putting two revolvers out. "For business, they're as good as any, though I got some a little fancier for show-off."

Cawinne picked up one of the weapons, hefted it, spun the cylinders experimentally and tried the hammer with his thumb. In his hands, the lethal piece of blue steel seemed to come to life. He slid it into the holster at his side and brought it out and up in a motion so swift and sure that the lean, gray face of the storekeeper fell open at the mouth.

"Damn me, West," he said, "that thing acts like it belongs at the end of your arm!"

"It's a mate for those I lost. I'll take both of them."

"I can make it a little off, that way," replied Smith. "Say we make it sixty dollars even, West?"

"Suits," agreed Cawinne, and paid him.

"How about a belt and holsters?" asked Smith, eyeing

curiously the stiff and faded leather about Cawinne's middle.

"Box of cartridges will be all. This outfit will be all right as soon as it's worked over with some oil. I'm used to it."

He loaded his two revolvers, slipped new cartridges into the loops of the belt, turned to Buck, and said, "Let's go."

They went on across the street and started up it, but a small figure lurked in the entrance of the Family Liquor Store, and Cawinne halted abruptly and turned on his heel.

"How are you, John?" he asked.

The trial of utterance contorted the other's dark face. When, finally he spoke, the words came out in a sudden burble of sound, like air through water.

"Long time I no see you," he blurted.

"And you don't know me now."

John Fee, called Fee Simple, looked at Cawinne doubtfully.

"You don't remember the old days on the Bar-G-Bar?"

A glimmer lighted the blank and tragic face of Fee. "West Cawinne," he said. "I no forget." Suddenly he began to cackle throatily in extravagant delight, at his perception in identifying Cawinne or pleasure at seeing him.

"Where you staying, John?"

Fee's lips moved soundlessly for a minute, then threw out, "South Fork, Crazy Cree."

"Same place Robideau," Buck declared significantly.

Fee looked away quickly. "Same place," he mumbled.

Cawinne asked, "You working?"

The half-breed shook his head. A wide and foolish grin wrinkled his face. He put his hand to his temple and made a winding motion.

"No work," he said. "No sense. You know, man sit on my head." He began to cackle again, enormously amused at the trick life had played on him.

There was no amusement in Cawinne's answering smile. "I'll have work for you soon, John, same as before," he promised. "I'm going to put some cattle on the old place."

"Mebbe so," the breed answered doubtfully.

When they left, Buck said, "I don't know as I ever did get the straight of it. Did a man really sit on his head?"

"That's it," responded Cawinne. "You remember old Lem Fee, the squaw man, who used to work for my father? He and the squaw took little John along to a dance one night and laid him out on a bench while they did a few turns. Johnny was just a baby then. When they came back to him, there was a drunk sitting on him."

"Well," Buck mused, "anyhow Jim Northcutt didn't do a bad job namin' him Fee Simple. It's like that damn lawyer to think up sump'n like that."

"I wouldn't mess around too much with that half-breed," he advised a little later as they walked on toward McCabe's livery stable. "Robideau's got him under his thumb. You can see that."

At the stable they asked McCabe for two horses. The old man regarded Cawinne in doubtful conjecture.

"Guess you won't be wantin' that roan again."

"Yeah, let me have him. Few times more and maybe he'll get tough enough so I don't have to turn him loose and go on foot when I'm in a hurry."

The hostler muttered in his corded throat, turned back into the barn and returned in a few minutes with the mounts.

"Guess you know," he said to Cawinne, "that you owe me for a bridle?"

The other nodded. "This old jug-head shied out from under it."

The two men mounted and turned their horses west and north when they had cleared the town.

"Bally," Cawinne asked after they had settled to a gait that ate up the miles without winding their animals, "have you been all along the old Indian trail at the foot of the mountains?"

"Yeah. Most of it. Long time ago, though. The Pondera Trail runs from north of the Smoky Water, no tellin' how far, down along the shoulder of the range, fords the North Fork of the Crazy Cree and turns up the South Fork. It goes clear on over the divide into Pondera County. Them slope Injuns made it, comin' to the plains to hunt buffalo. It's rough goin' all along, and no one travels it any more. When the Injuns picked it, I guess they was tryin' to keep clear of their enemies on this side."

"Rustlers are using it to drive cattle from the Crazy Cree range."

"You guessin'?"

"No," answered Cawinne, and went ahead to tell him in detail of the incident at Huger Gulch.

Buck's forehead wrinkled. "We should of thought about that. It's a pretty layout for 'em. Don't take 'em long, by hard drivin', to haze the stock off the back ranges of us fellows and get it in the canyon. And from Breedtown, if that's where they're from, it's not too much of a drive to Braden and the railroad, though it's rough as all get-out."

"They wouldn't run much chance of coming on to anyone, would they?"

"Be an accident," Buck answered, " 'specially if they're trailin' 'em at night."

He was silent for a time, then added: "We'd of caught up with 'em, I guess, but about the time we began to miss the stock, why, Marty McLean got killed and pulled us off the trail. When there's no cattle on the back ranges, they must go ahead and drive stuff out of the Freezeout."

"Generally, though," Cawinne amended, "there's some cattle in the hill country, and, besides, if the pickings are good enough part of the year, they don't have to worry about the rest."

They rode along wordless, then, while their saddles creaked accompaniment to their thoughts.

The sun had bored through an early-morning pall of clouds and beat industriously at a blanket of snow already worn thin and full of holes.

"Outside of seeing you still got your scalp," Buck remarked after a while, "I don't know about your pow-wow with Robideau. Learn anything?"

"Might as well have been talking to a turtle. If I found out anything, I won't know until I see how it adds up."

Buck grunted. "Nothin' like keepin' two and two to yourself 'til you find out if it makes four. Me, I think a man who'd steal a cow would gun a cowman."

Cawinne didn't reply.

"Have any trouble?"

"Not a bit. The only shooting done was just kind of a lesson to open the eyes of the law. Robideau popped off a chicken's head, pretty as you please, shooting left-handed, too."

"Left-handed, huh?" responded Buck, studying the other's face. "I guess he was just tryin' to show you he could beat you with one hand tied behind him. Question is: can you do as good, and does he know it?"

They had reached the southeast corner of Seldom Wright's Box-O.

Cawinne asked, "Did you look over this country around here yesterday?"

"Three of us," answered Buck. "John Bruce, Mary's Little Lamb and me."

"What say we ride on west, then, toward the Pondera Trail? I have a notion Seldom Wright might have been making for it, as a quick and safe way out, when someone plugged him. Afterwards, I'd like to turn south and have a look at the old home place. Haven't seen it since I got back, what with all this puzzle-working you roped me into."

Though they spread out and scanned the ground beneath them and the landscape roundabout, an hour's careful riding found them still without any indication as to the whereabouts of Wright's body, and Cawinne, who had been riding north of his companion, quartered to the south and joined the rancher. They turned their horses, then, almost due south and presently came to the long, low ranch house that had been headquarters for the Bar-G-Bar when the name of John Cawinne was one to reckon with.

The horsemen pulled up, silent, before the pole gate that gave entrance to the grounds, and later, still silent, they filed on through after Buck had swung the barrier open.

An air of desertion, of hopeful, sturdy effort come to

end, hung heavy over the place where John Cawinne had wrought. The vacant barn and empty barnyard, the bunk-house closed and silent, the soundless home and the spring-house from which a rivulet of water pursued its faithful and unheeded course, all spoke in quiet eloquence of times and people that had gone. A breeze, busy in the grove at the side of the house, set the naked trees to talking, and their murmur was like the echoes of personalities that once had lived and moved and charged with life the lifeless scene.

Cawinne dismounted at the barn and for a moment let his hand rest upon the wooden latch that John Cawinne's hand had worn smooth. Seeing him, Buck looked away, and as the younger man came back to his horse the older one flicked the ends of his reins uneasily against the horn of his saddle and remarked, "Place has been kept up pretty well, while you were gone."

"Yes," said Cawinne, and without entering either barn or house mounted his horse, and led the way back through the gate.

Once outside, he paused, absent-eyed, and rolled a cigarette. But when he had it going he said with a return of purpose:

"No use going any farther west, except to check up on my hunch that the cattle rustlers have been using the old trail, and we can do that some other time. I figure Seldom couldn't have got any farther south than this from the Box-O in the time he had."

"Uh-huh," Buck agreed.

"There's a patch of rough country four or five miles northeast of here. We just skirted it on the north on the way out. Did you fellows cover it yesterday, looking for Wright?"

"Some of that is part of Seldom's spread and some of

it is Often Wright's. The two places come together there," Buck answered, shaking his head. "We just gave it a kind of a lick and a promise."

"But you figure you have the rest of the country around Wright's place pretty well scouted?" Cawinne persisted.

"Oh, hell, West! You know how it is. We might have missed him a hundred times over. Same time, if you're lookin' for virgin territory, that section you speak of is pretty close to it."

"Let's go there, then," suggested Cawinne, leading the way.

Unprotesting, Buck began eating on a cigar.

They rode without speaking for more than an hour, until they reached the rough gullies that run back to the foothills from a point northeast of the Bar-G-Bar.

"Now look," said Cawinne. "If Wright hit out for the Pondera Trail, figuring his best chance for safety from the mob was to follow it on over the divide and catch a train, it stands to reason he would have set his horse to the south and west. If he did, he was bound to come into this section, provided he got this far. So let's fan out a little and push on almost straight for his ranch house."

"All right," Buck assented. "But we ain't going to have much time to look, West. Be dark in an hour."

"We have the hour, anyhow."

The chill, early-spring dusk was closing in about them, already giving to the horizons an aspect of dark mistiness.

"Holler if you find anything," said Buck, reining his horse to the left.

"Same to you. We ought to be able to cover a mile, maybe, before it gets too dark to see."

Eyes on the ground then, the two riders went their

separate ways, following ridges when they could, more often plunging down into steep gullies and straining up their farther sides.

Forty-five minutes later, Buck called to Cawinne across a coulee. "Might as well rack up, West. A man couldn't see a black cat in a pail of milk now." His figure was a silhouette against the fading western sky.

"O. K. Come on over and we'll go."

Horse and rider melted into the earth as they descended from the sky-line down toward a thicket that lay like a black strip in the bottom of the gulley.

It was from that thicket that Buck's yell sounded, hoarse and urgent.

He had dismounted from his horse when Cawinne's animal scrambled down, and stood bent over, staring.

"Lord Almighty!" he half whispered. "This is Injun's work!"

On the dark ground at the edge of a rotting drift there lay the butchered darker body of a man. It had been mutilated, Indian fashion, and ended at its upper extremity in a raw and bloody stump of neck.

"It's Seldom," Buck said awfully, "and someone's axed his head off."

CHAPTER TEN

SATURDAY NIGHT in Moon Dance arrives as the goal of
the week. It is release from discipline and reward for
drudgery and rebellion at routine. It is company in place
of loneliness. From sequestered ranch and solitary cabin,
off hayrack and mower and wagon, away from cook
stove and wash-tub come rancher and ranch-hand, white
man and breed, housewife and hired girl, to dissipate in a
night of drinking or dancing or conversation or love-
making, the impulses haltered since Monday. Beginning
at about three o'clock in the afternoon, a fresh life
animates Main Street. The stores hum with a cheerful
patronage. Little knots of men gather at corners to talk
of livestock and weather and politics. A perfumed vapor
fogs the barber shops, a compound of talc and tonic and
steaming leakage from the public baths. Whiskered and
untidy punchers line the walls, waiting their turns at
renovation. The bars are crowded with men eager to
ornament the plodding week with an evening of con-
viviality. The card tables in the rear are well patronized.
More than on any other day, the mood of the players is
one of careless sport. The post-office is a general exchange
of information, gossip, and greetings, and the place of
contact for beaux and belles without engagement.

The temper of festival catches up the townsmen. The
older and staider indulge their outlaw impulses by evening walks down town, where they pause at counters
and in doorways idly to pass the time of day. The
younger ones don their best, for Saturday, out of long
custom, is date-night, and later there will be a public
dance at which will be clerks and cowpokes, school girls

and hired girls and hoodlums and men of good manner, together with a considerable company of sprightly matrons and sportive oldsters who, departing early, will miss much of the wild spirit, the drinking and the arguing and the fighting, with which Moon Dance is wont to conclude the week.

The sounds of carnival were already in the air as Cawinne and Judge LaFrance sat talking in the latter's shop. The laughing voices of men and women, the clump of boots and the tap of slippers on the boardwalk, the occasional whoop of hilarity, the whining notes of fiddle and guitar from adjacent Woodmen's Hall, where the orchestra was tuning up, and the ring of horses' hoofs on the street made a muffled medley in the back room of the place.

"Anything at all you can put your finger on, West?" the Judge asked, peering earnestly into the other's lean face.

Cawinne shook his head. "It's all speculation, Judge," he said into the out-thrust horn.

"What about this butcherin' business?"

The younger man shrugged and made a gesture with his hands.

"Nothin' like that in these parts since the days of Crazy Horse and Sittin' Bull sixty year and more ago," the Judge continued inquiringly.

"I know," was the answer, "but it doesn't prove anything."

"Maybe so," replied the old man. "Still, people make up their minds quick, and then they want action. What if some of the boys took it into their heads to lead a bunch up the Crazy Cree on their own hook?"

"It would roil the water. But they aren't ready for that—yet."

"Let one more thing happen that points in Robideau's direction, and you're liable to find 'em ready and willin'."

"There's feeling," Cawinne admitted, "but no one's very anxious to go out there on the point. They all want to be back toward the drag."

Judge LaFrance sighed. "Nothin' seems to add up. I thought I had something." He picked up a newspaper from his bench. "Right here is an article from a place called Broken Rock, Kentucky, tellin' how four men was shot from ambush. One of our dead men was shot from ambush, and we had a Kentucky man, so I started foolin' around with two and two—"

"And came out on craps when Bally and I found Seldom dead."

The old Judge grinned ironically, his head bobbing on his palsied neck.

After a moment of thought he raised his pouched eyes to Cawinne's and ventured half inquiringly, "Here we are, knowin' pretty sure who's guilty, and with nothing to put our hand on. It couldn't be anyone but Robideau, West, or maybe one of 'em who runs with him, acting on his orders. It all points that way. Robideau potted old Marty to get hold of the gold-mine map, then he shot down Larion, and to cap it all off he killed Seldom."

"He had reason to shoot Marty," responded the other, "and reason to shoot Seldom, too, what with Seldom so anxious to organize a party against him, but why would he shoot Miles Larion?"

The Judge shrugged. "We don't know that yet, unless it was for the money he had on him."

"Marty was shot from behind, but Larion got his from in front."

"That might not mean a thing, West. Might be good

reasons that we don't know. Might be that whoever killed Larion had the drop on him, and Larion was just so fast he got a shot in anyhow."

"Yes," agreed the younger man. He took off his hat and ran his fingers through his dark hair and added, "Suspicions alone are no good, Judge. It's bad business, according to my rules, to sound off unless you've got your man in the bag."

"I always heard you played your own hand, and that suits me all right. But, Son, play it the minute you fill." He added, "I'd hate to see 'em talkin' against you."

"Most cases work out, if you just give them a little time. Takes patience in a case like this. Sometimes you go slower by pushing on the ribbons."

"I ain't pushin' on mine," the Judge declared, "but some of the rest ain't so strong on holdin' their horses. Even Bally gets some impatient once in a while."

"Where is he, anyway?"

"Prob'ly in a game. Maybe at the Family Liquor Store but more likely at Adlam's, where the stakes run higher."

Cawinne arose. "Might be back later," he announced.

"I'll be around until ten-thirty or so. But wait, West! Did you ever get them nuggets that Sven Svenson left with Tana, and are you havin' them assayed?"

"I'll attend to that. Haven't yet, though. There's lots of time, and I don't see that an assay is going to help much with these killings. So long, Judge."

Cawinne found Adlam's Saloon close and hot with the crowd at the bar and clamorous with rowdy voices, clanking spurs, ringing glass and restless feet. The room billowed with smoke and smelled of horses and stale cigars and spilled liquors.

He pushed through the jam to the rear of the place,

where clinking chips added their small voices to the up-roar. The chairs at the half-dozen tables were occupied. Behind some of them, out of the circles of light cast by lamps hung low over the green cloth, prospective players and interested spectators stood silent and absorbed.

At one of the tables, facing Cawinne, Buck sat, his hat pulled low on one side of his forehead. A dead cigar protruded from the side of his mouth. At Buck's right, Stud Manker examined his cards in hands close held. Pale as a turnip, Whitey Salter, in the chair next to Manker's, set five blues in the pot. The fourth man, nearest to Ca-winne, rapped for a pass, and the fifth, at Buck's left, tossed in his hand.

Buck rolled a fresh cigar around in his mouth, ma-neuvered it to base at one side, grinned genially around the table, and from an impressive stack of chips counted off ten. As he pushed them toward the center of the table, his alert eye spied Cawinne and a shadow of negation fled across his face.

Cawinne shook his head and came on toward the table.

Still smiling his mirthless half-smile, Manker bumped the raise by five. Salter stood it grumbling.

"Way I figure," said Buck easily, fingering his chips while he stole a glance at Cawinne, "a good hand's worth good money." He put out two stacks of blue chips. "I'll go for all you've got."

Manker studied the rancher's bold, unrevealing face.

"No wagons over me today, Mister," he said softly, and slid in his stack.

Salter was mumbling to himself while he closed and opened his hand, watching the cards intently as he un-covered them one by one. He looked in squinting inquiry at Manker, then at Buck, and finally thrust his chips in. It was showdown.

Buck put out a full house, Manker a heart flush and Salter kings and sixes.

"Sorry, boys," said Buck blandly, and with his left hand reached out to gather in the pot.

"Horseshoes," Manker stated in a voice that was half insult.

Salter's chair shuddered against the floor as he kicked himself back.

"Say!" he blurted.

Manker's gaze slid around, following the other's stare, and discovered Cawinne.

"Our playmate," he said through his smiling lips. "Pretty boy." Above the spread of his mouth, his eyes glistered with calculating malice.

"Evening," said Cawinne evenly.

"Howdy, West," greeted Buck. "Game's over, I guess, boys. I'll cash."

Manker's glance swung from Cawinne to Buck to Cawinne. Not quite on a line between them, he was still in a bad position, being the apex of a low triangle of which they were the base points. Opposite him, the two uninvolved players hastily had pushed back from the table.

His eyes dropped to the cloth where a lone white chip lay overlooked, and he picked it up, flipped it in the air, and caught it expertly in his cupped palm.

"Some day," he said with outward casualness, "maybe you and your friend'll both be sittin' in a game with us."

Pale eyes a-shimmer, Salter looked at him, as if lost for leadership, and growled in his throat.

"Maybe we will," agreed Buck indifferently. "See you outside, West," he added as if there were no point to the suggestion, and as the other turned back toward the front of the saloon he tarried to cash his stack, while his steady eye kept watch on the Breedtown gamblers.

When he reached the street, he blew noisily through his pursed lips.

"It ain't over yet, maybe," he told Cawinne, " 'less you hunt a hole tonight."

The latter shrugged.

"I tried to shoo you out of the place to begin with, because you keep tellin' me you don't want a showdown yet."

"Thanks."

"Have it your own way," Buck rejoined doubtfully, "but I don't see much sense in bein' too salty to take a run-out unless you're ready for the fireworks."

"They aren't in a spot to start anything, since Seldom was found with his head off."

"They're on thin ice, all right, but don't give 'em credit for too much savvy, even if Manker is cagey. If they was real smart, they'd lie low, like Robideau seems to be doin', instead of hangin' around town."

"How come you were making medicine with the enemy?"

"Lookin' for investment opportunities, and maybe for a little accidental information. Boy, you'd of thought they both was loco if you could of seem 'em bettin' threes into my flushes."

He steered the younger man out into the street. "Let's go over to the Mecca," he suggested. "Martha's waitin' for me there."

Mrs. Buck greeted them with one of those blunt declarations of policy characteristic of uneasy dictators and happy wives.

"You boys are going to take Tana and me to the dance."

In a black crepe dress with white jabot that modified but could not altogether disguise her heaviness of bust and limb, she made the slender Tana seem almost fragile and at the same time accentuated in her a bright and eager vitality.

The girl demurred.

"Please," asked Cawinne.

Buck regarded him thoughtfully. "Maybe, another time—" he started.

"Why, of course we're going," said Mrs. Buck, so assured that all objections collapsed.

With an air of elegance that even the tea towel about his middle could not diminish, Tandy Deck appeared from the rear of the restaurant.

"We might go to the dance, Daddy," the girl said.

"That is good," Deck answered in his mellow voice. He spread his hands toward the vacant counter and tables. "There is nothing to do here. You run along."

He turned to the others. "My lamb doesn't have enough fun," he explained, and his eyes were eloquent with a regretful devotion that saved him from absurdity. "I am glad she is going in such company."

He tilted his head for Tana's quick kiss. "Don't be too late getting in, Dear," he said.

The music blared out at them, wailing and insistent, while they were still half a block from Woodmen's Hall. In the hallway at the top of the steps, they edged through a crowd of youths and men whom timidity or awkwardness or simple disinclination kept off the dance floor. As the evening wore on, they would smoke endlessly and tell rude stories and bellow with laughter, or gaze with hungry eyes through the door to the swinging couples on the floor. Some of them, emboldened by drink, later on would filter into the company inside. A few of them probably would fight.

In the press of fermenting masculinity, Manker and Salter stood, conspicuous even among numbers, the one for his rowdy assurance, the other for the milkiness of his clouded face and the flickering glimmer of his eyes. A silence fell on them as Buck, Cawinne and the two women edged through the doorway.

Inside, on a make-shift platform at the west end of the hall, the abetters of Moon Dance's Saturday-night carnival belabored string and mouthpiece and key. Art Smithers, the convivial jeweler who doubled on the banjo, with his nimble wrist was fanning out a noisy meter. Lame Emory Wallace sawed on his complaining fiddle, with his broken foot beating out the time. A pale school boy punished snare drum and bass. Mrs. Salton, best musician in the group, had surrendered to the standards of the majority and banged forth chords to match the vigor of the dancers. Mike Looney's straining cheeks, through union with the trumpet, screamed a frenzied tune.

Into the wheeling dancers, Cawinne and Tana stepped. He danced only fairly, in the manner of a man whose life has been spent with men, but she looked up at him and smiled and said, "I guess it's so much walking on eggs that has taught you to dance."

Tardily, like one unaccustomed to the little graces, he answered, "Thanks," and, after an uncertain moment, "Are you really just floating?"

She drew away from him a little and looked up with a teasing smile.

"Mrs. Buck didn't know whether you'd agree to come, Professor."

Looking down into her animated, friendly face, he lost some of his gravity. A degree of youthfulness, light and engaging, came to his expression and his manner. With a sort of timid candor she confessed, "I wondered whether you could be like this," as they swung around the hall and he revealed that in the light, meaningful exchanges between man and girl even the untrained personality may possess some talent. She came forward in the clasp of his arm, and her head touched lightly against the strong ridge of his jaw.

Under the influence of a few drinks, Chuck Wilcoxsen always became the self-appointed aid of acquaintance, and he bellowed now, above the whine and beat and wail of the orchestra, "Everybody circle!"

"I check out here," announced Cawinne, bringing his arm from around the girl.

"No!" she insisted, smiling, "Please!" Her small hand tightened on his, and she brought him into the forming circle.

For the next twenty minutes, as the clamorous crowd demanded encore after encore, Cawinne danced with heavy, robust women and wispy, string-halted ones. He danced with women who talked incessantly and with others whose minds were monopolized with the effort of step and tempo. He moved about with friendly women and distant ones. He swung pretty women and plain ones, tall ones and short ones, bold ones and shy ones. While his eyes sought out Tana, in the exchanges of partners he seemed forever winding up against the bosom of some waiting female two or three removes from the object of his gaze. When, finally, the breathless dancers gave respite to the breathless orchestra, Buck sought him out.

"After the next one," he proposed, "let's stake the

girls out and go down the street for a minute. I could stand a little mouth-wash."

"Not for me, but I'll go with you."

Buck looked at him questioningly. Then he nodded and said, "I always hated the idea of cashing in with liquor on my breath. Don't hardly seem decent. Same time, no one wants to perforate me like they do you." He grinned at the younger man and, as the orchestra struck up, said, "Let's go."

The number was a waltz, which Cawinne danced with Mrs. Buck and Buck with Tana.

"You girls set here for a spell," Buck said when it was over, ushering the women to chairs. "West and I'll be back pronto."

They made for the door, and when they were almost there the rancher put an arresting hand on Cawinne's arm.

"Sump'n going on," he warned.

The jam of men in the small hallway had drawn back from the center to form the tightly packed circumference of a rough circle.

Cawinne pulled away from Buck and pushed ahead through the unwilling crowd. The latter watched him for an instant and then plowed after him, heedless of the resentment that the squirm and shove of his thick shoulders were exciting.

"I no say it."

Johnny Fee, a wavering defiance in his meek-dog's face, looked miserably from Salter to Manker.

The three occupied the center of the circle like a stage, Manker, the gross ex-athlete with a face reddled by drink, Salter, the albino, whose ashen countenance was gashed by the inflamed ellipses of his lids, and Fee, the defective, desperate with panic.

"Oh, yes, you will," Manker promised. His lips moved, wet and uncertain, over his words. His eyes were shiny with alcohol, and in his manner as he looked about him for appreciation there was the simple, zestful cruelty of a child. "Whataya know about it?" he asked his audience with exaggerated concern. "Fee Simple says he can't say, 'The skunk thunk the stump stunk'?" He made the halting isolation with which his drunken tongue managed each word seem like an emphasis for the benefit of Fee.

"Come on, Fee Simple," he wheedled.

"I no say it."

Manker reached out, his eyes suddenly ugly, to seize the unwilling half-breed by the shirt. "You will, damn you!" he said.

John Fee cast about him a look of terror, of appeal, of dumb and hopeless imploration to some god of circumstances he could not understand or appease.

Salter began to laugh, the rusty, choking laugh of a man seldom amused.

Manker's lips curled upward as he looked about him. He jerked the slight figure of Fee against his chest.

"Say it," he hissed in his face, "before I shoot your ears off!"

Like a hurt pup, Fee suddenly found voice. Words, syllables, and meaningless mouthings poured out of him, jumbled and swift, as if the dam of his utterance, giving way, had released the murky waters of his mind.

It was too much. Salter's strangling laugh shrilled upward to soprano. He beat his thighs with his heavy, gunman's hands. Manker bent double, griped by mirth.

It was thus that he postured when Cawinne, hitherto unnoticed by him, broke through the circle of watchers. Cawinne's boot swung hard and true.

Like a charging bull, Bally Buck followed his companion and in one grunting leap was at the side of Salter, who had straightened up in bewilderment, slow to comprehend.

"Stand still!" he warned the albino. "I got a gun in your guts."

Kicked off balance, Manker stumbled ahead and, catching himself, whirled around half-squatting, hand over hip, to find Cawinne's cool eyes within an arm's length of his own.

"So," he snarled.

The bashful males who had occupied the hall suddenly lost their timidity and stampeded into a crush at the narrow door to the dance hall. Others, too crowded for flight, pressed against the side walls with watchful eyes on the combatants. Manker's back was to the railing that guarded the flight of steps by which the hall was reached from the street.

"Fee's an old Bar-G-Bar hand, Manker," Cawinne said. "Mostly, we don't let each other get hurrahed around much."

Trickily, Manker's eyes flashed past the other's shoulder, as if at a surprise entry in the dispute and, in that split second, his hand stabbed for his hip.

Cawinne's right fist shot out.

Manker's head flipped back like a nigger-baby hit by a ball. His staggering body, receding as if before the blow of a ram, hit the flimsy railing over the stairs, brought it down in splinters, and hung for an instant over the drop to the steps below. Then it slid from sight.

Cawinne was leaping down the steps almost as the crash of Manker's body sounded. Behind him, with Salter's revolver clutched safely in his hand, came Buck, and, after him, hesitatingly, the other witnesses to the fight.

"I'm afraid you ain't killed him, West," said Buck as he joined in a swift examination of the injured man.

"He'll come around. Let's get him over to Doctor Kink's."

"I'll take care of that," Buck insisted. "You might need both hands, even yet." He raised his hoarse voice: "Here, you men, give a hand, will you? We'll take him over to the Doc's."

Cawinne pushed back up the choked and noisy stairway. The voices died to an excited murmur as the ranked faces above him spied him coming through. At the landing, he found Mrs. Buck and Tana. The former's aggressive assurance had left her. White-faced and shaken, she seized Cawinne almost beseechingly. "He's all right?" she begged. "He hasn't gone out to fight any more?"

"It's all right now," Cawinne assured her. "Nothing to worry about."

Big-eyed, unsmiling, the girl gazed at him with a distant wonder. There on the crowded stairway, hemmed about by an inquisitive and blood-hungry humanity, she seemed alien and alone.

With a return of confidence, Mrs. Buck grasped Cawinne's sleeve possessively. "This is as far as you go," she ordered. "That pale face is still up there, and we've had all the fightin' we're going to have tonight."

"I wasn't going any farther anyway," he said, and let himself be led back down the stairs.

Later, as they drank coffee and ate sandwiches that Tana served them in the rear of Motorists' Mecca, he said, "I wonder what became of Johnny Fee? I didn't see him afterward."

"You see him, Bally? You, Tana?" Mrs. Buck asked.
"Not me," answered Buck.

The girl shook her head. She had uttered hardly a
word since they had left the dance hall. As if she might
find something in a face, her troubled gaze went from one
to the other of them and kept returning to Cawinne.

"I think," Mrs. Buck volunteered, "that Fee Simple's
just too blamed scared of Robideau and his bunch to
be seen with you, West. He lit out, that's what. Maybe
you've made things harder for him by taking his part."

Absently, Buck fingered a knife. "Three times is out,"
he mused aloud, "and already, West, your count with
them is two."

CHAPTER ELEVEN

I T WAS NOT EARLY, but Moon Dance lay forsaken and still in the gentle morning sun, for the day was Sunday. In an hour the pious would begin starting for worship, and, still later, the sportive of the night before, their hang-overs somewhat relieved, would lounge at street corner and drug store and disappear periodically for pick-me-ups. The one or two wretches, afflicted beyond endurance, who had left their beds to wander ill and thirsty up and down Main Street, served to accentuate the dreary emptiness of the town. Likewise, the tardy show of activity at Motorists' Mecca and the Moon Dance House, where breakfasts were being served to a few who had risen early and a few who had not been to bed, by contrast made the street seem deader.

In Judge LaFrance's harness shop a dirty-faced alarm clock clucked to the drowsy time. The three men who had gathered for a conference there were thoughtful and still. West Cawinne was seated backwards in a chair, his arms folded across its back. Bally Buck lounged against the workbench and fiddled with the elk-tooth fob that adorned his Sunday vest. Judge LaFrance sat tilted against the wall and looked at the other two rheumily over his small-lensed, gold-rimmed glasses. Before breakfast, he was irritable and sharp-tongued.

Out of his reflection, with an edge of impatience in his voice, he asked, "And what the hell do you want to get Robideau for, Buck? Like some of the rest of the hotheads, you just want to shoot in the dark."

A slow smile pushed wrinkles into Buck's rugged, good-natured face.

"It 'ud be a sight better for us to shoot in the dark than get shot in the dark," he insisted. "Besides, if we don't shoot pretty quick, some else is going to."

The Judge snorted and pointed at Buck with his trumpet. "I was thinkin' that fool thought for a while, but will you tell me who's going to lead the bunch against Robideau if you or West don't?"

Buck reamed a hairy ear with a stubby forefinger. "That's sump'n, all right," he conceded. "Some of the boys, like Blackie Cox, are doin' a lot of talkin' but probably don't hanker to be at the front of a posse that's huntin' Robideau. Same time, you never know. We ain't doin' ourselves much good by waitin' around in the face of what everybody knows."

"What if we brought him in?" asked Cawinne. "We haven't any evidence to convict him on, and I don't aim to see him strung up without a trial."

"Maybe he wouldn't care about askin' for a trial, time we got him in," Buck suggested slyly.

"If we get him in, that'll be the way," the Judge supplemented. "On a door."

"The trouble is, this case won't play dead," said Cawinne, chafing his chin with the knuckle of a forefinger. "A man doesn't have time to look into what has happened because of what keeps happening."

"West," the Judge asked, "do you think it all ties up?"

Cawinne grinned regretfully. "So far, I'd say I've chased down side roads, mostly. It's a sure thing that falling into the gorge and getting shot at by Svenson and tangling with Manker and Salter have just kept me off the main line."

He considered a minute and then pointed a forefinger

at Buck. "Even if it seems cutting things pretty fine, I want to find the rest of Seldom Wright."

"Good Lord!" Buck groaned. "A regiment maybe couldn't do that, and here you put it up to me. Let me just go and shoot myself instead."

His mouth twisted into a grimace of extreme reluctance as he eyed Cawinne. "We got three men dead and no ideas," he said. "Let's just say they all shot theirselves, before we get to suspectin' each other."

"Aw, shut up, Buck!" commanded Judge LaFrance testily, with the privilege of the old. "Even when you're not trying to be funny my mind balks every time you open your mouth. Anyhow, this is a sorry time for thinkin'. Let's go over to Duke Deck's and get some coffee and cakes."

Goldie Lampkins, the angular and buck-toothed waitress, was clearing away a stack of dishes as they entered, and after she had carried it to the kitchen she came to wait on the trio. Save for them, the restaurant was empty of patronage, but the nickel coffee urn behind the counter fretted for customers, giving off a rich bouquet, and from the kitchen came the odors of bacon and pancakes.

Buck winked at the Judge, who appeared to have come into better humor at the mere thought of breakfast, and said to the ill-favored Goldie:

"Us two and this here officer of the law have business with Miss Tana Deck. Is she up and about yet?"

Goldie started to answer, but mid-way of her reply the door to the rear swung open and Tana and Duke Deck both came into the room.

The latter strode forward with the flourish of a Southern gentleman welcoming gentility.

"Judge LaFrance and Mr. Buck and Mr. Cawinne," he said with his fine exaggeration of manner, bending in his greeting, "it is a pleasure to have you. The top of the morning to you."

His hand swept in a gesture of gracious good-fellowship and knocked a sugar bowl off the counter.

"Lamb," he said, turning to his daughter, "ask Miss Goldie to tidy up this mess, will you?"

The girl started for the kitchen, whither the waitress had gone, but Buck, always more direct than tactful, blurted, "You tell her, Duke. Shucks, a man would a heap rather be waited on by a pretty girl than the owner of the joint, even."

Deck's expressive mouth parted in a look of obliging compliance. He said, "To be sure, Tana, will you wait on the gentlemen?"

She came forward, smiling a half-shy greeting. For work, she had put on a starched white dress that was like a uniform. Above the severity of it, the blue of her eyes, the flush high on her cheeks, and the fragile overbloom of her mouth gave to her face the wrenching beauty of a solitary flower.

Buck grinned appreciatively. "Blue eyes and dark hair and high color! Kid, you do a man good even if he is old enough to be your father and then some. Don't she, West?"

Cawinne answered "Yes" at his plate, and she said, with doubt and mischief and reproof in her eyes, "Are you old enough to be my father, too? I thought you were so hard you just looked that way."

Cawinne flushed, and Buck, looking at him contemplatively, smiled with one side of his mouth.

"Wheat cakes and coffee and a couple of eggs and

some sausages for me," ordered the Judge, whose deaf ears had not caught the conversation. He looked at Tana in aged affection.

"Make it two," said Buck.

"Three," added Cawinne.

They ate silently and swiftly, as hungry, outdoor men do. The Judge had knocked the heel from his pipe, Buck had bitten the end off a cigar, and Cawinne was rolling a cigarette before the next customer arrived.

Two-Wattle Thompson, a broad, scarlet-faced, amiable rancher from the Smoky Water, signaled a friendly greeting, but Blackie Cox, starting to gesture, too, arrested his hand when he recognized Cawinne and brought his loose lips together in a line of hostile dislike.

The newcomers sat at the counter two or three seats removed from Judge LaFrance, who was nearest to them. After they had ordered, Cox began talking, low-voiced, to his companion.

"I guess it's time to go over to the hotel and get Martha," said Buck. "We got to be starting home. I don't hardly know the place any more."

Cox's voice had strengthened. Low enough to have about it a suggestion of confidence, it was loud enough to be overheard.

"No mystery about it, if you ask me," he said to the uneasy Thompson. "Who's going to hack a man up except an Indian? Couldn't be anyone who butchered old Seldom Wright except that half-breed, Robideau."

Buck looked at Cawinne, and his mouth said less than his eyes. "Why'n't you ride out with us and spend the night? You ain't going to be doing anything today."

Cox insisted, "Could it?"

Cawinne answered Buck's question: "Thanks, but I better stay here."

"What ought to be done," said Cox, louder, "is for some real men to go after that killer."

Isolated in his deaf world, Judge LaFrance puffed peacefully on his pipe, his eyes far away. Tana Deck, unaware of tension in the room, had moved up to the head of the counter and was gazing out on the deserted street.

"I'll be comin' in early tomorrow," Buck promised, "case you still want me to go ahead with that job of tryin' to collect Seldom's parts."

Emboldened by their disregard, Cox announced, "All this flat-footin' in the face of facts is simple four-flushin'."

Buck's face was dark with blood. His eyes, as he fixed them on Cawinne, glinted with grim expectation. The latter rolled another cigarette and said calmly to him, "Better come in then. I'll be needing you."

Incredulity wrote itself into Buck's congested face. For a long instant, he kept his narrowed eyes on the younger man, and then, as if at the end of endurance, he looked over at Cox and grated, "A while back, some people was powerful sure it was Seldom Wright murdered Miles Larion."

Cox turned to him. "Natural mistake," he defended, his gaze shifting to Cawinne's impassive face, "but the cards are up now."

He was silent for a moment. When he spoke again, there was insult unmistakable in both word and tone.

"What we need around here, Buck, is some officers with guts."

Startled, the girl turned from her contemplation of the street.

Astonishment and disappointment and rage struggled

in the look that Buck gave the unmoving Cawinne. The rancher slid off his stool, his face black.

Cawinne's out-thrust hand held him back. "Hold up!" the younger man commanded. He rubbed out his cigarette against his plate, dismounted deliberately from his his stool, and moved leisurely over to Cox, his face grave and unrevealing.

"Just so I don't get you wrong," he suggested evenly, "supposing you say that again."

Sensing trouble that his ears did not catch, Judge La-France boomed, "What's up? What's up?"

Tana Deck stood transfixed behind the counter, as if all the tension of the moment had been communicated to her. Lips slightly open, she stared at the two men.

Cox's hands slid off the counter. He made a half turn on the revolving top of the stool.

"I was sayin'—" he started, and then his eyes met Cawinne's. His tongue came out nervously and wet his lips. He put his hands back on the counter.

"You get on the prod mighty easy," he said tardily, his eyes downcast.

"I guess maybe I didn't hear you right. Did I?"

Cox squirmed. His big mouth twitched a little, and his furtive eyes ran from his outspread hands to Cawinne, to Judge LaFrance, to Tana Deck, and back to his hands.

"I guess you didn't."

He slid a half-dollar across the counter and called to Tana in the manner of a man who attempts to escape a loss of face by ignoring the issue. "Here's for breakfast," he said.

Slowly, then, he lifted his tall frame from the stool, paused to take a toothpick from a dish at the side of the register, and let himself out the door.

"Your friend," suggested Buck to Two-Wattle Thompson in a choked and evil tone, "ought to try usin' his head more and his tongue less. It 'ud be a change for both of 'em."

Thompson's red face deepened to tomato. "Same goes for others," he said, looking Buck in the eyes, " 'specially those who think if you eat with a man you got to wipe on the same towel."

Instantly, Buck's expression softened. "Good boy," he relented, grinning.

Turning, he saw Tana standing silent and white, and he said to her in a bantering voice, "Mr. Cawinne drove off a customer, Honey, and with his breakfast only half et, to boot."

There was stiff uncertainty in her voice. "Mr. Cawinne," she said while she held her fists thrust into the pockets of her skirt, "seems to have a knack for trouble."

The rancher started to respond, but something in her eyes checked him. He shrugged and spread his hands as if to deny an alternative. "O. K., Kid," he said, and smiled with engaging sympathy into her clouded face as the silent Cawinne made toward the door.

CHAPTER TWELVE

I T WAS LATE SUPPERTIME at Motorists' Mecca. The crowd of cowhands, ranchers and townspeople that earlier had constituted a fair patronage had thinned out, and Goldie, the maid, looking drawn and haggard but working with the mechanical efficiency of one who knows only labor, was clearing off the last of the tables.

West Cawinne, who had eaten the evening's special of pot roast and brown potatoes in thoughtful silence, gulped the last of his coffee, pensively rolled a cigarette and wearily dismounted from the stool at the deserted counter. He and Buck had spent the day fruitlessly in a search for what remained unfound of Seldom Wright's body.

He started to go out, his boot heels clumping on the worn wood floor, but as the voices of Duke and Tana Deck came to him from the rear of the place he paused irresolutely, considered, and turned back, pushing through the swinging door.

Deck, dishing food onto two plates with the nice attention, if not the dexterity, of a particular woman, welcomed him with a nod and smile. At his greeting, the girl turned from her task of tidying the long serving table and moved her head in grave acknowledgment of his presence.

"Even prisoners must eat," Deck volunteered in wordy friendliness. "I am preparing these plates, in accordance with my contract with the county commissioners, for two unfortunates, Shorty McGorty, a sheep herder and his son, Young Shorty, who had the bad judgment to get drunk and engage in a public brawl this afternoon. Our marshal, Clarence Lamb, promptly arrested them." With an exaggeration that he evidently found humorous, he added, "They are having opportunity now to reflect on their trangressions in the fastness of the bastille."

He spooned potatoes carefully on a plate, surveyed the two servings, and wiped his hands on the damp dish towel about his waist.

"There, Tana. I believe I have everything ready."

"But Daddy," the girl protested in affectionate vexation, "you've forgotten the meat!"

"Ah, so I have," he agreed. "Now it wouldn't be much of a meal without meat, would it? The commissioners might terminate our understanding, on the grounds of breach of contract. Bring the kettle over, Lamb. We shall have time for a little more cordiality soon, Mr. Cawinne, after I have delivered the provender to the prisoners."

"I just wanted to say hello."

The girl looked up, a distant friendship in her manner. "You needn't go," she said. "We'll be through in a minute."

With one hand, he drew the rim of his big hat through the fingers of the other. "I'm sorry," he said, looking down at it, faintly frowning, "that that trouble with Cox had to come up yesterday."

Tana busied herself covering the plates with paper napkins. Her face had shadowed at his words, and, though her tone was light, when she spoke it was as much in denial as in inquiry.

"Did it have to come up?"

"Yes," he said briefly, and put on his hat and turned and went through the door. The girl's lips opened, as if she would call him back, but no words came, and he strode up the aisle to the outside, where he paused under the wide, low roof that reached to the street.

A warm wind blew gustily in the dark spring night, carrying from the barren plains the promise of grass. Up and down Main Street, occasional lights glowed cheerfully in shop windows. A tired saddle horse, hitched at the side of the restaurant, shifted his weight with a creaking of leather.

Perhaps it was the noise of the saddle, perhaps the sixth sense that those in constant jeopardy develop, perhaps the merest glint of metal where the porch joined with the corner of the building that caused Cawinne to leap back toward the wall, his right hand striking at his hip.

A pencil of flame streamed from the corner and an explosion shattered the night.

At that instant, Duke Deck, stumbling at the threshold, lurched out of the door of the restaurant, swinging the jail tray crazily in his effort to maintain balance. From up the street behind Cawinne a man came running, his voice bellowing.

Revolver up, Cawinne sprang to the right, to remove Tandy Deck from the line of fire. But even as he did so, a shot came from behind him, and the runner, who had checked himself to aim, broke again into a heavy gallop, shouting, "I got him, West. I got him for you."

But it was not the assailant hidden at the corner whom he had hit. Duke Deck staggered half around, the tray clattering from his wilting hand, and fell headlong against Cawinne. He groaned once as the latter let him down, and then melted into limp collapse, like a leaking balloon.

Doors flung open in the lighted shops along the street. There was the sound of men running and shouting questions. The fast clatter of a horse's hoofs shook echoes from the street and faded out with distance. Out of the restaurant Tana came flying, crying, "Daddy, Daddy, is anything the matter?"

Wordless, Horace Fladd, the great smith, ended his run and stared dumbly at the wounded man. His revolver hung in his hand.

"Your shot went wild, Horace," Cawinne said quietly, without reproach.

"Quick!" he ordered then of the gathering crowd. "One of you get Doctor Kink. Duke Deck's been shot. Here, some of you, lend a hand!"

Not until then did he think to sheathe the weapon that his right hand clasped.

They carried the wounded man to the kitchen and up the narrow stairway to the Decks' sleeping quarters above.

Wordless, the girl had run ahead to light a lamp, and now, as the men laid her father on the bed, she dropped beside it, in her eyes the hopeful, unbelieving, tragic imploration of the young facing disaster.

Hurried steps sounded on the stairs, and Doctor Kink, puffing from his run, entered the room with the messenger who had summoned him. But already the patient was beyond his help. For an instant, death had threatened the physical beauty that had attended Deck all his life. His face strained with anguish while Tana sought to soothe him. His body turned in unlovely writhings. But at last he lay quiet, his fine features peaceful, his body composed, like an undertaker's masterpiece. His last breath was a tired and gentle sigh.

Unwillingly, Doctor Kink shook his head. "Nothing can be done," he said, low-voiced, and let his hand rest on Tana's rigid shoulder.

She buried her face in the bed. Her fingers clasped her father's dead hand. Sobs wracked her.

"Oh, Daddy, Daddy," she cried against that remorseless force that only the old and defeated can see as friend, "why did this have to happen to us? Why did it?"

In a corner of the room, the big blacksmith who had wanted to be a gunfighter cried like an inarticulate boy. Hands at his sides, he stood there, weeping openly, his simple, friendly face pulled and twisted by his grief.

The dozen men who had followed the body of Deck up the stairway shifted uneasily, like children before the mysterious and moving, and only Goldie, her teeth bared in sympathetic distress, had words of consolation. She had come clumping hastily up the stairs, her plain and pallid face set in apprehension, but when she entered the room and beheld Tana some quality of the heart swept away her ungainliness and touched her with a profound dignity.

"There, Honey. There, little Honey," she whispered, and dropped down to put a comforting arm about the girl's shoulders.

Abruptly Tana leaped to her feet, and she was no longer a girl now but a woman, with a woman's fierce and desperate resistance to the adversities that mature her.

She pointed to Cawinne. "Oh go!" she commanded. "Go and never come back! Wherever you are, there are ugly feelings, and violence, and—and death." She gestured toward the figure on the bed, and the force went out of her. Slowly, she brought her hands to her bowed face.

"It was me done it, by accident," the stricken Fladd managed to confess.

Goldie arose and put her red hand on the girl's shaking back and looked mutely at Cawinne.

The eyes of all of them were on him now, solemn and distant and contemplative, as if here in the presence of death was something alien or explanatory.

Cawinne looked at the girl and at the still faces about him and moved to the stairway, summoning Doctor Kink to follow.

"I'll be at the hotel or Judge LaFrance's, if you need me," he said when they had reached the landing.

"I'll see to everything," the doctor replied gruffly and turned as if to go, but Cawinne reached out and seized him by the coat.

"She has friends, if the money's short," he said in rough insistence, and Doctor Kink gave him a long and probing look and went back up the stairs.

Cawinne ran down the steps and swung up the street toward Judge LaFrance's shop. Bally Buck was hurrying out as he arrived.

"My God, West!" the rancher called hoarsely.

"Wait!"

"I got to see little Tana."

"No use right now. Goldie's the one."

Buck paused uncertainly and turned back.

As they entered, Judge LaFrance made a fierce sweep with his trumpet and raised his aged bones from his chair.

"Who done it, Kid?"

Buck threw out, "And why?"

"It was Fladd that shot Deck, aiming at someone who took a crack at me."

The Judge's voice was full of anxious fury. "Tell us everything," he demanded.

Briefly then, in short, harsh sentences, Cawinne told them of the occurrences at Motorists' Mecca.

"And you didn't even get in a shot?" Buck cried unbelievingly.

"Couldn't," Cawinne retorted cryptically.

"Who shot at you?" the booming voice of the Judge asked.

Cawinne's habitual air of composed gravity was tinctured with a sharp authority.

"I don't know. Couldn't see."

Buck swore violently. Arising, he jerked his hat down on his head and hitched his belt. "Whoever it is," he suggested, "let's go get him."

"You want to go out looking for an unidentified horseman on a night so dark you can't see a horse ten feet away?" Cawinne asked critically.

"God Almighty, West! All we ever have is suspicions, and all we ever do is wait. Come on! By Joe, I'll go myself if you won't."

"Go, then!"

At the edge in Cawinne's voice, the Judge hobbled over to a wall cabinet, reached in and abstracted a bottle. "Drink 'ud do us all good," he said placatingly. "West's right, Bally. You couldn't find a white elephant tonight. Besides, it ain't as if anything was lost by waitin'. Hold your horses."

Buck grunted, unconvinced, and up-ended the bottle.

"What about it?" the Judge asked presently. "Was someone tryin' to get you, West, before you pinned something on him?"

Cawinne didn't answer.

"One thing we know, and that's that the whole damn settlement will be wiped out if we don't get to the bottom of this thing pronto," Buck complained.

The other two were silent. The old harness-maker passed around the bottle again, and for half an hour and more they sat quiet, each thinking his own thoughts.

From their reflection they were jerked by the noise

of running feet. Someone pounded frantically on the door.

A voice screamed, "Let me in! Let me in!"

Cawinne was on his feet like a cat. He swung the door wide.

Into the shop staggered Goldie Lampkins, with blood running from her mouth.

"He came and got her," she shrieked. "He took her away. I was alone with her and he hit me. He took her away."

"Who took who?" Cawinne barked.

"Tana. Tana Deck," she cried. "A man in a white hood."

Cawinne's voice was like the crack of a whip. "Which way?"

"I don't know. I don't know. Oh, he took her away!"

Cawinne held himself just long enough for three quick sentences bitter with self-criticism. "I should have known. I should have watched. It's her connection with the mine."

Buck's big hand was on the door knob. "Dark or light," he rasped, "by Joe, we look now!"

CHAPTER THIRTEEN

TANDY DECK's whole life was a record of polished ineffectuality, of graceful mistake, of beautiful incompetence. Whether in physical activity or social intercourse or business procedure, his manner was so finished, his utterance so suave, his appearance so handsome, that the unfailing presence of error seemed the result of some fantastic confusion in the assembly of his being. In boyhood he had loved sports and had erred with such grace on diamond and court that the village prophets of Iowa had nodded in sage assurance of his success. As a student he was obedient, eager, ingratiating, and wrong. He tried bookkeeping in his early manhood but sought other fields after his employer found that the neatness of his figures was equaled only by the number of their discrepancies. The ambition to be a rancher, a flashing cowman with Angora chaps and a square of silk around his neck, drew him west, where he contributed to the lore of the range by demonstrating with what finesse a man could leave a horse unintentionally. By turns grocer, hotel clerk, salesman, make-shift teacher and small-time promoter, he had wandered from locality to locality, everywhere elegantly incapable, in all pursuits exquisitely inept.

Another so afflicted might have reckoned and despaired, but Tandy Deck had an airy confidence inversely proportioned to the trifle of his talent. Always, everything would be all right with him. Past and present glowed, not with the dark illumination of experience or circumstance, but with the radiance of things ahead.

The golden day was coming. "You just wait!" he had said a thousand times to his wife, before she had died of waiting. And "You just wait!" he said in playful earnestness to the daughter she bore him. "You'll be in silks and satins yet, my lamb."

Whatever credit a father may claim for the virtues of his child, he could claim in uncommon measure. She was knowing and capable and brave, this girl of his, and there was about her a stabbing, piteous femininity compounded of compassion and eagerness and flowering beauty. But for the rest, there was on his record only the entry of failure. Even the small success won by the restaurant at Motorists' Mecca was the work of his daughter. Its related activity, the sale of gasoline and oil, which he had claimed as his special enterprise, had never flourished, and month after month the pump and the barrel had stood unused and empty. Gentle, well-meaning, hopeful, handsome, gracious and utterly incompetent, he had been a constant promise, with never a fulfillment.

And fate, for once consistent, terminated his life on a note of that contradiction on which it had always been lived. To match his grace and his ineptitude, his great intentions and his feeble executions, his polish of manner and his poverty of resource, she had him die by accident, the undeserving victim of a bullet intended for a rascal.

But the Reverend Howard Logan, pastor of the Moon Dance Methodist Church, if he realized the irony of the life that had run its course, ignored it in his funeral sermon, preached at the grave in the little hillside cemetery that lies half a mile east of town. Instead, to the little crowd gathered about the coffin, he spoke of the deep affection of father for daughter. He talked of the beauty of parental love. He dwelt on the characteristics of kindliness and simple honesty that had bound the deceased brother to the community. He advised his hearers to have faith in the purposes of God and the bounty of His love, however harsh the circumstance. And finally he prayed in quiet earnestness for the restoration of the daughter from the kidnaper and for her resignation to the loss which served Heaven's inscrutable ends.

So, on a dreary afternoon chill with a northeast wind, in a cemetery flanked by starveling trees that a lover of beauty had set out more in hope than expectation, Tandy Deck was deposited with the company of the dead.

But not death, or sermon, or chill afternoon, or lonely grave long could divert Moon Dance from the question of the hour. Where was Tana Deck? It was the subject of speculation wherever men and women met, inside or out, at home and at work, at the Ladies' Industrial and Adlam's Saloon.

Four days had passed since that wild night that Goldie Lampkins had banged hysterically on the door of Judge LaFrance's harness shop, four days of feverish search and anxious hope and eager inquiry—and one day, too, of blind reprisal, for Breedtown lay in ashes.

On that first day, word of the abduction ran from store to store and house to house and, inexplicably, by what the range terms the tomato-can telegraph, to the sequestered ranches that embrace Moon Dance on the west like a new moon; and with the news the suspicion developed, moment by moment, into the certainty that Breedtown had supplied and abetted the abductor. Long before noon, men were forming in the streets in excited, angry knots. Dusty new arrivals, stiff from hard rides, kept adding themselves to the churning groups. A nervous expectancy, like the wait for an explosion, gripped

the town. Leadership began to shape the fuming sentiment to point. "To Breedtown!" men commenced to
shout, while two rose to recognized command. One of
them was Estes Rell, a gaunt old freighter with skeleton
for face, whose sweeping mustache looked like an adorn-
ment added by a prankish boy; the other Blackie Cox,
in whose flushed, wild countenance was pictured the
essence of the passions he was fanning. At the last, as if
all had come to the decision at once, men began to run
for mounts. Townsmen without steeds stormed Jerry
McCabe's livery stable. From their horses in the middle
of the street before the Moon Dance House, Rell and
Cox bellowed impatiently for action. At a little past
midday, a hundred horsemen galloped off on the trail up
the Crazy Cree to Breedtown.

Bally Buck, returning from a swift ride to the eastern
drainage of the Smoky Water, toward which the tracks
of a shod horse had pointed, pulled up before Judge
LaFrance's shop five minutes after the cavalcade had
gone.

Hunched in the open doorway, the Judge signaled to
him imperiously and came hobbling to the edge of the
walk.

"You go on," he said, motioning.

"Go where?"

"To Breedtown."

"You told West you'd send a couple of men up
there!"

Judge LaFrance gestured impatiently with one hand.
Deep in his pocket, the other showed as a fist against
the cloth.

"I sent 'em," he fumed. "It ain't that. Didn't you see
that bunch start, led by Rell and Cox?"

Buck leaned forward, squinting into the lined face of

the justice of peace, while his horse pawed restlessly at the earth.

"You mean Breedtown's It?"

"They won't be lookin' much for Tana. That ain't the main idea."

Buck gnawed at his heavy lower lip. "What could a man do?" he asked sharply. "Besides, West told me to kind of get things organized here."

"Since when did it get so I couldn't hold the ribbons?" the ancient Judge queried belligerently, chin thrust out. "There's nothin' you can do at this end. All West's instructions are being carried out. I got men scourin' the Freezeout and the Crazy Cree. A bunch under your own Rusty Jones is huntin' the back country, and West himself is in the Smoky Water. Maxie Roser has wired sheriffs of every county for two hundred miles around. You go on. I got more man-power now than I got places to put it."

"I'm tryin' to find Tana, not turn a stampede," Buck objected.

The Judge's voice softened. "Bally, we can't have a pig-stickin' at Breedtown. There's women and kids there, and some good-enough breeds, too."

Buck blew gustily through regretful lips and took up the slack in his reins. "O. K.," he conceded, "but not even West would savvy this job."

"You'll do as good as any. Some'll get beat up, in spite of hell and high water, but Cox and Rell won't be so keen on rubbin' out all comers if they know there's an honest witness around."

"No use wishin' for Cawinne, anyhow. He's wolfin' every trail between here and the Smoky Water."

He turned his horse abruptly and touched its belly with his spurs.

When Buck reached it, the column had slowed from its first impetuous gallop to a jogging and determined trot. Before it, the canyon of the Crazy Cree notched the blue barrier of the Rockies. Around it, occasional meadow larks lifted their fluid tribute to the spring. Under a warm sun, the universe moved to the rhythm of a new season, in which the voices of the men, the creak of saddle leather, and the clump of hoofs in the soft earth seemed rude and out of time.

Rell's drawn and bony face with its comic decoration of mustache turned toward the rancher as the latter came to the head of the procession.

"Look, Blackie!" the freighter said.

Cox slued around in the saddle and saw Buck.

"Howdy," the latter announced. "I'm trailin' along."

Cox's face was full of ill-natured suspicion. Before he spoke, he twisted about and surveyed the troop behind him as if to assure himself of his enforcements.

"Trailin's all right," he warned then, "but me and Estes are doin' the leadin'."

"Yeah." Buck's tone was one of matter-of-fact acceptance.

"Damn right!" Rell retorted. "And we got our own ideas."

Cox added, "Them that don't like it can pick up their chips."

Behind them a rider chided, "And go home," and a second put in jeeringly, "And stay there."

Buck answered mildly, "O. K., boys. You're the doctors. I'll tail along, anyhow. Guess we're as likely to find Tana Deck there as anywhere." As if by afterthought he added, "Might be sump'n interesting happen, anyhow, to tell about later."

Cox's long face widened at the nostrils. Out of the corners of his eyes he regarded the rancher darkly.

Rell's voice was thin: "A man wouldn't want to see too much, or say too much, either."

Buck began to whistle softly.

The company grew silent, except for occasional guttural exchanges between the riders, and for hour after hour kept hoofing on while the canyon of the Crazy Cree opened before them like the jaws of a vice. Dusk like powder smoke was drifting in among the high hills when Breedtown came into view.

Cox turned in his saddle as they topped the slope that led down to the huddle of cabins. "All around it!" he commanded of the men behind him, accompanying the order with a wide sweep of his arm.

As if by prearrangement, about half the company fanned out to right and left, while Rell and Cox, with Buck and two-score followers, rode ahead.

The settlement seemed shuttered and lifeless save for a half dozen lean dogs that came out to run growling about the horsemen, but here and there slow plumes of smoke, rising in the spring twilight, and here and there the amber of lamp glow in the dusk testified to presences inside.

"Peaceful, ain't it?" Rell growled, and while Buck sat his horse he and Cox swung to the ground and strode to the door of the first cabin in which a light shone.

Cox banged on the door with his revolver and, when it opened timidly, kicked it wide with his boot.

"What's your name?"

The sloe-eyed part-blood looked at him silently, and at the company behind him, his gaze running like liquid jet under the close bank of his lids.

Cox swung his weapon in a swift half-circle. The breed staggered. A trickle of blood weaved down his forehead from his broken scalp.

"Frank Chouquah," he said, licking his lips.

"Where's Robideau?"

"No know."

"No know," mimicked Cox through his teeth, and raised his revolver like a bludgeon. The breed cringed.

"Maybe he don't," Buck suggested from his horse.

"Where's Manker and Salter?"

"No know."

Despite the shrinking of the man, there was something stony and calculating in his manner, as if, against a sure and different day, he was storing up the memories of this one.

The pistol barrel cracked against his skull again, and he went down in a sudden heap.

Inside, a woman began to shriek Indian curses.

Cox turned away, his mouth twisted and savage.

Buck's voice was keen with controlled indignation. "You better hope you ain't killed him."

Around him, men had dropped from their saddles. For an instant they had looked on hungrily, as if at a lesson, and now they began streaming to other cabins, whooping as they ran. They jammed before entrances, scrambling for vantage points. They broke through doors. They fell to with pistol barrel, fist and boot, abandoning as their fever climbed the questioning that at first had been a formal prelude to the satisfaction of assault. Routed from their retreats inside, button-eyed children squalled through the broken doorways, pressing small hands to pinched flesh. Squaws stumbled out, dazed from buffetings. After them came the flung bodies of their men, who hit the ground and lay still or moved

little and looked on wordlessly, out of bloody faces, while
the avengers surged from shack to shack. Above the cries
of the victims the voices of the invaders rose in a roar
that rang back from the hills.

Buck, beside himself at last, spurred from group to
group, crying curses on them. His words boomed, hoarse
and insistent, and were lost in the storm of their passion
like a shout in the wind.

Surprised, outnumbered, cowed, the victims of the raid
had not time or temerity to attempt a defense, but one
fat breed, agile as a cat, leaped through a doorway as a
knot of besiegers bashed in the panel. In the light that
streamed out of the cabin his knife flashed high above
his head. Behind him, a pistol streaked an arc, and the
defender, stunned at the peak of his motion, slumped
slowly to earth like a statue sinking.

"Resistance, by God! String him up!" cried one of
the mob.

"Get a rope!"

"Kill the Injun!"

On the instant, the temper of all was the mood for
murder. A man ran for a lariat while others bent the
senseless half-breed forward on his buttocks.

Buck spurred into the midst of the squirming huddle,
knocking men right and left as he drove his horse on.
Above the other cries his voice rose, a rough and furious
bellow.

"I know you all, you yellow-bellies! Kill one man and
I'll testify against every mother's son of you!"

The crowd stilled, beaten back by his wrath, until one
of them pointed and screamed, "There she goes!"

Fire blossomed in the gathering dark. At half a dozen
points it came to life, thin and sharp, as the guardsmen
on the outside came sneaking for arson. Rooted in the

dry pine of the cabin walls, it sprang up and out in the stunned moment that Buck watched. It shot from log to log and from wall to roof and flung banners in the sky. The crackle of the wood became a blowing roar. The raiders howled in exultation, until the night swam in red and black and they ran for the horses that danced snorting at the edge of the settlement. Dark and prodigious, their shadows leaped ahead of them.

In the face of this further danger, panic-stricken Breedtown began to gather itself for flight. Hoarse guttural, shrill soprano and childish squall picked up, like an antiphony, the fading war song of the raiders.

"Down to the river!" Buck shouted, riding his frantic horse from house to house. "Get the babies! Here, you, give this man a hand!"

The night fanned brighter, like a blown ember, and burst into a scorching brilliance against which the fugitives shielded their faces.

Like a general in the face of disaster, Buck fought the terror that gripped them, shouting commands, directing their retreat, rallying their resources, while fire singed his face and his mount reared in wild alarm.

A slack-bosomed squaw hung at his stirrup.

"My man!" she cried, pointing back.

Before the doorway where he had fallen, so close to the blaze that his clothes smoked, lay the fat defender of his home.

Buck wrenched his unwilling horse about and drove spurs deep into his sides. He leaped off as his mount lunged snorting into the heat, slipped a noose about the half-breed's feet, remounted, took a turn about the horn with his rope, and rode toward the river, dragging the unconscious man while he held his horse to a rearing walk.

"All here?" he shouted at the river bank.

The dispossessed colony stared at him silently, their eyes shining dark and stubborn and desolate in the flare of the fire.

For an instant, Buck waited for an answer and, when there was none, wheeled his steed, circled the blaze and came to the top of the slope. The departing invaders had halted there and now sat their horses silently, fascinated by the spectacle they had created. Their exultation was gone now, and their violence, too. Red in the glow of the flames, their faces were slack and lifeless.

Buck looked back. On either side the burning town, the canyon walls were light as day. Above it, a shifting nimbus hung. A frantic figure, black as an ant, etched itself against the blazing back drop as an anxious occupant, bolder than the rest, dashed out toward the cabins.

Cox, watching with the others, spat and said, "A man's a fool to fry himself over a bunch of breeds."

Buck amended, "A man's a fool to keep a fool from bein' a murderer." Gingerly, he felt of his blistered cheeks.

"Some never do get much sense, Buck."

The rancher eased around until he looked square into the long, sullen face.

"I got enough sense to know it's your fight now, even if you haven't, and I don't feel so much like takin' any more of your talk."

Cox glanced around him.

On his other side, a rider grinned sardonically and said, "Guess Buck's right, Blackie. He's your meat. We don't care for none."

Buck's steady glare demanded an answer.

"Hell, no sense in trouble! Breedtown's done. Let's get goin'." With that, Cox wheeled his horse and set off down the canyon. Wordlessly, the men followed him, their fury for justice done with the satisfaction of dark desires. No more would the fate of Tana Deck disturb them. It was as if the deed had been done, the punishment meted, and the case closed.

Buck left them when they came to the fork beyond the river and urged his jaded horse homeward.

He glanced over his shoulder once, back toward Breedtown. Above the shadowy escarpment of the mountains, a splotch of red still hung, like a wound in the night sky.

"The fools!" he muttered to himself. Then, with stubborn hope, "Maybe West's found Tana."

Although Buck was not present to see it, the altered temper of the sackers of Breedtown was manifest the next evening. Shrewdly striking in the first flush of reaction from the raid, Robideau and his satellites, Manker and Salter, came out of hiding and visited Moon Dance at dusk. They came jogging up the street, their horses abreast, and pulled up before Adlam's Saloon. By a frightened boy Robideau sent word that he waited outside.

Of the scant handful of patrons in the saloon, only four came out, to lounge uneasily against the front of the building, but word of Robideau's call filtered quickly up and down the street, and within ten minutes a score of men, most of whom had had no part in the raid and answered now to mere curiosity, had grouped themselves on the board walk.

Not until then did Robideau speak. The strong jaw under the trimmed mustache barely moved to his words.

"We onerstan' that you look for us," he said in his clipped speech, "and we are here."

One by one he regarded his hearers as if for an answer. On either side of him his companions sat, vigilant and wordless. In the silence, the creak of leather sounded as the trio's horses shifted under their burdens. Inquiringly, Robideau leaned forward in the saddle. His right arm hung limp at his side. In the gloaming, the faces of the three were darkly shadowed, but half a dozen of the men in the forefront of their audience noticed that Manker's face was bulged and black with bruises. It was an observation that in the days to follow gave Moon Dance still another subject for speculation.

"No?" asked Robideau with biting scorn when none had answered to his challenge. "No one would have the business with us?"

He brought his horse's head up, but before he wheeled and jogged down the street he announced, "If anyone wants to see us, we go to Louis Swan's Horse and Cow Saloon."

For two hours thereafter, Robideau, Manker and Salter sat in the Horse and Cow, drinking slowly and keeping their eyes on the door.

But no one came. No longer had the sackers of Breedtown the indignation, or the courage, to face them. And to other and more thoughtful men, who would have confronted them under other circumstances, their every presence in town appeared, in degree at least, as an exhibit of their innocence of the kidnaping of Tana Deck.

CHAPTER FOURTEEN

For every man who spent his indignation in the sack of Breedtown, there were two who searched earnestly for Tana Deck. Bellowing his outrage, Judge LaFrance on that first day of the abduction saw to the distribution of his volunteer forces and afterwards, for lack of a more promising place to go himself, rattled his old bones over the trail to the upper Smoky Water and Indian Pete's Palace, where he looked into every nook and cranny. At the office in Cawinne's absence he directed the hunt with a fierce insistence that recognized no fatigue, in others or himself. Bally Buck rode far and fast, thrusting his belligerent way into every hiding place within his old-timer's knowledge. Led by the laconic Rusty Jones, his men scouted the foothill country from the Smoky Water to the Crazy Cree. John Bruce and half a dozen others rode deep into the knolled and gullied Freezeout, spying into every fissure. Maxie Roser, fat publisher of the *Moon Dance Messenger*, working at Cawinne's direction, filed wire after wire to sheriffs and police chiefs, giving descriptions, asking aid. George I. Smith, the hardware man, and Hugh Jerome, the banker, canvassed the town and in half a day gathered twenty-five hundred dollars, to be given as reward. Mike Looney shut up his barber shop, borrowed a horse, and hunted like a bird dog at last free from a kennel. Grim and taciturn, Cawinne scoured the north country and, between trips, searched every house of dubious repute or unknown quality in or near the town. Outraged householders, starting to protest, fell silent after one look at his face and gathered outside in murmuring family groups while he explored their premises. Directions, abrupt and brief, he gave to Judge LaFrance or Maxie Roser in impatient halts at the harness shop or the *Messenger* office while his horse fretted as if with his own anxiety to be back on a trail that hourly grew colder.

The duly constituted authorities of the law put in their feeble hand. Podge Wilkins, the sheriff, came from Cottonwood, wearing his powers like a label. He asked a multitude of questions, squinting wisely through his glasses, obtained a great deal of information, mostly from people who knew little about the case, and, leaving a forlorn deputy on the scene, departed after two days with the promise of action. The town marshal, Mary's Little Lamb, his lower lip out-thrust like the snout of a pitcher, talked to whoever would listen, hinting darkly of impending developments.

Ranchers and ranch hands, business men and clerks, boys and men took their volunteer parts in the search. For miles around, they spied into hill cabins, they explored possibilities in canyon and coulee, they pushed into grove and thicket, they followed false trails, they shadowed strangers and put to question a dozen men of doubtful reputation or unestablished character on the desperate chance of a clue.

Men and women too old for active effort waited and hoped and inquired ceaselessly. The Ladies' Industrial held an hour of prayer. Youngsters went about their sports half-heartedly, burdened with the anxiety of their elders. Mrs. Buck, who had come to town to stay with Mrs. Scott Hardy, halted suddenly half a dozen times a day, confusing the ringing of her inner ear with the tolling of the public school bell, which, by arrangement, was to be sounded on the instant of a break in the case, by day or by night.

Wild rumors stirred Moon Dance, disputing Cawinne's conviction that the purpose of the abduction was the discovery of the Early Day and hence that kidnaper and victim probably were close about. Captor and captive, by one report, had gone up the canyon and over the divide to Braden and had taken passage for the coast. The abductor had slipped through to Canada, taking his prisoner with him. He had been arrested in Spokane, in Portland, in Winnipeg. Weighted, Tana's body lay in the big hole at the bend of the river south of town. She was held in the camp of roving Indians west and north in the mountain wilderness.

Each report brought its flurry of excitement, which no sooner died under the slow hand of truth than another took its place. A half-dozen times, the impetuous were on the point of running for the bell rope in the school tower.

Bearded and black with dust, Rusty Jones loped into town on the third day of Tana's disappearance, leading a pinto horse.

"Where's Buck?" he demanded, drawing rein before Judge LaFrance's place.

The Judge shrugged. "Why?"

"I got a stray horse here. Caught him over against the mountains, makin' for the Crazy Cree."

LaFrance screwed his trumpet deeper into his ear.

"So you mean to say he's a Breedtown horse. Sure?"

"Reasonable sure."

"That cayuse is marked up like a blackboard," the Judge observed, pointing to the brands that welted the beast on shoulder and thigh.

"Yeah," agreed Jones, and cut himself a chew of tobacco from a worn plug.

"Take him over to Jerry McCabe's," the judge ordered. "West and Bally'll want to see him."

But neither of them could identify the beast, and repeated inquiries about the town brought no proof. Jones' assurance, however, mild as it was, inclined them both to believe him. "I tell you," Buck insisted, "that old hand could see a goat on the Crazy Cree today and spot him next summer in Yellowstone Park."

"Even if it's a Breedtown stray, it doesn't prove much," Cawinne observed.

"No," agreed Buck. "It don't. A horse might stray any time, any place. It's just a kind of possibility. And not much of a one at that, because if Robideau or Manker or Salter is holdin' Tana, what was all three of 'em doin' in town last night?"

For a day the finding of the animal was the topic of conversation. New theories of the whereabouts of Tana and fresh substantiations of old ones were drawn from the discovery. Flagging energies and sinking hopes were renewed by the mere possibility that of horse and rider and captive the horse at least might not have been swallowed by the unrevealing earth.

But when another day passed without a succeeding development, as horsemen who had set out with fresh confidence in the morning returned at night silent and dejected and stiff from long hours in the saddle, a mood of despair, deeper because of that last little flurry of hope, began to settle on the town. People still put the constant question, "Where is Tana Deck?" but more now in resignation than expectance. If hope abided in the breasts of Moon Dance's rank and file, it was largely the hope of finding and meting punishment on the kidnaper, for men and women, talking in grave and regretful

tones, began to concede that Tana Deck probably was
dead. Her body lay among the silent mountains, in the
cover of some copse, or under deep waters. No matter
what the uncertainty of its whereabouts, the wordless
days themselves bespoke a fate of which each unen-
lightening hour was added evidence.

The fifth day found Mike Looney back at his barber
chair and Scott Hardy returned to his desk at the Moon
Dance House. Maxie Roser, looking spiritless and flaccid,
wrote a despairing little editorial on the incomprehen-
sible way of things. Smith and Jerome talked privately
about the refund of the money they had collected as a
reward for the return of the girl. Jones still rode, but
only because Buck told him to. John Bruce went back
to his ranch, the deputy back to Cottonwood. Passive,
pensive, defeated, Moon Dance began drifting back into
the pattern of day by day.

Three men kept on, resolute and grim, as the others
dropped out of the search. Fierce in manner, acid in his
judgment of the quitters, Judge LaFrance by word and
deed fought off the gnawing dread that began to show
in his eyes. Buck, who never in his life had surrendered
to adversity, refused to give up now. Drawn and racked
by fatigue, he swore to continue the hunt to its conclusion. More taciturn than ever, Cawinne kept to a
saddle that he had vacated only for impatient moments
since the night of the kidnaping. Rest, sleep, food, these
things he took sparingly, as the full measure of his endurance ran out. His spirit showed in his face, so bleak and
dark that both friends and strangers, conversing with
him, fell into the lean language of strain.

Looking at his haggard face as he drew rein in front
of the shop after Tandy Deck's funeral, Judge LaFrance
was moved to remonstrate.

"Kid," he said, crippling out to the edge of the board walk where Cawinne sat his horse, "why don't you get some rest? A man'll crack, going it day and night."

"Any news?"

The old man shook his head, shivering in the chill wind that swept in from the northeast. "Where you bound, then?"

"North."

"Wait, you durn fool!" the Judge commanded. "It'll be rainin' icicles in a half hour."

He hobbled inside and came out with a slicker and rain hat.

"You're bustin' to go, and I can't keep you," he said, looking at the younger man with an expression of regretful and affectionate pride, "but I can make you take these along. We got enough on our hands as it is, without nursin' a man with pneumonia."

For a bare instant, the other's face softened. "Thanks," he said, and the harsh mask of resolution and anxiety closed again over his features as he turned his mount and touched it with his spurs.

The Judge watched him for a long minute, rounded about then, rubbing his chilled hands, and limped back to the door. Inside, he pulled his worn leather chair closer to the heat that radiated from the round-bellied stove, and let his ancient body drink it in. He leaned back presently, nodding. Slowly sleep erased from his withered face the deeper etchings of care. Blue-veined and still slightly tremulous, his shrunken hands lay folded in his lap.

Thus, as if all his fears and his defiance had gone out of him and left him peace, Buck found him two hours later as he came into the rear room streaming with rain water.

The rancher put a gentle hand on the shriveled shoulder.

"Where's West, Judge?" he asked in the other's ear.

The old man awakened bewildered, staring red-eyed over his glasses at his visitor.

"What say?"

"Where's West?"

Judge LaFrance sighed. Slowly, the grooves of worry cut themselves again in his face.

"Gone north again," he answered after a little. "Raw out, ain't it?"

Buck unbuttoned his dripping slicker and shook its skirts.

"Yeah," he answered. "Nice day to be buried in. People like to froze to death at Duke's funeral."

Judge LaFrance shoveled coal into the stove from a battered scuttle.

"I wanted to talk to West," Buck said when he had finished.

The Judge grunted. "Guess he didn't have anything particular in mind for you or he'd said so. He was in a hurry."

"Been in one, uninterrupted, for five days now," Buck said as a matter-of-fact.

"What say?" asked LaFrance, turning his horn.

"I said," Buck answered in louder tones, "that West'll be gettin' to know every jack-rabbit between here and the Smoky Water."

"Big scoop of country. Lots of places to hide, or be hid from," the Judge defended.

"Anyhow," replied Buck, "it looks like West is puttin' all his chips there. By Joe, I hope he's right. One place is as good as another, the way things look."

He pulled his wet hat over his eyes.

"I'm takin' Martha back to the ranch tonight," he said into the trumpet. "Time I get something to eat, we ought to be startin'. Be back tomorrow."

The Judge nodded in assent, and his visitor clumped stiffly to the door and let himself out. From the shop, he splashed through the chill and driving rain to Motorists' Mecca, where Goldie Lampkins came to wait on him. She gave him the dumb, inquiring look of an anxious animal.

Buck shook his head gravely and toyed with a teaspoon. "Nothing," he said unwillingly, as if in shame before the mute appeal of her eyes. "How you makin' out with the place?"

Her glance fell to the counter, on which, palms down, she had spread her red, working-woman's hands.

"All right, I guess," she answered lifelessly. "What do you want?"

Her appearance had not improved with Tana's absence. Save for that one unuttered question, every sign of animation seemed to have left her thin and angular face. Her hair straggled aimlessly away from her forehead. Outside her thin and bloodless lower lip, her upper eyeteeth shone. At the corner of her mouth, where the abductor's fist had torn it, the healing skin showed red.

"Whatever you've got," answered Buck. "Beef and spuds and a wedge of pie suits me all right. And plenty of coffee."

He ate slowly and thoughtfully, oblivious of the few other customers who had braved the rain. When, finally, he had finished, he paid his bill, put his slicker back on, pulled his hat down hard, and hurried to the livery barn, where he helped old McCabe hitch the team to the buckboard.

"No time to be travelin'," the aged hostler grumbled as if he himself were being called into the wet, chill night.

"I got another slicker in there," Buck replied, un-offended, "and plenty of wraps besides. I got to get home once in a while, if only so the dogs will know me."

He stopped the team before Scott Hardy's house, wrapped the reins about the hub, strode up on the porch and knocked at the door.

Mrs. Hardy, a gray and wispy woman, came to the door full of objections to the trip, but, after repeated assurances from the Bucks that they were well outfitted for the storm, she consented to their departure, pro-vided only that Mrs. Buck took an umbrella. Even then, she kept them interminably while, with frequent God's-will-be-dones, she discussed Tana and her virtues and the mystery of her whereabouts. When, finally, she had exhausted both praise and piety, Buck took his wife to the rig, climbed in stiffly after her, and clucked to his team.

"I'm glad I took this umbrella," she said, opening it after they had arranged robes and slickers against the pelting rain.

They were quiet then for long minutes while the horses, eager to be home, answered also to the spur of the storm on their rumps and splashed through the mud at a brisk trot.

Mrs. Buck sighed after a while and said in a small voice, "That was the saddest funeral. No kith or kin there. Couldn't it have waited a little, Bally?"

"Steady, boys," Buck said to his team. "It could of, Martha, but it seemed best to go ahead with it."

"Everyone was wondering about little Tana."

"Yep."

"Bally, hasn't anyone any ideas? Are you keeping anything from me?"

"Now, Honey, you know I wouldn't do that. Everybody's got ideas, looks like, but nobody knows anything."

"You know the idea everybody in Moon Dance seems to have?" she asked falteringly, as if merely in giving expression to the possibility of death she was adding to its likelihood.

"We ain't payin' any attention to that."

"The poor tike. The poor, sweet, little tike."

Buck transferred the reins to his right hand and put his left arm about his wife's plump shoulders in rough caress.

"There now, Martha, don't you cry," he said with that show of confidence that devotion can muster from despair. "Me and the Judge and West will find her yet." Clumsily, he patted her shaking back.

She nodded dumbly and wiped her eyes on the robe that lay over her lap, and for an hour they drove on, silent and miserable.

"No need to tire yourself holdin' that umbrella any longer," Buck said solicitously then. "Rain's stopped."

The storm clouds had broken and scudded away, and the heavens showed fleecy in the intermittent illumination of a high small moon. The wind had died, too, leaving the night soft and still. Their first energy spent, the horses went slower now, the sounds of their hoofs muffled in the soft earth.

"Sure smells fresh and sweet," Buck remarked. "Air's so still you can almost hear it sing."

He jerked the team to a halt.

"Honey! Honey!" he cried, a choking fullness in his voice, "It is singin'! That's the bell a-pealin'!"

CHAPTER FIFTEEN

E VEN SOONER than Judge LaFrance had predicted, the
rain came. The whistling wind sprayed it, swift
and sharp, from a northern horizon curtained with shifting clouds. Banners and pennants of vapor scudded low
in the sky. Long trailers reached down, fingering the
earth regretfully as they yielded to the gale. The world
contracted, to flicker darkly in the driving mist.

Cawinne put on the slicker that the Judge had given
him, buttoned it tight and, forcing his hat low over
his eyes, spurred his unwilling mount into the teeth of
the storm, over the trail that he and Buck had taken on
news of Miles Larion's death. When thicket or gully
showed to right or left, he rode to it, to explore with the
methodical thoroughness of a man who has concluded
that a missing object must be under hand, since all other
possibilities have been exhausted. Once, where a footprint was impressed vaguely on the bare bank of a
rivulet, he dismounted for a closer scrutiny, but after a
moment got back on his horse and pushed on.

A mile from the Smoky Water ford, he cut to the
left and came to the stream some two miles west of the
point at which the bodies of McLean and Larion had
been found. In the cover of the aspen and cottonwood
that straggled miserably along the banks of the tortuous
river, his horse moved more willingly, and, working upstream, he had frequently to restrain it, while he took
time to examine every cut-bank and coppice that might
conceal a man and a girl.

By the time he reached the foothills of the upper

Smoky Water, the rain had slackened, though the wind still screamed, raw and rough, out of the north. Down from its aspen grove, across a clumped and stony slope, the ruined mansion called Indian Pete's Palace glared at him out of the thinning mist.

Thirty years before, when the visionary humanitarians of the invading race had decided that the education of Indian youth would elevate and transform tribal standards, Peter Runs A Mile had been sent to an Indian academy, there to absorb the major virtues of the alien culture for the benefit of his people. Back on his native heath after his exposure to the civilizing influences of the whites, he revealed that he had acquired a thirst for whisky, developed his Indian's love of the wide gesture, and discovered ways of gaming hitherto unknown to his delighted compatriots. More than that, through the kindness of a rich and addled eastern dowager, who had been fascinated by his innate dignity, he had acquired a considerable fortune through a provision of her will.

Whatever its failings, the influence of his education was strong enough to make him want a house, and almost immediately on his return he began casting about for a place befitting one of his erudition, affluence, origin and impulse. What made him decide on the long-forsaken ranch house of the defunct Empire Land and Cattle Company, no one seemed to know, not even Pete himself. It had been a great place once, a gathering center for blooded Englishmen, for dukes and earls and spendthrift sons of rich and titled fathers, who came to the American West with an airy if inoffensive confidence in the combination of cattle and aristocrats, and who left it, for the most part, poorer if not wiser, their assets checked off against the liabilities of inexperience, irresolution and noble prodigality. Poorly situated in the remote and stony

hills of the upper Smoky Water, crippled by errors of
judgment and lack of will, the Empire outfit was among
the first of the foreign syndicates to realize the insensi-
bility of cows to caste. Its money ran out, its hands
found other jobs, its principals vanished. Only the house
remained, a sequestered and decaying reminder of other
and gayer days. About it, even in Pete's time, still sounded
the echoes of that grander time, and it was, perhaps,
the lingering shadow of that vanished substance that
prompted Pete to acquire it. Or perhaps it was only that
his roving ancestors had liked the site, as a multitude of
half obliterated teepee rings in the vicinity of the house
gave evidence.

Pete demolished a part of the house, a part of it he
restored, and to all that he let stand he added touches that
were peculiarly his own. When he had finished, there
stood a bold and scowling structure so ugly that it met
even Pete's standard of the impressive.

The remainder of the Indian's monetary inheritance
went fast, but hardly faster than the outward marks of
his eastern training. Back among his own people, he felt
the pull of the old ways, of the campfire and the hunt
and the free life. When, finally, his money was gone, he
returned to the teepee and the existence of the nomad.
The one physical fruit of the humanitarians' experiment
was his grotesque house, which no one wanted except
for its materials and which some lingering loyalty to the
life that the academy had attempted to graft on his
Indian roots kept Pete from selling for junk.

And so for years, until fire destroyed it, the structure
stood empty and disintegrating, its lower floor used as a
refuge by cattle in fly-time and cold, its upper story
netted with cobwebs and tracked by field mice. Gales
blew out the windows that adventurous boys did not

break. The aspens, once cut back, regained their losses and shouldered the building resentfully on side and rear. The paint peeled off, the chimneys fell, and the shingles shed in patches under the pull of the wind. Abandoned and doomed, the great house glared out of its empty eyes with a hulking and sullen defiance toward the world and particularly toward the occasional horseman who traveled the trail below it.

So it glared at Cawinne, who had pulled his horse to a stop as he came upstream to the crossing. Half shielded by the low, blowing growth that crowded the ford, he surveyed the crumbling structure in absent speculation for a minute before turning his gaze up the twisting canyon of the Smoky Water as if in consideration of a continued search along its banks. He rode across the stream, but abruptly, like a man under the compulsion of a sudden and significant idea, he looked again at the old house and after an instant of scrutiny drew his mount to one side in the full cover of the willows.

He tied the animal there when he had completed a quick and guarded study of the terrain about the Palace, and slipped back to the trail. Concealment was difficult in the clearing that the road had worn, and after a moment of deliberation he lay flat on his belly and wormed his way across a shallow dip that led across the trail to the underbrush at the other side. Once there, he arose, ran down the stream for two hundred yards, crouching where the thicket thinned, and cut to the left behind the shelter of a low ridge.

Thus concealed from the house, he reached the aspen grove that stretched eastward from it. There he stopped to doff the encumbering slicker, which he dropped at the side of a tree. Before proceeding, he hitched up his belt and, throwing his gloves with the coat, tried his revolvers in their holsters. When he moved again, it was with quick caution, zigzagging, stooping, halting for rapid observations. Between himself and the glaring windows of the decaying mansion he kept the clustered quaking asp.

When he came finally to the east wall of the house, he stood close against it for an instant while he looked and listened. Nothing sounded except the cry of the gale and the complaint of the shaken ruin. He slid to a window, thrust his head beyond its edge and peered into the crepuscular interior while his eyes sharpened to the gloom. Noiselessly, alertly, he put a foot over the low casement and climbed through.

Inside, the wind sounded muted and mournful. Murmurous with years and desolation, the mouldering pile muttered accompaniment to its mood.

Motionless in a murk that the pearly oblongs of windows and door made it more difficult to penetrate, Cawinne took careful stock. He had entered what had been the living room. Running across the entire front of the structure, it was a wreck of fallen plaster, rotting casements and splintered floorboards that cattle had littered. From it, a crumbling stairway climbed to the upper story, and on either side of it doorways gave to the rear.

In that musty twilight no life stirred. The shadows of corner and nook that the gray day hesitated to explore were still as death. There was only the old house breathing, crowding its broken body with the dismal and forsaken spirit of itself.

Picking his way through the debris, Cawinne moved silently through a doorway to the rear. The next compartment, which once had been a dining room, was as empty and dilapidated as the first. From the room behind it, almost lost in the melancholy whispering of the house, came a small thumping like a heel moving to music.

He went through another doorway into the one-time kitchen, and as he did so the dark soul of the Palace for an instant seemed naked and revealed in the scuttling figure of a pack rat which scurried from behind a broken box, beady eyes aglint, and paused before diving into a hole in the floor to thump its scaly tail on the boards in a gesture of suspicious and furtive defiance.

Cawinne went on. Everywhere were gloom and ruin and decay. The pantry and the porch at the rear of the house and the bedrooms and closet at its western side were vacant and still. Nowhere was there sign or signal of life, except for the mourning of the place at its own demise.

The round of the first floor completed, Cawinne came to the stairway that stepped to the second and stopped to examine it. Fresh patterns of footprints showed on the dusty wood, but whether they were the prints only of Judge LaFrance in his frantic, first-day search, or the marks of intruding boys, or the sign of a fugitive and his captive, no tracker could have told even had the light been better.

Cautiously, Cawinne began to ascend, testing each step before he put his weight on it, looking from side to side at the top of the long, steep stairway, for it had no turn or landing and appeared to open both to right and left at its upper end, where a window, cut in the end wall, admitted a leaden light.

The ancient lumber complained even under his careful tread, but its voice was only one in the creaking chorus of destruction, and he climbed on, watchful but un-hesitating, to the top.

A wide hall, somewhat better illuminated than the

ground floor, ran back from the stairway to a second window in the front wall. On the left-hand side a sagging door, whining on its hinges as the draft moved it back and forth, gave to what once was a bedroom. Two entrances, from which the doors had been removed by earlier visitors, penetrated the other wall.

Cawinne paused to run his eye from doorway to doorway and from footprint to footprint along the patterned floor, but the tracks were confused and the light feeble even here, and after a moment he glided to the room at the left and peered in. In the forsaken chamber there was only a broken iron bedstead, half covered by peeling wallpaper on which great clusters of roses had faded and run. As the wind stirred in the room, the once gaudy tatters added a sighing rustle to the Palace's weary murmur.

Noiselessly, he moved to the other rooms and found them tenantless, and he stood irresolute and dissatisfied, in the hallway. The gloom deepened as he waited, and the rain began to drum on the roof with new insistence.

Less cautiously, he descended the stairway and crossed the front room to the window and stepped out, but there in the dripping gloam he paused again uncertainly. Head toward the ground then, like a dog questing for a scent, he began a circle of the house, keeping close to its walls. Even so, he might have missed the stone but for an unseen wire that caught the toe of his boot and threw him forward on his hands. He started to rise, but there it lay, a heavy conglomerate placed tight against the foundation, and, dim in the dusk, half effaced by the rain, were the prints of boot heels.

He cast a quick glance about and, satisfied, locked his fingers under an end of the rock and wrenched it back. Behind it, a hole opened in the foundation like the mouth of a burrow. For a bare instant he paused, then slued around, thrust his feet in the opening and wormed himself back. Inside, the ground had been cut away, and he felt for footing as he let himself down the earthen wall. His boots touched the floor as his head came level with the opening. He released his hold and looked around him, but his eyes could not penetrate the darkness save close at his right, where the meager light from the entrance revealed a crumbling stairway. Later he was to wonder why he had not discovered it on his tour of the first floor, and still later he was to find that Indian Pete, with his red man's dislike of the subterranean, had floored it over.

Slowly, as his eyes came to focus, the darkness grew into a pattern of shadows, and he perceived that he was in a roughly finished cellar, in which the extravagant operators of the Empire Land and Cattle Company undoubtedly had stored their vintages.

He took a step away from the hole in the foundation, but turned as if on second thought, and grunting, brought the stone back across the opening.

The voice was thin and tight with strain.

"What do you want now?"

A face, as he wheeled around, swam pale and disembodied in the thick murk of the place.

"It is West Cawinne—"

The words came out in a quick, breaking little cry. "Oh, I didn't know! I couldn't see—"

For an instant they stood silent and motionless in the shock of discovery, and the splash of the rain from the dripping eaves sounded loud in the underground room.

He said stiffly, "We'll leave now, Tana."

Urgently her hand clasped his arm. "Wait!" she whispered. "Wait!"

"For what?"

She drew him back, away from the hole by which he had entered.

"Shh!" she cautioned. "He will be coming. It is his time."

"Who will be coming?" he whispered back, but she breathed a "Shh!" again, and they stood motionless, waiting in the deep shades. Her hand, resting still on his arm, shook with the waiting, and her breath was light and fast with suspense.

He looked at her and saw her more plainly now, for the darkness was fading, and his hand shot out and seized her and brought her head to his. "Get him down here! Get him to talk! He won't see me!" he whispered, and slipped into the darker shadow of the stairway, away from the light that the moving stone was admitting.

A voice spoke from the hole in the wall.

"You want now to tell where the mine is?"

As if for assurance, she glanced fleetingly in Cawinne's direction, then back to the entrance.

"How can I know you will let me go if I do?"

The voice grunted with astonishment. "You will go, all right. Come close, so we can talk."

"No."

"I come in, then."

After a minute, a body stuffed out the light from the hole, dropped to the floor and turned to face her. Re-admitted, the gray illumination outlined a figure hooded with a flour sack in which eyeholes had been cut. The figure advanced on the shrinking girl.

"So you will talk?"

"How do I know you will let me go? Whose word do I have?"

"It is enough if I say it," said the other, and suddenly, quick as any cat, as if all the time he had seen the man hiding in the shadow, he lunged at Cawinne.

They went down heavily in a sprawl, shattering the rotten staircase as they fell, but in Cawinne's hand before his back struck the ground and a swift agony paralyzed him was the other's six-shooter. He lay flat and still, grunting a little with the pain in his back, straining to bring his tortured limbs under the command of his will, while his opponent's hands clutched fiercely at his throat.

He got one breath, in a harsh, strangling wheeze, and now, as the stout fingers closed the passage and the world began to wheel, his right hand came up like a study in slow motion, and the revolver in his fist barked one hollow bark in the dank chamber.

The slug knocked a guttural exhalation from the man and rolled him over in a momentary convulsion, but he scrambled to his feet, still full of fight, and from the broken stairway seized a timber. His wild swing cleared Cawinne by inches, but the timber thudded sharply against the magazine of the revolver and sent it spinning from Cawinne's clenched hand.

The force of the swing threw the man off balance, and to recover, he stumbled away from his foe. When he turned back, his bludgeon upheld, it was to face again the dull bar of the revolver, held now in the hand of Tana Deck.

The speed and fury of the struggle had numbed the girl, but as the revolver had spun from Cawinne's grasp she ran and snatched it up and rushed protectively between the two men.

The hooded figure hesitated and then moved forward one slow step.

"Shoot!" barked Cawinne, hitching himself desperately to one side to remove the girl from the line between them. "Shoot him!"

The man hesitated again, and a slow gasp came from him, and he held his make-shift weapon motionless overhead like a mechanical man in which the spring has run down.

"Go!" warned Tana. "Go!"

Uncertainly, as if waiting for nature to rewind him, the man stood there, his slitted hood shining ghostly white in the murk, and then he gasped again and the club slid out of his hands. He rocked unsteadily on his feet and, turning, stumbled toward the opening in the wall.

"Hold up!" ordered Cawinne from the floor, but he went dumbly ahead and lifted himself laboriously into the mouth of the hole and crowded through.

Slowly, Tana sank to the floor. A long shudder shook her. "I couldn't shoot him," she cried in a whisper. "Oh, I couldn't shoot him! It is blood! Always blood!"

Jerkily, she raised herself then and turned to Cawinne. "Are you hurt?"

"No," he said, and that one bare word had in it admiration and wonder.

"You are hurt," she denied in growing anxiety, and stooped by his side.

But the lean, hard fibre of him rapidly was throwing off the quick paralysis that the blow on his spine had induced, and he found after a little that he could get to his feet and walk.

"Come," he said.

"Are you—all right?"

"Yes," he said, but before he tried the opening he thrust his hat out as a test. When it was undisturbed, he brought it back, clamped it on his head and raised himself into the exit, seeking, as he crawled through, to rub off the blood that his hands had felt.

With quick vigilance, he looked about him in the gloom, then reached back and gave Tana a hand and she clambered up and out.

The rain still whispered on the sodden earth and the old house muttered to the wind, but of their visitor there was no sign.

CHAPTER SIXTEEN

AFTER CAWINNE had looked and harkened, Tana raised
her eyes wonderingly to the wall of the Palace
that rose at her side. She turned to Cawinne with an
unuttered question in her manner.

"It's Indian Pete's Palace," he explained, understanding all at once that she did not know where she was.

"I tried and tried to guess," she said, her voice low
and husky with tired relief, "but I never could. You
see, I was blindfolded when we had left Moon Dance
behind." She paused, as if the memory of that trip still
held terror for her. "We got here at night, and I fought
with all my might, but finally found myself in that dark
cellar just the same."

"Come," he said, and guided her away from the scene.

In the quaking asps, he picked up the coat he had
dropped there and slipped it close about her slim shoulders, for, though the wind had lessened, a fine, keen rain
kept sifting from the shaken heavens. Low in the west,
the darkening sky pearled before the hidden sun.

Weighted and silent with their thoughts, they descended the ridge and came to the stream where
Cawinne's horse stood hunched among the twisted trees.

Down through the gathering dusk, Indian Pete's Palace
stared black and bleak, and Tana, glimpsing it as Cawinne
helped her into the saddle, shivered convulsively, losing
before that somber gaze the confusion in which she had
sought to arrange dress and slicker as she took her seat
astride.

"I'll see it in my dreams forever," she said then, as if
to herself.

"I'll think," she whispered a little wildly, still in the way of self-communion, "that the masked man is looking out of it, and the eyes in the old, dark house will be his eyes, staring at me."

Cawinne glanced up at her and spoke softly. "Tomorrow will be different."

He added, "The two happiest people in Moon Dance will be the Judge and Bally Buck."

"But I want to talk about it," she insisted in a voice small and restrained. "Just telling someone will help, as if I were putting part of the load on another's shoulders."

She was silent, though, for moments, while horse and man plodded in the sodden trail.

It was as if she noticed for the first time then that he was afoot, and she slipped to the side of the saddle as if to dismount. The horse came to a stop at the shift in its burden.

"I'm going to walk and you're going to ride," she announced. "I don't know what I'm doing up here. You are the one who is hurt."

"No," he answered commandingly. "The walk will help me. I'm all right."

"But I can see that you aren't," she insisted self-reproachfully as her mount, with Cawinne's hand at its bridle, resumed stride. "Let's both ride then."

He looked up at her and smiled and shook his head. "This old snorter won't ride double."

"And besides," she added, "I have your coat and you are wet through and have to walk to keep warm, even if walking hurts you."

"I'm warm enough," he answered, and they both fell silent again until, in that low, quiet voice of reminiscence she said self-accusingly, "I shouldn't have been so afraid. No one intended me any harm. I wasn't in danger. All that was wanted was the location of the Early Day, and I didn't know where it was. But I was afraid, terribly afraid, and down in that cellar I would cry to myself." The edge of hysteria had crept into her tones. "And I got so I looked forward to the visits of the masked man, just because it gave me someone to talk to."

"I would have found you sooner," said Cawinne in a manner that he purposely made matter-of-fact, "if only you had yelled while I was searching the first and second floors of the Palace."

"I heard you walking," she admitted, "but I had heard people walking before and I had shouted until my voice was gone, but no one had ever come and I just supposed whoever was in the house was someone who wanted to keep me prisoner."

After a moment she resumed, "The very first day that I was in the cellar, someone poked around the building for a long time. He had a slow step, different from the steps I heard once or twice later, and I shouted and shouted, but it was just as if he didn't hear me."

Cawinne interrupted in swift understanding: "He didn't."

"Didn't?"

"He couldn't. That was old Judge LaFrance, probably without even his trumpet. He scouted the Palace first, and we never thought to do it again, not considering that maybe his deafness would keep him from finding you."

He looked up into the oval of her face, now made vague by the gathering darkness, and smiled without amusement but with some quality of regret and regard that brought a wistful answering smile.

The night closed in, damp and chill. Around them in the unwinking dark was no sound save the insistent whisper of the rain.

After a while, Cawinne brought the horse to a halt, stepped back to its side and unbuckled a side pocket.

"You're frozen," he said. "I can hear your teeth chattering."

Uncertainly, her hand closed upon the bottle he thrust upon her.

"Take a swallow, anyway," he urged.

She drank from the flask then and, half choking, handed it back, and he pulled at it too before returning it to the saddle.

"Maybe you'd better walk for a while," he suggested.

At her "All right," he lifted her from the saddle.

"Hang on to me," he suggested. "The going's hard, and you're tired enough to fall."

Obediently, she slipped an arm through his, and they walked together on the wet earth. The patient horse, a shapeless movement in the dark, splashed steadily behind them.

Presently her small hand touched his open palm, and his fingers closed upon it, and, as if the intimacy of their solitary journey through the unrevealing dark lightened the guarded burdens of her heart, she asked about her father.

Simply, he told her of the funeral and of the things the Reverend Logan had said about Tandy Deck, and of the general sorrow at his passing.

Head bowed, she listened, and when he was done she said in a small voice steady with resignation, "It all seems so far away, so very far away."

He went on to tell her then of the efforts that Moon Dance had put forth to find her, of the anxiety of the Judge and Bally and Mrs. Buck and all her friends, of the firing of Breedtown and of the continued operation of Motorists' Mecca under the direction of Goldie Lampkins.

Afterwards, they walked on wordlessly, each busy with his own thoughts, while her hand lay warm and confiding in his.

She asked, after a long silence, "How did you happen to give the Palace a second search?"

"I wasn't going to," he responded. "I was spying around the thickets on the off chance of running into you. We were all desperate, and the only thing I felt sure of, somehow, was that you had been taken north and still weren't very far away. Then when I got opposite Indian Pete's Palace, I noticed something."

"What?"

"It was pretty cold, and the wind was firing that rain from the north. In weather like that, it was almost certain that some of those wild Smoky Water cattle would be in the Palace keeping warm, with their noses poked out of the lee side windows. But I didn't see a cow, and I got to wondering how come they'd been scared off."

"I see," she said gravely.

She seemed free now of the beginning hysteria that had marked the start of their journey, and he suggested quietly:

"Tana, you must have an idea who your kidnaper was."

Gradually, as the significance of that question occurred to her, her hand stiffened in his, and she drew it out, and her voice when she answered had tightened with emotion.

"I have no idea. Absolutely no idea. Every time I saw him he was masked."

He did not respond, and as if his silence expressed doubt and criticism she added in tones strangely loud and positive, "I have no idea, but if I did I wouldn't tell you. It would only mean more trouble, more shooting, more blood."

It was a long minute before he answered and then he said only, "Yes."

Her hand dropped from his arm.

"Maybe you'd better get back in the saddle now," he proposed.

"Why must it be so?" she asked in a half whisper, as if inquiring of herself. "Why must it be so with you?"

"Up!" he said, and made a stirrup of his hands.

"Why?" she breathed again, her hysteria reduced to that one low, accusing question.

"What does it matter?" he asked shortly. "It's just that when a man gets started in a certain way, he can't let up."

"Oh," she retorted, as if comprehending all at once, "your reputation!"

"Have it that way if you want it."

As he spoke he glanced upward at the slim, vague silhouette of her figure, and suddenly she reached down and touched him impulsively on the shoulder in a gesture conciliatory and half regretful.

"What I said the other night, the night Daddy died—"

"It's all right," he interrupted.

She straightened in the saddle. "Thank you," she said stiffly, as if to put an end to all that had passed between them.

Like worn travelers occupied with thoughts of destination, they moved through the night. The rain had ceased, and overhead the moon broke clear, shining high and bright from a sky patched with clouds like drifting down. Red in the shadowed bowl of the valley, the scattered lights of Moon Dance came into view.

Still silent, they reached the town and passed through the sleeping outskirts and came upon Main Street, on which, like one vigilant eye in the thick of slumber, the lighted window of Judge LaFrance's shop kept watch.

"I want to see the Judge," she said as they drew near his place, and Cawinne led the horse to the side of the street and helped her down.

Half asleep in his chair at the rear, Judge LaFrance peered over his glass and a flood of relief came over his face at the sight of Cawinne, who had entered first as the girl hung back, suddenly hesitant, and motioned for him to go ahead.

"For some reason or other I been sitting up kind of late, Kid," the Judge said lamely to Cawinne, as if to explain away his presence in the shop. "Ought to have been in bed hours ago."

His puckered eyes sprang wide.

"Praise be to God!" he boomed. "Little Tana, back home and safe!"

In a moment she was crying on his shrunken shoulder.

CHAPTER SEVENTEEN

HUNCHED ON A STOOL behind the clerk's high desk at the Moon Dance House, Scott Hardy propped his chin on his closed fists. His large brown eyes, as deceptively gentle in appearance as a Jersey bull's, gazed in absent speculation through the soiled front window of the hotel to the street, at the edge of which two old cottonwoods were knobbed with bursting buds. Occasionally his long upper lip lifted stiffly to let out a small *pfft* as he sucked at a front tooth.

Before him in the lobby four men were playing solo for drinks. Their rough voices made an intermittent, echoing rumble in the high, dark paneled room. Cowmen all, they slapped their cards down hard, as if the very force of the play would establish the trick winner. When one went broke, the other three jeered good-naturedly, and all repaired to the hotel's little frequented bar to drink at his expense.

A dour, extreme man given to such frivolity only on occasion, Hardy declined their insistent invitations to join them. After a while, Bally Buck left the card table, clumped across the worn green linoleum that covered the floor and lounged against the counter, his heavy forearm resting on its top.

"Got it figured out yet?" he asked of Hardy.

The latter kept looking moodily out the window and gave two meditative sucks at his tooth before replying. "What?" he asked then, as if the answer were of no consequence.

"Whatever it is you're figuring on."

Hardy sunk his chin deeper in his cupped fists. When he spoke, the knuckles against his lower cheeks gave his mouth a look of infantile pout.

"Well-meaning people sure as hell bust a button to get right with the Lord once they're afraid they've been wrong."

Buck regarded the averted face quizzically.

"Ain't that what they call philosophy?"

"Fact."

Buck fished in the pocket of his open vest, drew out a fat cigar, wallowed it around in his mouth and lit it with a match struck on the seat of his faded trousers.

A solo player's "I'll try one" broke into their silence.

Hardy resumed: "They bust a button and get caught with their pants down."

"Meanin'?" asked Buck, squaring around toward the speaker.

The hotel man looked at him, long and slow, as if the situation were plain without explanation.

"Meaning," he answered, "that Robideau could pretty near come into town now and get an even break."

"If he tangled with the kid?"

Hardy nodded. "This town's never seen the time it would ride a man very hard for killing another in a fair fight, provided both was in good standing."

Buck scratched his stubbled jaw. "It ain't likely the boys are forgettin' the murders and rackin' up," he observed tranquilly.

"Ah hell!" contradicted Hardy. "To most of them it's just like everything was over and past now that Tana Deck's back. And even those that maybe don't feel quite that way are just aching to make it up to Robideau because they acted in a way unbefittin' the actual evidence. Burning Breedtown was so damn extreme, they've got to swing the other way to get their consciences eased down." His wide mouth lifted at a corner as he turned his gaze on Buck. "The fools! Bunch of jug-heads around here didn't even have a hand in the burning, are now popping with Christian regrets because they had a sneaking sympathy with Cox and Rell that night on the Crazy Cree. Robideau wasn't the one that suffered anyway, as you might have known, but even if he was it was just damn good and well what he deserved. Makes me sick!"

Buck blew a cloud of smoke toward the cobwebbed ceiling. "You're overdoin' it," he said placatingly. "The boys are a little short on memory all right and some of 'em may be strayin' in their minds, but Robideau ain't in a position to start anything. Just one bow in his neck, and a crowd will be remembering McLean and Larion and old man Wright."

He turned to follow Hardy's gaze as the latter tapped him significantly on the forearm.

Outside, into the scene framed by the front-window casement, there came a figure low and hefty and close-knit and yet somehow easy and fluid in movement, like an animal.

An absorbed solo player was counting: "Eleven, twenty-two, thirty-three, forty-three, forty-seven—"

Hardy pushed back from the desk and spat down on the floor. When he looked up it was to gesture to Buck as if a point had been demonstrated.

"Not wasting any time taking the hand of good-fellowship," he commented dryly.

"All dolled up pretty, too," Buck added. "Nice new flannel shirt, hay brushed off his pants, boots shiny and hat shaped up."

"That flock of brass on his belt and hat band shows the breed."

"And no guns—in sight anyway."

"That's what the parson would call the true sign of the spirit of repentance," Hardy said out of the side of his mouth. "It ought to get him in good with the Ladies' Industrial."

Buck moved leisurely away from the counter, hitching his forty-five into position as he did so.

Interest jumped to two points of light in Hardy's slow brown eyes.

"You said he couldn't afford to start anything," he reminded Buck.

"Right," agreed the rancher, still moving away.

Hardy started to climb down from the stool.

The other held up a restraining hand. "I'm just going to speak a piece, anyway," he said.

"Maybe you'll need someone to help knock a knot on his head," the hotel man answered hopefully.

"Too quick on the trigger, Scott. You won't do for a pow-wow," Buck negatived over his shoulder.

Slowly, Hardy climbed back on his stool, grunting aloud to himself, "That sounds funny, coming from him."

Buck paused at the card table for a minute while one of the players gustily related an episode of the game. Then, shaking his head at requests to sit in again, he walked with an air of leisure out of the door onto the street.

Except for a handful of men clustered in the block to the north, the street was deserted. Gone back to their tasks were the celebrants who had crowded the town the day before, rejoicing at the return of Tana Deck.

It had been a great day. From thirty miles around, the rural residents of Powder County had streamed into Moon Dance, apprised of developments by that same quick telegraphy that had brought them news of the kidnaping. By buckboard and lumberwagon, by buggy and saddle, they came to town to celebrate, increasing in numbers as the remoter sections reported until, by late afternoon, stores and saloons were taxed with their patronage and the rough two-by-six walks sounded steadily to not always steady feet. As if the restoration of Tana were a dizzying stroke of personal good fortune, ranchers and ranchwives had quit work, cowpunchers deserted their posts, teamsters unhooked their horses in the field, and hired girls abandoned their chores to give expression at Moon Dance to a wild exultation. Business men and their employes joined in, for the most part reluctant to withdraw from the spirit of carnival to wait on trade. Judge LaFrance forsook his awl and bench to hobble up and down Main Street, telling all inquirers how Tana and Cawinne had come to his shop the night before. The solitary Wright came in from the ranch, his ape's face wrinkled in a delighted smile. Blackie Cox got drunk and allowed Cawinne a grudging measure of praise in the face of the general sentiment. The sitting rooms of Moon Dance's homes buzzed with callers and conversations. Mrs. Jack Smith's millinery and ice-cream store was thick with a fluttering humanity. Loud and genial, men stood two and three deep at Adlam's and the Family Liquor bar, deliberately drinking more than they should out of a jubilation that scorned all ordinary restrictions. Half a hundred women, uncertain whether to congratulate or condole, went to see Tana Deck, who met them in the bare little living room over Motorists' Mecca. No less jubilant if more restrained than the rest, the Reverend Howard Logan went to his study and there gave thanks that his prayers had been answered. A dance at Woodmen's Hall, lasting well into the dawn, brought

an end to the festivity. Long before it was over, tired
and groggy revelers had started heading for home, welcoming, now that their spirits were spent, the thought
of bed and the routine of day by day.

It had been a day of wide gesture, of generosity, of
ready friendship, and as a consequence a day of faint but
recurring regrets. The very openness of heart began to
make men regard with revulsion that savage attack on
Breedtown, particularly since no evidence linked Robideau or his satellites with the abduction. A feeling of
guilt pricked members of that indignant and impulsive
company that had followed Cox and Rell up the Crazy
Cree. The stay-at-homes who had sympathized with the
raid had a secret sense of wrong-doing. Both classes
suffered from the half-acknowledged conviction that
decency demanded amends, not so much to the real
sufferers from the Breedtown attack as to those who
had provided cause for it. In contrast to the self-accusers,
a few men like Scott Hardy, who had neither participated
in nor encouraged the sack of the settlement, rebelled at
the unexpressed but perceptible sentiment that a wrong
done Robideau required apology or redress.

Whatever their impulses, Powder Countians generally
were entertaining them privately as Buck swung up the
street with the stiff, rocking gait of the cowhand toward
that single cluster of men. Like the street, the stores were
almost deserted. Here and there a shopkeeper made a
pretense of rearranging stock for customers he appeared
too listless to serve. One team stood at a hitch-rack at the
side of the Moon Dance Mercantile Company. Tattered
wrappers, torn sacks and empty whisky bottles, ignored
by tired swampers, littered the walks. Nursing a hang-
over, Moon Dance had drawn into herself, leaving the
disorder of yesterday until tomorrow.

Buck clumped with easy confidence along the waste-strewn walk, his thumbs hooked in his belt. Low on his right side his worn old forty-five depended.

As he approached and halted, the knot of men fanned out a little, and Robideau stood facing him at the end of an irregular aisle.

Jay Coffey, a rancher from south of the Crazy Cree, was one of the group, and he shifted uneasily, as if in embarrassment at the company he kept, and grunted a greeting. The others—three breeds, a dry-lander from the Cottonwood country, and a strange cowpoke—were silent. Their eyes went from Buck to Robideau to Buck.

As the two principals faced each other wordlessly, the lines shifted. The breeds edged to Robideau's side. Coffey moved around to stand with Buck. As nonpartisans, the dry-lander and the cowhand held their positions.

It was Robideau who spoke first. Black and hard as obsidian, his eyes under their heavy lids were the only life in an impassive face.

"Is it trouble, Buck?" he asked in his close, clipped speech.

"Not without you make it so."

"Breedtown, I don't forget what you did for my people there," came out of that mask of strict composure.

"I ain't lookin' for thanks, Robideau," Buck responded. The bluntness of his words contrasted with the mild evenness of his tone. "I just been comin' up the street sayin' to myself that if people forget things easy, still it don't take much to remind 'em."

Robideau answered "Uh" like a teepee Indian.

"There's some, now, ain't in exactly a healthy position to start anything."

For reply, Robideau spread open his strong, dark hands and looked down at his holsterless thighs.

"Cawinne," he said, his eyes as lustrous as a serpent's, "he fears too much."

A surge of blood swelled Buck's thick neck and stained his face.

"When Cawinne sends messages, they'll be wrote on lead, Robideau," he said a little louder. "This is my own idea. If you're not a whole damn fool, you'll remember."

Abruptly, as if there were no more to be said on either side, he strode ahead, brushing Robideau as he passed. Silent, the men watched him for a moment as he bow-legged up the street toward Judge LaFrance's.

Inside the harness shop, Buck asked, "Where's West?"

Standing stooped at his bench, the Judge turned, pushed awl and leather aside, and reached for his ear trumpet. Through the wide window behind him the sun like a flattened orange pressed the western horizon.

"What say?" inquired LaFrance.

"Where's West?"

"Went down to Cottonwood early this morning. Didn't say what for."

"I just wanted to tell him Robideau's in town."

Judge LaFrance's white eyebrows lifted as he looked at Buck over his small-framed glasses. "I didn't think it would be long," he said. "Things move ahead."

"What about it?" Buck asked into the trumpet.

The Judge opened his hands expressively.

"Robideau," he said like a schoolmaster, "is no fool, whatever else he is. Sure as he starts anything the community'll rise up and tie a knot in his tail."

"Same way I figured," Buck agreed. He added significantly, "Feelin' ain't near as strong as it was, though, and maybe it'll lighten up some more."

A frown grooved the old justice's seamed forehead. "Oh, well, hell!" he said with regretful resignation. "One

way or another, it'll come out some time, anyhow."
Suddenly irritated, as if vexed at inconsistencies within
himself, he asked sharply, "Ain't that what we expected
when we got West to take the job in the first place?"

Buck nodded soberly. "Yeah, only we didn't know him
as well then." By way of good-bye, he said, "Be in tomorrow," and went on out the door.

He walked down the street and crossed to Motorists'
Mecca. Robideau and the men with him had disappeared
and in the early dusk the only figures were occasional
townsmen bound home from work. A light blossomed
yellow in the restaurant as Buck approached, and Tana
Deck came forward to greet him when he entered. He
sat at the first stool, removed from the other customers,
whom Goldie Lampkins was serving.

After their greetings were said, he asked, "Bring me
whatever's special tonight, Tana, and come and talk to
me while I eat." His eye swept the counter and the
tables behind him. "Things ain't so rushin' but what
Goldie can get along alone."

She returned with his food after a minute and stood
quiet, half smiling, half pensive, as he grinned affectionately at her. In the yellow illumination of the lamp,
her face appeared strained and white, the flesh about her
mouth almost translucent.

"Work is a great cure, Girl," Buck advised out of
the corner of his full mouth, "but go into it kind of easy.
You'll land in the hospital bunch yet if you don't watch
out."

"I'm all right."

"Know Robideau's in town today?"

The words struck her into startled immobility. In her
eyes as Buck glanced up was the liquid, melting look of
an animal too sorely wounded to flee the hunter.

Hastily, the rancher added, "West's in Cottonwood. Been there all day."

She put her small, sturdy hands on the counter, and her gaze fell in confusion before his. Her fingers moved in an uncertain pattern on the wood as she framed her words. "Bally," she asked, for the first time in her life addressing Baldwin Buck informally, "is he—are they—must they surely meet some time?"

She spoke in a small voice, like one trying to breathe life into a lost hope, and all at once, as she looked up, her heart shone in her eyes, naked and fearful and unashamed.

As if he had seen something that was not for him to see, Buck's glance dropped from the still, drawn face, and when he spoke the truth was not quite in him. In abrupt annoyance he ejaculated, "By Joe, Tana! Who can tell about that?"

CHAPTER EIGHTEEN

BUCK stood in front of Motorists' Mecca for a while, smoking and breathing deeply of the night air which, here in the northwest, the darkness keened with winter though half of May was gone. The occasional passers-by he hailed silently, with a lazy motion of his heavy hand. For half an hour he stood thus, a thick, solid, bold figure, lost now in some speculation of his own. Then he pitched away the stub of his cigar and ambled up the street to Adlam's Saloon.

"Hi, Jake," he greeted Jake Schwartz, the fat and tidy barkeeper who came from the rear, carrying his swollen belly lightly. The place was vacant except for him and a drunk who drowsed at a table.

Buck shook his head at the question in Schwartz's glance. "Don't want anything, Jake. I'm just passin' time."

Jake folded his great arms and rested the burden of his bulk against the bar.

"He ain't been in all day," he volunteered. His voice was high and girlish, as obese men's sometimes are. When he spoke, the crowded slit of his mouth barely opened, as if to let pass the chosen words and no more. "Tell me he's gone to Cottonwood."

Buck nodded and flipped away the match with which he had lighted a fresh cigar. "Don't matter exactly," he replied. "He don't need anyone to ride herd on him."

"Enemy's gettin' right spunky," Jake observed. The gleam of a pair of shrewd eyes, deep in pockets of fat, gave life to his round, dull face.

Buck nodded again. "Some."

Jake brought together the pudgy fingers of his spread hands. "I hope I don't miss it," he said, and added, "Be too bad if your boy got to thinking it was easy."

As the drunk stirred he picked up a towel and mechanically began wiping the spotless counter, as if the subject were at an end. "Some celebration yesterday, huh?"

"He ain't one to get it in his neck," Buck answered. "I'll be seein' you."

He clumped out of the saloon and drifted down Main Street, and, from it, down the side street on which stood the stucco offices of the *Moon Dance Messenger*.

The place was yellow with light and noisy with the cough of a gasoline motor and the grind of a flat-bed press.

As Buck entered, Maxie Roser looked up from a form he was adjusting on a stone. A smudge of printer's ink in the fluttering illumination of a lamp overhead gave an evil leer to his ordinarily amiable countenance.

"Workin' late, ain't you, Maxie?" Buck shouted by way of greeting.

"You damn well know we do on Wednesday. First run's got to be got off and some type set. Tomorrow's press day."

"Yeah," replied Buck with the outdoor man's good-natured scorn of indoor work. "Mighty tough."

Roser jerked his thumb toward the rear, where a printer stood on a platform feeding sheets into the press.

"Been all right this week," he remarked, "if Handy hadn't gone on a bust."

He added as an afterthought, with no attempt at humor: "So would we have been every other week."

He dropped his make-up rule into the pocket of the

canvas apron he was wearing and untied the apron and took it off.

"Anyhow, I've had enough for one day," he said. "Handy'll be through with that run in a minute. Let's set!"

First, he turned to a rickety table, crusted with the drippings of other washings, and laved his hands in a battered basin in which the water was stringy and opaque from use. He dried them on a black and stiffened towel, and, spying the smear on his face in a dingy mirror above the table, eyed the towel dubiously and made an indifferent pass at the smudge with a scrap of newsprint that he wetted on his tongue. Then he led the way around a proof press and dusty cabinet of type to the space he used as office. Undivided from the rest of the building, it was a litter of crumpled paper, discarded journals and hasty scissorings. On an old roll-top desk an Oliver typewriter clung precariously against the encroachments of a pile of unopened exchanges, trade catalogues, correspondence, and odds and ends of boiler plate. About the whole place was the mixed odor of printer's ink, paste, gasoline, musty paper and tobacco smoke.

"I'll get this devil's nest cleaned out some day," Roser said in an off-hand apology for the disorder as he salvaged a chair from the waste. "Take it easy for a while. The Judge usually drops in on Wednesday nights if he can't scare up someone for a game of cribbage."

"Speak of the devil—" he added, for Judge LaFrance came crippling through the door.

The press came to a groaning stop and the motor coasted into silence as Handy Mason finished the run.

"Hello, Judge. Come in!" Roser shouted. " 'Night, Mason. Bright and early in the morning, remember!"

Judge LaFrance eased his infirmities into the seat that Roser offered.

"Copy falls right into the office," the pudgy editor said. "What's hot? I already got that Mr. Robideau, sometimes of Breedtown, was a pleasant visitor in our midst today."

Buck sprawled out in his chair and hooked his thumbs in his belt. "You tell us for once."

"All right," answered Roser. "Old Often Wright, being the only known relative, heirs all of Seldom's spread, including the McLean place. That give you an idea?"

The Judge, fumbling with his trumpet, grunted "What say?" and the editor repeated his words into the mouth of the horn.

"Motives is beginnin' to run all over the place," Buck complained.

Judge LaFrance raised a palsied hand and stroked the sagging flesh under an eye. "Worth looking into, anyway," he said dubiously. "We'll tell West."

"We'll tell him, but he ain't going to tell us anything," Buck grumbled. "He plays lone wolf too damn much."

"It don't call for cussin', Bally," the Judge answered. "He's got a lot on his mind, and if he don't choose to tell it all, it's all right with me."

"I know," the rancher agreed unwillingly, "but it looks like he might drop us some sign once in a while. We hired him, didn't we?"

"Not to spout," the Judge objected. "Give him his head and let him run."

Buck sighed. "O. K., only that don't give us much of a look-in, or any chance to help him. I like to be dealt into a game, not watch it."

After a silence the Judge said, "He probably don't know what he thinks himself."

Roser had been watching them silently. He put in now, "What is there to think?"

He took a piece of paper from the litter on the desk, uncovered a stub of pencil and shoved the pile back until he had a spot to write on. "Just try to line them out."

In parallel columns on the paper he wrote:

Dead Ones	*Live Ones*
Marty McLean	Often Wright
Miles Larion	Robideau
Seldom Wright	Stud Manker
	Whitey Salter
	Blackie Cox
	Estes Rell

"I'm putting Cox and Rell on the list just on general principles," he explained as he finished his roster, "because they're no-good hounds."

He turned around, the paper in his hand.

"Take them one at a time," he suggested, "figuring all ways."

The Judge pressed tobacco into his battered pipe, held a match over it while his unsteady lips puffed with strenuous ineffectiveness, and bent forward, trumpet to ear.

"Shoot!"

"Take the dead ones first. Who'd shoot Marty Mc-Lean, and why would he do it?"

The editor looked questioningly from one to the other of his auditors.

Buck worried aimlessly at a crack in the floor with the toe of his boot.

"Lot of people might have potted him, on account of the mine."

"All right, supposing first that Seldom Wright killed him, so's to get hold of the mine and his place, too," the editor pursued. "Would Seldom have been fool enough, then, to gun Miles Larion, too, especially after their run-in in town?"

"And if he did, who got Seldom?" the Judge asked.

"Wait a minute, now. We'll come to that. Miles Larion's next. Who wanted him dead bad enough to shoot him?"

"Seldom had a motive there, just like he did with McLean," Judge LaFrance volunteered.

"A motive, yes," agreed the publisher, "and also a darn good reason to let him alone. Seems to me the reason was a lot better than the motive. He could be sure that if he went after Larion everyone in town would know he did it."

Buck and LaFrance nodded soberly.

"Who else, then?"

"Good many people thought Larion was a little too staggy," Buck answered.

"Who thought it strong enough to knock him off?"

"Cawinne said he had a big roll on him, too. Won it in a game. It was gone when they found him, you know."

Roser ran his hand over his pink, dimpled face. "That opens the field to anyone who knew Larion had the money and was coyote enough to kill him for it. So where are we?"

When the others did not answer, he went on: "Now this note that Larion had telling him he better meet the writer at Hangman's Tree. What does it mean? Was Larion mixed up in some dirty work?"

"Can't believe it," Judge LaFrance answered in his loud and toneless voice. "Why would he be in it?"

Roser raised his short arms in a gesture of ignorance. "You have to remember, though, that he had the note," he insisted. "It must mean something."

"You guess," Buck replied to his look of inquiry.

"I don't know any more than you do," the editor responded in his mild and friendly voice. "Just asking this way, though, might get us some place."

He added, "That finishes up the dead ones. Now let's turn to the live list. Often Wright's first on it."

The Judge took his pipe from his teeth and said judicially, "There's a reason there for him to kill Seldom, if he knew he would come into Seldom's layout, but I'd say it wasn't in him."

"You get in some crazy tangles if you figure Often killed Seldom so as to get hold of his spread," Roser commented. "If you say he killed Seldom all of a sudden, on realizing what he'd gain by it, you have to look somewhere else for the killers of McLean and Larion. And if you say he worked it all out, deliberate like, you've got to figure he and Seldom were in cahoots at first to get the McLean place, and later that Often decided he wanted it all himself. And that still leaves Miles Larion unaccounted for."

"Besides," Buck broke in, "the brothers wasn't exactly friendly. I figure they couldn't have got together. Whatever one asked, the other was pretty sure to do the opposite."

Judge LaFrance took off his hat and stroked the sparse white of his head.

"You ought to of been a lawyer, Maxie," he growled. "You sure can get a man mixed up."

"Now as for Robideau," went on the editor, "I can't get much sense out of thinking he shot anybody."

"He's sure as hell up to it," Judge LaFrance declared.

"But what would it get him to kill McLean and Larion both? What was there in it? I don't know him, but you fellows say he's dumb like a fox."

Bally Buck offered, "He would of liked to put a slug through Seldom, hot as Seldom was to get him strung up, and maybe he done it, too."

"And murdered McLean and Larion to boot?"

The rancher moved his head wearily. "That don't make sense, I guess. He wanted to know where the mine was, that's a cinch, and he was present when old Marty told about havin' the map, so there's a right good motive there, but Larion just don't come into the picture."

The Judge knocked the ashes from his pipe. "Manker or Salter would be up to it, but I guess they would be acting on Robideau's orders. And Cox or Rell could do a little killin', if the break was with 'em, but there ain't much sense in figuring on them, either."

Roser crumpled the paper in his hand. His fat, meek face was puckered, as nearly as ever, into a frown.

"There you are," he concluded, "and we haven't even touched on the case of Tana Deck, which must fit in here somewhere. No wonder West's mum."

Presently Judge LaFrance said thoughtfully, "Maybe it ain't good for us to know all that's going on in West's head, and in particular you, Buck. You want to shoot too quick. Been left to you, or me either, we'd gone gunning for somebody before this."

Buck complained, "If a man don't make a few free draws in this game, he gets to suspectin' his friends."

"West ain't our kind," the old justice of the peace pursued. "He's been an honest-to-God officer of the law, and he wants everything certain and regular before he begins throwing lead. Meantime, he keeps his mouth shut and don't spread any false ideas. Right, too, God knows if any men swung in the vigilante days for things they didn't do."

Roser leaned forward until his round stomach rested on his thighs. "They tell me," he observed inquiringly, "that Cawinne is God Almighty slow to take offense."

The other two looked at him.

"You'd expect a man like him to be hair-trigger. Some are saying he hasn't got much stomach for this business."

Judge LaFrance poked his finger under Roser's nose. "If he did," he defended sharply, "he'd be a fool or a born butcher. One killing'll last a lifetime, if a man's got any feelings."

"That's right," Buck interrupted with a strange diffidence, like a man on the verge of disloyalty. "Same time, it kind of worries me, too. Best gunfighters I ever saw was men without the feelings of a mule. It don't speed a man's hand, thinking how he hates to ventilate another."

"West has stood up plenty times before."

"As far as we know, though, never against a gunnie like Robideau," Buck amended. "One split second and that breed will fill him as full of holes as a prairie-dog town."

The Judge's lips came together in a tight line of anxiety and resolution.

"Anyhow," said Roser, "I guess they won't tangle as long as Moon Dance keeps Robideau in the dog house."

The Judge grunted, "He's out."

"I gave him a little reminder today," Buck related, "knowing West didn't want a shoot-out until and unless he had the goods on him." He looked down at his right hand and flexed it experimentally. "It's a good thing he was reasonable," he added. "He'd of had time to cut his initials in me."

The rancher stood up and stretched.

"I got to go home tonight," he informed them, "and get things lined out. I'll try to be back in the forenoon, though I don't know it's much use, seein' we followed all the signs and found the range empty."

"Anyhow," said Roser by way of conciliation as the Judge brought his old bones out of the chair, "we know we got a good man, even if he is a kind of a dude."

Judge LaFrance tucked his horn under his arm and answered with repressed ferocity, "Dude or dirty-neck, I'm putting all my stack on him."

CHAPTER NINETEEN

B UCK'S FRETFUL BEWILDERMENT was hardly relieved
the next day by a conversation with West Cawinne. Riding toward town, at midday, he had met the
latter jogging along in apparent aimlessness, and they
had pulled up their horses and exchanged the bluff greetings of the plains.

"Missed you yesterday," said Buck. "There was a
gentleman in town, from Breedtown."

"I guess he wasn't looking for anyone in particular?"

"No," Buck answered sourly. "Just acceptin' apologies
for bein' mistreated. I kind of let him know he wasn't
ready for grace yet, as Parson Logan would say."

They had stopped near a sluggish little stream, and
after their horses had drunk they dismounted and sat
idly on its banks while the animals, their reins trailing,
cropped the tender grass.

"Maxie Roser and the Judge and me did some high
power augurin' yesterday," Buck volunteered inquiringly, "but we didn't get anywheres."

"That makes us all even," Cawinne answered soberly.
After a while he added, "Blackie Cox deposited fifteen
hundred dollars in the Cottonwood State Bank the other
day."

"So?" ejaculated Buck, his eyes a-squint with thought.
He went on, giving voice to speculation as it developed
in his mind. "He never had a hundred dollars cash before. And he was first to Miles Larion, who by your
reckonin' had maybe up to twenty-five hundred dollars
in his pocket. And he was almighty anxious to do away

with old Seldom Wright, like someone tryin' to shift
the blame. What's more, he was present when old Marty
McLean told about findin' the Early Day. And to boot
and finally, a little matter of killin' wouldn't bother him,
long as he didn't risk his hide."

Thus on the way to a solution, Buck asked, "Well?"

"Two things don't fit," his companion responded. "In
the first place, I've been talking to Jake Schwartz, the
barkeep, and according to him Blackie Cox is the one
man that couldn't have killed old Marty. Cox stayed
around the saloon for a long time after the others had left
on the night Marty was killed, and when he did go he was
too well loaded to do much navigating."

"Yeah?"

"In the second place, no matter how good Cox is with
a gun, I can't see him shooting it out with a hand like
Larion."

"Well, hell," Buck objected. "Maybe he didn't. Maybe
he had the drop on Larion and Larion was still fast
enough to get his six-shooter smokin'."

"Maybe," agreed Cawinne without conviction.

Buck brought out a big cigar and lit it meditatively,
then leaned back, relaxed, against the sloping bank of the
stream.

"You were going to see Sven Svenson and try to dig
something out of him," Cawinne reminded the rancher
presently.

"I couldn't do any good with that sheep herder,"
Buck replied. "I been over to his camp twice, West,
thinking I might pick up some sign, and once I even went
so far as to take a bottle along with me, hoping a little
oil would loosen up his tongue. But it wasn't no use. He
drank the whisky, but it didn't oil him a-tall. There's
only one or two people in the whole county that crazy

galoot'll talk to. One of 'em was old Marty McLean because he let him run his little bunch of sheep on his range
when all the rest of us was in favor of tyin' a can to
him. Sven might talk to Tana, far as that goes, but I
don't think anyone else'll get anything out of him. I
tried sneaking up on his blind side, West, and I tried
bluffing, and I tried to sweeten up to him, but if he's got
any idea who done Marty in, he ain't sayin' anything.
He ain't sayin' anything, either, about the Early Day."

"Did he say anything about ghosts? They were on his
mind that night I spent at his camp."

"Naw. He just said, 'Yah, sure,' to all questions, ex-
ceptin' when he strayed off like a loco horse onto ranges
that was clear out of my territory."

"I guess you know that map he drew for old Marty
and Tana wasn't a proper map at all."

"So?"

"Tana told me he just drew a couple of lines that
didn't mean anything and then passed out."

Cawinne added, after a silence, "It was because the
map was no good that Tana was kidnaped, or anyhow
I think that's the way it was. Whoever ran off with Tana
hoped to get the secret of the mine from her, as you
know."

Buck fished on the bank for a pebble, and with his
broad thumb flipped it at a frog that had come to the
surface of the stream and floated there regarding them
with its wise, bulging eyes.

"That there is a leopard frog," the rancher observed
presently. "Won't ever get much bigger'n it is right
now."

The observation apparently stirred memories, for he
was silent for a long minute, and when he spoke again
his tone was reminiscent.

"My old man, now," he said, his eyes half closed in his heavy face, "he always said if he had any reason for feelin' sorry he settled here, it was because he couldn't get frog legs."

Cawinne tilted his hat against the spring sun and brought out papers and tobacco and fashioned a cigarette.

"But," Buck resumed, "Mom always said if she was glad for livin' here it was because there wasn't any bullfrogs around. It was funny about Mom. She was scared of frogs, the way some people are of cats. And when it came to talkin' about cookin' frog legs, she fair got sick. She said the meat was creepy, and not meant to be et."

Buck chuckled. "One time, thinking how good frog legs were back in Illinois, the old man he went out and caught him a bunch of these leopard frogs, like that one there. He just brought home the legs, but that was enough for Mom, and darn if she didn't climb a horse and go to town."

"And the old man ate them by himself?"

"Naw," the rancher corrected. "The old man was never much of a cook, and them frog legs got him down. I was just a pee-dad then, but I remember watchin' 'em, not much bigger'n a weed root, hoppin' around in the pan. They wouldn't stay still for nothin', but kept jumpin' just like they was on the end of the frog.

"Finally," Buck went on, chuckling again, "it kind of got on the old man's nerves, and he threw 'em all out, and I never heard him say he wanted frog legs again."

Meditatively, Buck knocked the ashes from his cigar and concluded, "He always said, though, that Mom robbed him of one of the best nachural appetites a man ever had. And when he'd say that, Mom would look up and say she wished she had as good luck with his unnachural appetites, meanin' red-eye, of course. That always put an end to the conversation."

Yawning, the rancher abruptly raised his back from the bank and came to a sitting posture.

"Well, what do we do now?" he asked with a sudden sharpness. "Just set some more?"

"Hard to tell," replied Cawinne thoughtfully. "I'm telling you true, Bally, I can't get a tail-hold on this business. Anyone of half a dozen might have shot old Marty. But which of them shot Larion, if any, and why? And who put a bullet through Seldom Wright, and why?"

"I don't know why you shy away from Robideau," the rancher answered with an edge in his voice. "Why can't it be him?"

"You think he'd cache himself in the bushes and shoot Marty from behind?"

"It don't look like it, I own," the older man retorted, "but still it might of been someone actin' for Robideau. How about Manker or Salter? They wouldn't mind shootin' the old man from behind, and they might do it that way, too, even if Marty was slow on the draw and drunk to boot. And Robideau or one of the others could of got Larion and old man Wright. It don't fit the case so bad."

"Why would they want to get Larion?"

"Money, maybe, if they knew he had that roll."

"And Seldom was shot with a rifle, maybe from ambush, too. That doesn't sound like Robideau."

"Sounds like Manker or Salter though."

"Well, maybe, but it's a long throw."

"Someone shot at you from behind, too. Guess you ain't got any idea who that was?"

"No."

"Hell!" said Buck disgustedly.

"Long as we're out this way," suggested the younger man, unoffended, "let's mosey by Often Wright's place."

"O. K.," Buck responded with sour resignation. "We were figurin' last night he had a motive, too, comin' into Seldom's spread the way he is."

"But—" began Cawinne.

Buck held up a broad hand forbiddingly. "Stop it!" he demanded. "We already figured it out. I know. It couldn't of been him, either."

Cawinne smiled at the other's disgusted vehemence, and they went to their horses and, mounting, rode for Often Wright's E-Lazy-R.

"It ain't much to look at," said Buck as they topped a rise and came into sight of the house and outbuildings. "Often thinks more of his stock and his machinery than he does of himself—which ain't bad ranchin' in a way. Anyhow, he's done pretty good. Maybe, now that he gets Seldom's outfit, he'll figure he can build a house and quit livin' in a shack."

At Buck's hail a half-grown pup padded from behind the corner of the house and regarded them with friendly inquiry, but no answer came from the sagging sod-topped cabin.

"Looks like he's away," Buck observed, but at that moment an answering hail sounded from the barn, and Wright, moving with loose-jointed ease, started across the barnyard toward them.

"Git down," he invited. " 'T'ain't often I have visitors, somehow or other." His mobile mouth, stretched in a grin of greeting, riffled his face into wrinkles.

The pup barked at him with mock ferocity and play-fully fell on a ball of hair that a fitful breeze had rolled before him.

Wright kicked irritably in the direction of the pup.

"That damn dog!" he complained. "I guess I'll have to get shet of him. He's a tail-puller. Got most of the hair yanked off the old gray mare's behind. That's some of it he's a-playin' with now."

"Some day," Buck consoled him, "the old gray mare will let him have it in the snoot, and he won't be a tail-puller any more."

"Well, git down, anyway. He's pretty foxy, though."

"We're just riding, trying to pick up some sort of trail," Cawinne explained as he swung to the ground.

"You wouldn't know, now, just where we'd find some nice, fresh sign, would you?" asked Buck, dismounting too.

"I wouldn't, for a fact. There's a pretty lot of it already made, ain't there? Come on in."

"We haven't got time, Often," answered Cawinne, slouching lazily against the shoulder of the roan. "We're just riding by, and thought we'd say howdy."

"I guess you know," he added smiling, "that you're on the suspect list now, coming into Seldom's spread the way you are."

Perplexity gave to Wright's face its monkey's look of bewildered inquiry.

"You're a-meanin'," he asked incredulously, "that because I get his outfit, I done away with Seldom?"

"No," Cawinne corrected, "but when things seem to kind of stack up, you've got to consider them, too. But I don't think you killed him, Often. It doesn't stack up far enough."

"I always claimed it was Robideau, and I claim so now," Wright said stubbornly. "I'll say it before his face, too."

"Maybe so," Cawinne agreed. "But we haven't got

enough to pin it on him. Can't you give us some kind of lead that we don't know about?"

Wright shook his head. "You know," he explained, "Seldom and I didn't pull very good together, and so we didn't see each other much."

His mouth drew forward into a wide, protuberant pucker, and out of his puzzlement he said earnestly, "If you're a-suspectin' of me, I'd welcome you to go through the house or ask me anything you're a mind to. Ain't anything to hide."

Cawinne shook his head. "I told you it didn't stack up far enough."

"A man ain't necessarily guilty just because he heirs something," Buck put in.

The pup, which had crept forlornly away when Wright kicked at it, had regained its spirit now. It jumped up on Wright, the ball of hair still in its mouth, and the man hit it sharply across the nose with his hand, commanding, "Get the hell away from here!" Whimpering, the dog retreated behind the house.

"Now, me," said Buck with pointed casualness, "I like dogs, and if I didn't like 'em I wouldn't have 'em around the place."

"Damn nuisance," Wright muttered.

Cawinne mounted his horse.

"Want to talk to you more some other day, Often," he said by way of good-bye. "Maybe we'll run across something that'll point the way, even if you can't think of anything now."

"Any time," Wright said, smiling his ape's smile.

Once away from the house, Buck observed, "Now I bet there is a mean man with his stock. Notice the way he hit that dog, which wasn't doin' anything a-tall? It's hard for me to shine up to a man that'll abuse an animal."

Cawinne dismissed his complaint. "As a rule, I don't believe he does abuse the pup. You saw the pup wanted to play, as if he was used to it. He just got on Often's nerves today, I guess."

They fell silent during the ride to town, and Buck took his leave later with a brief "So long" and the promise to see the younger man in the course of the next day or two.

Cawinne had his supper at the Moon Dance House and, declining requests to sit in on a game, went up to his room shortly thereafter and sat thinking and smoking for an hour or more, his strong, sharply cleft face reflecting his hard and fruitless examination of the facts he had gathered.

Finally, with a sigh, he went to bed, but sleep kept at the fringe of his consciousness. In his mind events, observations, contrasts, possibilities ran in a circle that he could neither stop nor direct.

The burglary at Seldom Wright's . . . a buckeye lying in the bushes . . . sweat rolling down the face of sheepskin-coated Robideau . . . Sven Svenson's "ghoosts" . . . a man who could see in the dark of the cellar at Indian Pete's Palace . . . Buck's mother and her fear of frogs . . . a dog playing with a ball of hair, and a man striking it across the muzzle.

Suddenly he sat up, for suddenly the tangle had fallen into a pattern, a pattern so fantastic and yet so logical that the shock of it brought him wide awake.

Dawn found him searching in the swamp grass along the creek where he and Buck had sat the day before.

CHAPTER   TWENTY

"Buck'll be in if you wait a while," Judge La-France said. "He ain't missed comin' to town since God knows when."

With a palsied hand he jabbed the key at the hole in the door of his shop, and, finally successful in inserting it, moved into the atmosphere of stale smoke, new leather and harness oil. "Come in."

West Cawinne followed him through the door.

"I wasn't looking for Buck," answered the younger man, his voice pitched for the deaf ears. "I'm just killing time."

"Till when?"

"It doesn't hardly seem decent to go calling this early."

The Judge looked at him sharply. "Goin' callin', eh?"

"Thought I would."

The Judge kept looking at him, but Cawinne did not pursue the subject, and the former with a dissatisfied grunt turned to the business of filling and lighting his broken old pipe. Cawinne shook tobacco into a paper and manufactured a cigarette.

"I saw Buck yesterday," he volunteered idly.

"He tell you about Robideau being in town?"

"Yeah."

The Judge grunted again and eased himself into a chair. "Set," he invited.

"West," the Judge said between the stumps of teeth he had clamped on his pipe, "it ain't none of my business, or theirs, but some of the boys are wondering a little why

you should take such an interest in Fee Simple, him bein'
more or less mixed up with the crowd you're supposed
to be gunnin' for."

Cawinne blew a thin plume of smoke and watched it
as it billowed in a shaft of light that slanted through the
front window.

"I know you're going to do what you damn please,"
LaFrance conceded in the face of his silent resistance,
"but it might not hurt for you to think about it, West. I
bet you set him up to a meal five-six times in the last
week or so."

"That isn't making Robideau fat, or anyone else except Fee."

"No," agreed the Judge doubtfully.

"What's the hurt?"

"Damn if I quite know, West, but it does look kind of
funny, you settin' up a man that's runnin' with the
enemy. Might make some of the boys think you ain't as
serious as you might be."

"Let 'em think," said Cawinne. He added, as if it
were the end of argument and the justification of behavior, "Johnny Fee worked for my dad, and he's in
hard lines."

"Uh-huh," answered Judge LaFrance, nodding understandingly. "Let it lay then."

He turned as the door knob twisted and Bally Buck
came in.

"You're almighty early," the Judge said by way of
greeting. "Martha chase you off the home range?"

"I needed some stuff from town. Goin' right back.
Anyhow, I always get up early to ride herd on the wild
oats."

"Hi, Bally," said Cawinne; then, to both of them, "I'm
pulling out. See you later."

When he had gone, Judge LaFrance, his eyes still on
the door by which he had left, confided to Buck,
"There's something up, Bally. That kid's harder to read
than the back of a square deck, but there's something
up, or I'm loco."

"If there is, it's come up recent. I was with him till
late yesterday. He didn't know nothin' then."

"He knows something now," insisted LaFrance, "and
I bet he's bound to find out some more. He'll get him,"
he added with a return of his dogged confidence.

"You think it's just one?"

"In a place where murder ain't done every day, three
in a bunch makes it look like the same hand, Bally, even
if the killin's weren't all done the same way."

The rancher shifted impatiently on his booted feet.
"Hell, if he's really gettin' down to business, I want to
be along."

He started impulsively for the door, but halted at the
commanding movement of LaFrance's horn. "Ain't no
use," the Judge boomed at him. "He don't want you,
and when he don't want you, he ain't going to have
you."

"O. K.," answered the rancher grumpily, "but damn
if people didn't used to think I was good for sump'n
besides augurin'. You're probably wrong, anyhow."

While the two friends talked, Cawinne went to the
livery stable.

"Same thing, the roan, McCabe," he said to the aged
hostler. "I'm going to buy that jug-head from you, when
I get on the ranch, just to remember you by."

McCabe, already more respectful since the recovery of
Tana Deck, now bared his stained and broken teeth in a
grin. "Sure thing, West," he said. "I'll sell him to you all
right." Then, more cautiously, "You got to remember

he's a mighty fine horse. You couldn't expect to get one like him for nothin'. Lots of bottom there."

He said the last words over his shoulder as he disappeared into the stable, with what agility his rheumatic legs would permit, to reappear presently with the saddled horse.

Once clear of town, Cawinne reined the animal to the north and west on a rutted trail, since abandoned, that led to Often Wright's E-Lazy-R. For a mile or more, the route meandered along the valley and then, with an appearance of resolution, climbed the westward bluff to the bench that lifts in easy stages to the foothills and the mountains.

Like a sleeper waking to the day, the country was answering to spring. The hardiest of the cottonwoods in the valley had unrolled their sticky leaves. Red willow and black birch were tipped with green. In the swales, violets and johnny-jump-ups lifted their shrinking beauty in the shielding grass. Meadow-larks, yellow-vested and black-lapelled, showered the silence with their songs. No bigger than chipmunks, young gophers sported around old burrows. A complaining crow flapped overhead, pursued by two king birds jealous of a nest in some bullberry bush. In the distance, the ridges showed green with new grass. Underfoot, the earth yielded to the tread of the roan. Above, the sky hung close and cloudless, blue as lupine.

Cawinne let the horse fix its own pace, and it was on toward noon when steed and rider eased down into the shallow coulee where the solitary Wright kept headquarters for the E-Lazy-R. It was the place of a man concerned with profit and not with pleasure. The barn, reared against the slope of the hill, was large and stout. The fences about it were in good repair. The hen house

near it was tight, and the adjacent tool shed sturdy. Off
at the side, a circular corral gleamed with the tan-white
of poles freshly barked. But fifty yards up the coulee, so
alike that one could not tell bunk house from ranch
house, stood two decaying log shacks, the human habi-
tations, drawn low and crooked by the years, roofed
with sod out of which thistle and pig-weed were spring-
ing.

Cawinne found Wright outside the barn, repairing a
door that he had laid flat on the ground.

"Hi, Often," he said, pulling up.

So engrossed in his work that he had not heard the
walk of the horse on the springy ground, the older man
half started to his feet, a look of bewilderment on his
flexible face. When he recognized Cawinne, his mouth
relaxed into a friendly grin.

"Surprised me right smart, Cawinne," he observed.
"Didn't look for you, two days runnin'."

Cawinne got off the roan, letting the reins drop to the
ground.

"Go over there and set in the shade," Wright invited.
"I aim to get this door hung before noon. Damn bronc
sprung it off its hinges. Then maybe you'll go in and
lick the pot with me?"

"Thanks," said his caller, sitting down with his back
against the barn. As he smoked he petted the pup that
came up to him, sniffing in friendly inquiry.

Wright labored silently and rapidly, pausing only now
and then to volunteer a chance reflection or to eject a
thin stream of tobacco spittle through his mobile lips. He
was a painstaking workman, and it was not until the door
swung easy and true that he picked up his tools and, with
a "Come on in" to Cawinne, made for the shack that he
called home.

Inside, he stirred a pot of beans that was simmering on a cook stove. The stove was old, and he had to be careful not to disturb its position on three legs and a make-shift wooden block as he poked wood into it from a half filled box that sat by its side.

"If you haven't et, you better," he said inquiringly to his caller.

"Cup of coffee's all," Cawinne answered. "In town, we don't get started as early as you do."

Wright got out two potatoes from a sack behind the door and, having given them what evidently passed in his judgment for a peeling, began slicing them into a greasy skillet.

"Sit down! Sit down!" he insisted as Cawinne stood near him, hands on hips. He motioned to a battered chair held together with haywire.

The other furnishings of the one-room shack were no less rude—a make-shift bed from the bottom of which protruded the hay used as padding, an old table listing on its legs, an apple box that served as seat, a row of nails hung with rough clothing, two open shelves, a bootjack flung in a corner, the chair and the stove. The pine floor had splintered with the scuff of boots. Overhead, the tangled roots of weeds growing in the sod rough had worked through.

"How's the investigatin' business comin' along," Wright asked as he turned the potatoes in the pan.

"Slow, mighty slow."

The other grunted, not unsympathetically, and spooned coffee into the boiling pot.

"I got all the suspicions corralled, I guess, but I can't find a fact in the bunch."

Wright's long lips pulled forward, half open and stiff with perplexity like the mouth of a monkey. He stabbed his fingers into his hair and scratched. Upon his guest he fastened an intent, slow, searching gaze.

Then, out of his simian face came the half complaint: "A body gets some provoked, waitin' for vengeance."

Cawinne's head moved in sober agreement.

"You better hitch up," invited Wright again, scattering knife, fork and spoons on the bare table. "Got beans and potatoes and some left-over spider bread, besides stewed fruit. If I'd knowed you were comin' I'd put on some meat."

"No thanks."

"I don't get around enough to hear nothin' myself," the rancher said, returning to their previous subject. "Celebration the other day was the first time I been to town in a long spell, and nobody comes by to visit me, seems like."

Cawinne moved up to the table as his host poured coffee into tin cups.

"Often," he inquired, sipping at the hot brew, "you think Seldom could have killed Miles Larion?"

Wright put down his fork and studied the other's face. "Reckon so," he said slowly, "but he didn't."

"No?"

"He was up to something like that, all right, but Seldom wasn't no fool-man. What would he get out of killin' him? Nothin', without you figure personal feeling, which wouldn't make old Seldom risk his neck. And after that trouble with Larion at Moon Dance, he knew it would be riskin' his neck, all right."

"Yeah," agreed Cawinne. "No other way to figure."

The rancher returned to his food, eating greedily as a hungry dog.

"I say Robideau killed Larion," he said finally, shunting a mouthful of potatoes to the siding of his jaw and motioning at Cawinne with his fork. "And of course Robideau done for Marty McLean and Seldom, even if you can't lay it on him square."

"Why would he kill Larion?"

"No tellin'. He just done it."

Thoughtfully, while his jaws moved like pistons, Wright lifted the pot of beans and gave himself another helping. He forked a mouthful and added a bite of bread before he spoke again. Then he said, "If I could use a pistol-gun, I would be a-layin' for Robideau myself, and not doin' so much talkin'."

Cawinne stamped his cigarette out on the floor and reached into the buttoned pocket of his open jacket.

Wright, glancing sidewise at him as his lips closed over the fork, first gasped and then spewed his mouthful of beans over the table with the gust of his words.

"Christ Almighty!" he cried, and lunged backwards, sprawling over the apple box as he fell.

In Cawinne's hand, half over the table near where Wright's face had been, a small water snake squirmed against the hold of thumb and finger.

Wright scrambled to his feet. "Get that thing out of here!"

Cawinne turned the tiny serpent between his fingers.

"Your brother, Seldom, now, was afraid of snakes," he said casually.

Wright's contorted face went tight and still, as if someone had slugged him in the belly.

Then, like a man beside himself, he leaped for the corner of the wall against which he had backed, his hands clawing for the rifle that stood there.

Cawinne's shot split the inches between his hands and the weapon.

"Hold it!"

Wright faltered.

Cawinne warned, "I got you, Seldom. Don't make me shoot."

Wright's face was gray. His mouth hung open. He wet his lips and said in his throat, "You got nothing on me. Take that snake and get out of here!"

"You might as well own up."

"You got nothing on me."

"Come along!"

"Shoot, damn you! I ain't movin'!"

"Then I pack you in." Cawinne motioned peremptorily with his revolver. With the other hand he had returned the snake to its pocket.

Resistance seemed suddenly to drain out of Wright. "O. K.," he mumbled, and stepped forward, drooping, but as Cawinne moved back he whirled and dove for the corner.

He lurched as Cawinne's slug tore through his shoulder, but, righting himself, scuttled ahead like a wounded gopher making for a burrow.

His hand clutched the rifle.

"I'll show you," he shouted, wheeling, to be knocked back on his heels by Cawinne's second shot. The rifle wavered in his hands and, exploding, drilled a hole in the stove pipe.

Cawinne said, "That's the way you wanted it."

The wounded man sank slowly and tumbled forward on all fours. The rifle clattered on the floor.

Cawinne holstered his weapon and laid Wright out flat on his back.

"Take it easy," he advised.

Wright panted for breath. "Goner," he wheezed, "goner."

He struggled to sit up and, failing, seized Cawinne by the arm. "Damn you, you got me!" he gasped.

"It was the whiskers, Seldom," Cawinne said, not ungently.

"That damn dog!"

The wounded man writhed stiffly, like a man stretching, and strained out a grunting moan. As the spasm passed, a little tremor riffled over him, touching legs and torso and face, and when it had gone he lay relaxed and still. Slowly, as if at the pull of sleep, his eyelids came down.

"Where's Often's head?" Cawinne was asking. "Where's Often's head?"

As he spoke, the eyelids lifted and the flickering life in the haggard monkey-face for an instant burned brighter. The words came slow and halting. "Ain't no use—hiding things from—you—now—in the barn—buried." Wearily, he closed his eyes again.

His blood had soaked his shirt and began to stain the floor. His breath fluttered in his throat.

"Just when everything—was right," he whispered. "McLean's place—mine. But I didn't—didn't—"

Whatever it was that Seldom Wright meant to say went unsaid. As his lips struggled for a word, death came with a quivering of the eyelids, a convulsive shudder, and a last, long rasping sigh.

CHAPTER TWENTY-ONE

Adlam's Saloon is almost directly across Main Street from the Family Liquor Store. By strict attention, Bally Buck managed to travel the distance with few deviations from the straight line, and came into port with little more than the ambulatory list of the cowpuncher born and bred. To Jake Schwartz, who was polishing a glass behind the bar, he gestured peremptorily, then turned and summoned the half-dozen others in the place.

"On me," he said.

Blackie Cox was there, and Estes Rell, the gaunt freighter, and Jack Rawlings, who clerked at the Moon Dance Mercantile Company between sprees. From a table in the gloom at the rear two breeds came forward, leaving a game of pitch. On the face of one of them a knife scar gleamed white from temple to jowl.

Rell, whose chief claim to notice lay in his ability to make a horse scream in anguish at the cut of his blacksnake whip, raised his drink and turned toward Buck his skeleton of a face with its long wisps of mustache.

"What are we celebratin'?" he asked, and brought his glass before his eyes to study the amber sparkle of the whisky.

The question nettled Buck. "Shove it back if you don't want it," he said.

Jake held a glittering glass to the light.

"It ain't like you, Rell," he purred between his fat cheeks, "to ask about the reason for a drink."

"Go to hell!" retorted Rell, and drained his potion at a gulp. His corded throat jerked up and down with the swallow.

The two hybrids wiped their mouths and looked at Buck in silent expectancy.

The rancher spilled some silver on the bar.

"Fill 'em up."

" 'Smy round," spoke up Rawlings, the clerk, and fumbled in his pockets.

"I'm wolf, and I'm howlin'."

"O. K., O. K.," Rawlings agreed hastily. "No offense."

Cox, who had stood wordless and surly at the upper end of the bar, lounged down it, toward the rancher.

"Kind of on the prod, ain't you?" he asked.

Buck studied him, slow and unsmiling.

"What if I am?"

Schwartz caught Cox's eye.

"Buck sure can howl," he volunteered in his thin soprano. " 'Member the last time someone tried to drown you out, Bally?" His eyes were still on Cox.

Rawlings had edged toward the door, and, with a muttered "I gotta be goin'," stumbled outside.

Cox shrugged. "Nothin'," he answered Buck. "Interested, is all."

The concession brought about in Buck the drunk's easy change in attitude.

"I got plenty to be on the prod about," he confided. His speech had commenced to get a little thick. Stained with the crustings of a dead cigar, his mouth hung slack.

Cox motioned for another round.

Talking low to himself, Buck heeled back to a chair at a poker table. Cox and Rell followed. Waiting silently, as if uncertain what was expected of them, the two breeds finally sat and hitched their chairs timidly toward the table.

"You got something to howl about, all right," said Rell. "Killings cleared up, and all."

Buck gazed fixedly at the table top. "I'm howlin'," he declared moodily, and spat the wet butt of his cigar on the floor. With fumbling deliberation he brought another from his vest pocket, bit off its end, and lighted it.

"Understand Cawinne's going to stock up his place, right away," said Cox.

Buck drew a deep and wheezy breath. Still staring vacantly at the table top, he asked as if of himself, "Looks like, don't it, when you hire a man you ought to know what he's doin'?"

His slow gaze found his glass and saw that it was empty.

"Damn you, Jake, will you keep 'em filled up?"

Jake came around and left the bottle.

"I said," repeated Buck, "looks like you ought to know what a man you're payin' is doin' for his money."

He waited for an answer and, receiving none, demanded, "Don't it?"

One by one, his lack-luster eyes put them to inquisition.

"Sure does," said Rell.

Cox agreed, "You're right."

"Sure," the two breeds said in chorus.

Buck drained his glass and splashed himself another drink. When he had returned the bottle, he banged his great fist down. The table tilted with the blow, and Cox thrust out a hand and settled its legs on the floor. Rell steadied the bottle. Buck's spilled drink made dark spots on the green cloth.

"That's what I say!" the rancher proclaimed in accompaniment to his gesture. "By Joe, a man works for
you, you want to know what he's doing."

He slouched back in his chair sullenly. His head had
commenced to nod jerkily. When he looked up it was
with sudden suspicion.

"You with me or against me?"

"All the way," answered Rell.

"Sure," Cox seconded.

"Damn liars."

"Have it your own way," Rell answered, "but with
Blackie and me it's all over and forgot."

"All'ss forgiven?" Buck asked dully.

Buck's drink slopped over the brim of the glass as he
brought it to his mouth. He drank noisily. A trickle of
whisky ran unheeded down his chin.

"All'ss forgiven."

He reached out at either side and pawed the two
affectionately.

"Good fellas," he pronounced. "Have a little drink!"

When they had refilled their glasses, he reached out
and clutched Rell by the forearm.

"Know what?" he asked. "That damn Cawinne—"

"I just see your wife drivin' by, Bally," Schwartz
called from the head of the bar. He had been occupied,
until the previous moment, by a scattering of patrons
who gazed back curiously toward the group at the table
while they put away their drinks. As he spoke, his round
face was clouded, like a distressed child's.

"Let 'er drive!"

Buck's gesture was half lunge as he returned to his
subject. "Look! I'm goin' to tell you sump'n only two
people know. Only me and the Judge."

Schwartz came around the end of the bar.

"Better get out and get some air, Old Timer," he wheedled, putting his hand on Buck's shoulder. "I tell you, the missus is in town."

Cox glared at Schwartz, his long horse lip twisted with displeasure. "Leave him be! Is it so a man can't take a few drinks, even in a saloon?"

Rell's face was expressionless as a corpse's. His voice was flat. "Buck's all right. Hear?"

Buck complained, "Go 'way, Jake! Leave me alone!"

Schwartz gestured hopelessly and, turning back toward the bar, addressed the ceiling in his woman's voice: "Mostly, a man's sorry afterwards for spillin' his guts."

If he heard him, Buck ignored him. "Look! I'm goin' tell you sump'n. Everything's settled, ain't it? You and me and everybody knows that. Old Seldom Wright killed Marty McLean to get his spread, or maybe the map, or likely both. Then he shot Miles Larion just because he didn't care for'm, and then he rubbed out his own brother to get out of it." The rancher's manner was heavy with emphasis. "All makes sensh, don't it? Plain as pie, ain't it?"

Cox's eyes were steady on Buck. The latter overpoured his glass and passed the bottle round.

"But," he exploded, and banged the table again, "it ain't all over. Cawinne says no sir. Someone elsh in it. Sump'n maybe old Seldom told him before he died, or sump'n he saw at Indian Pete's, or sump'n he just figured out. Someone elsh in it, he says."

Cox's face was dark.

"I always said he was a fool."

Buck glowered at him, with eyes half paralyzed. With extreme deliberation he got up and leaned over, one outspread hand using the table for support.

"You're the fool," he said thickly. "I'm goin' to let you have it."

Quickly, Rell put a restraining hand on the rancher. "He don't mean it."

"Naw," Cox half apologized. "If you say he ain't a fool, then he ain't one."

Buck sat down again but, still aggrieved, pointed his finger accusingly at Cox.

"Boy'ss shmart," he insisted. "Shmart as hell. Don't ever think he's a fool. Rest of us give up and say't's all over, but not West. Not that kid. He'll get 'im. Don't ever think he won't. Don't ever think he'ss a fool."

"He'll get him, but there's no one to get," Rell corrected, speaking with a sober man's indulgence of a drunk. "You just said that yourself."

"Tha's right," answered Buck as if before a new thought. The weight of the contradiction appeared too heavy for him, and he sank back in his chair.

"Same time," Cox reminded him, "you got a right to know what a man's doin'."

Buck came forward, insisting, "That's what I say." He propped his unsteady head on the table with his forearms. "You ought to know what he's doin'. And that's what makes me mad. Think me or the Judge know what West's doin', or even what he's thinkin'? Never a damn thing, 'til't's all over. We say, Seldom's dead, ain't he? Why you 'spect anyone elsh? Who's it? And he just smiles and says wait now, day or two, you'll know. Thing's ain't ready yet, he says. But what it is, he wants to be the whole show, tha's what."

Swaying in his chair, the rancher reached out and captured the bottle. Three drinks of whisky he poured on the table before he had his glass full.

"Yeah," Rell volunteered. "I heard you was gettin' kind of ringy, not bein' dealt in."

"You heard right," Buck mumbled. As if in the face of a vast injustice, he added, "And we're payin' him."

The drink he had poured went unnoticed. He got up, reeling, and started for some destination of his own, and fell heavily at his second step on the solid floor of the saloon. Mumbling unintelligibly, he tried to rise, but the effort was too much for him and he let his head back on the planking.

Cox and Rell got up. The two silent breeds moved back to the pitch table. "We'll leave him to you, Jake," Cox said, and he and the freighter walked out.

When they had closed the door, the fat bartender spat after them, "A polecat and a coyote!" He walked down the bar and around it and summoned the two breeds to Buck's side. The rancher's mutterings had slid into the deep, labored snore of intoxication.

Said Schwartz, "You, St. John, and you, Romain, get Buck into the back room!"

Willingly, they pulled and tugged at the limp body of the rancher and, dragging more than carrying, got it into the rear and stretched it on the floor.

Schwartz bent over and took from the pockets a wallet and a handful of change.

"Here," he said, "a dollar for you now, and another after you take him to the Moon Dance House. Don't go yet. It's still light, but as soon as it's dark, get him over there. Take him the back way, see, and up the back stairs. No need for the whole town to know Buck's on a bust. Scott Hardy'll fix him up with a room. Wait now till dark."

The breeds nodded.

Schwartz started to go, but turned back to display the wallet and money in his pudgy hands. "I got his roll, see? No use friskum."

Over his unconscious, mumbling protest, they took Buck off the floor when night had fallen and, each under an arm, started down the alley. It was not so hard to move him now. Though wobbly and directionless, the rancher supported a part of his weight on his reluctant legs. Nevertheless, the two hybrids were hot and panting when they reached the back stoop of the hotel.

St. John went in to summon Hardy, who swore slowly as he saw the slumped figure. "I'll get a light," he said, and went back in, to return with a kerosene lamp. "O. K., boys, follow me. And take it easy."

Sweating and straining, the pair got Buck up the narrow, dark staircase.

"Bring him up to Number 15," Hardy directed, leading the way.

When they had put the rancher in bed, Hardy dismissed the two. He pulled off Buck's boots then, and removed his hat and holster and, after opening a window, went out and closed the door.

Five minutes later, Buck rolled to the side of the bed, sat up, and pulled his boots back on. He chuckled once to himself as he did so. "Yippee!" he said softly. "What a drunk!"

He walked in careful silence to the door, opened it, and tiptoed up the hallway to Number 19, from under the door of which a ribbon of light showed. Without knocking, he turned the knob and went in.

Fully dressed, West Cawinne lay on the bed. He sat up as the visitor entered. "I was afraid maybe you were making it too realistic," he said, and smiled.

Buck laughed shortly, let himself down in the lone rocker the room afforded and brought his palm across his forehead ruefully.

"I'm half shot now for a fact, West."

"Yeah?"

"It was a success, though. A hell of a success. Even Jake fell for it."

"Who was there?"

"Cox and Rell."

"Anyone else?"

"Uh-huh. That scar-faced breed I think they call St. John and another that runs with him. Jack Rawlings was there for a while, too, but not long enough to figure."

"They were enough, without him."

"I acted it out just like you told me to, with a few little finishing touches that was my own idea."

"You got it over?"

"All along I acted like I was considerable riled at you for bein' so close mouthed, and us payin' you at that. Then just to be like an honest-to-God drunk, I lit into Cox for sayin' you was a fool. Him sayin' that gave me a good chance to tell 'em, by Joe, that you'd run down anyone else that had a hand in the killings. I made that pretty strong."

There was a glint of amusement in Cawinne's eyes. "It oughtn't to have been very hard, acting like you were put out with me."

"Oh, hell, West!" the older man protested. "I been put out some, all right, and I've talked about it some, too much, I guess. But it wasn't hard actin' like I thought you'd get to the bottom of this thing, either." He grinned a little sheepishly.

"Good thing you did talk," Cawinne said, grinning

back. "The only reason this might work is that everybody knows you haven't been what you could call satisfied. So your kick today fits in pretty well."

"Another thing," Buck interrupted. "Playin' drunk there for the boys, I made it pretty plain that no one, not even me and the Judge, thought there was anyone to catch, now that Seldom's dead. I was kind of lookin' both ways there, predictin' you'd get someone in one breath and sayin' there wasn't anyone to get in the next, but it sounded real reasonable, comin' from a drunk."

Buck paused thoughtfully. "By Joe," he resumed, "I would say for a fact that there wasn't anyone else mixed up in the case if I could just forget one thing, and that one thing is Seldom staying there at his shack as innocent as you please while a party was on its way to string him up for puttin' a hole through Larion."

"He wouldn't have been waiting for you to warn him."

"No," agreed Buck. "It sure don't look that way."

"There's one other item about that play down at the saloon today," said Cawinne. "Did you tell them there'd be a break in a day or two?"

"I got that over all right. Said you'd promised action real soon."

"That ought to push things, if they can be pushed."

"I wish I could see your hole card," Buck said almost plaintively.

"Sometimes you can run a man down, and again you have to lead him where you want him, if he'll lead."

"In my case," the rancher answered reproachfully, "it's sure as hell a case of the blind leadin' the blind. Maybe I got a good idea who you're after, but I can't see why, or how this play's going to work."

"Maybe it won't," Cawinne asserted. "It's just a wild

chance, but if it doesn't I'm afraid we might as well
rack up."

"Meantime, you ain't sayin' nothing'?"

"It's no good to cut the picket rope on a lot of speculation. If this idea works out, we'll have the proof. If it
doesn't, we won't, and if it doesn't I don't want to have
pointed suspicion toward a man who may be innocent."

"More lone-wolf stuff," commented Buck, not without
respect.

Cawinne smiled fleetingly. Sitting there on the bed in
his shirt sleeves, with his dark hair rumpled and his face
still and severe and his big forty-fives off his thighs, he
didn't look like a gunfighter.

Buck asked, "Anything going to happen soon?"

"If it happens, it'll be soon."

"I got to go up the river a ways in the morning, but
I'll be back before noon."

"Time enough."

The rancher got up. "I better sneak back to my room.
Like as not, Scott Hardy'll be up to see how I'm sleepin'
off my jag, and I better be there." He waved his hand in
parting admonition. "You better stir up sump'n, or I'll
go on a sure-enough bust and cuss you proper."

CHAPTER TWENTY-TWO

AGE AND HARD EXPERIENCE had given to old Judge LaFrance a set expression of testy readiness for what might be said or done, but there was on his face now an uncommon look of perplexity and gentle concern. He was seated in his shop, in the worn leather chair that he used more and more as time drew on, and Tana Deck leaned forward from a low stool at his side, her pink young mouth close to the horn that he held at his ear. Her eyes searched his stubbornly.

It was warm outside, but the Judge's thin blood was slow to respond to spring, and he had lighted a fire in the round box of the stove. Particles of dust, raised in its building, eddied in the light.

The Judge looked at the young face, at the expressive mouth with its delicate fullness, at the disturbed, questioning eyes, at the soft hair that framed the features.

He sighed then and, contrary to habit, said in a voice so low that it could barely be heard, "You're all wrong, Tana. Good men don't like bloodshed, and West Cawinne is a good man."

She cried rebelliously, "Then why must he always be getting into trouble?"

Judge LaFrance took a worn pipe from his pocket, filled its choked bowl with a pinch of tobacco, and struck a match.

"I've knowed West Cawinne since he was a toddler," he answered thoughtfully. "He always was a nice kid, polite to people, and friendly, and unselfish, and like that. I remember I made him some skate straps once when he

was only so high"—the old man gestured with his unused
match, now too short for service—"and I wouldn't take
any pay for them. I never did, though I guess I made a
thousand for the kids around here. But when Christmas
come around, he stopped at the shop with a can of tobacco and wished me well. None of the other boys ever
did that."

The Judge stayed his tongue to relish his memories.
Absently, he struck another match, and forgot it, too.

"Money was always scarce with the Cawinnes," he
resumed slowly. "It was with nearly everybody in them
days, and when old John died—and there was as fine a
man as God ever let the sun shine on—when old John
died, West didn't have anything except a ranch with a
lot of paper and no stock on it. He didn't have any people even, because his mother had died earlier. There
wasn't anything for him to do except hunt a job."

The girl rested her small, smooth chin in her hand.
The absorbed attention she gave him appeared to stimu-
late the Judge. He went on in stronger voice.

"He left here and traveled south, and the next thing
we heard about him he was making a big reputation as an
officer of the law. That didn't surprise us who knew him
as a kid, and who knew his folks, too. Whatever he did
he was bound to do well. I suppose he got into the officer
business by accident, like all of us seem to settle into our
ways of life. But when he had money enough he come
back to redeem the ranch and buy a few head of stock.
That shows he don't like man huntin'."

"But he went right back into it," the girl accused.

Judge LaFrance's voice boomed now. "Yeah, he did.
Because we asked him to. Because we downright begged
him to. I never asked a man to do anything like I asked
West. Makes me ashamed, sort of, to think about it."

"Why did you beg him?"

"Someone's got to do something when a killer gets loose."

"Someone else would have done it, though."

The old man agreed with a thoughtful nod. "Someone would, I guess. But that's just where you don't understand."

He paused a full moment, as if rallying his thoughts. When he resumed it was to speak slowly, like a man defining an accepted but unstudied fundamental.

"Lot of people don't understand the western man and the west, and you couldn't hardly be expected to, Tana, at your age. I don't know that I do myself, entire, though I never lived anywheres else. But first of all about the western man was that he wasn't waiting for anyone else to do what he could do himself, or expecting him to either. The country'd never been settled by lily-livers.

"Look!" he said, warming to his subject. "In the beginning there were the old trappers and later on the settlers comin' over the Oregon Trail, and they didn't have anyone except themselves to depend on. They had to get over rivers and cross deserts and fight Indians and rustle grub and stand the cold and heat, with nothing to help 'em except the brains they had in their head and the strength they had in their body. Along come the gold camps and the cow towns and Indians worse'n ever now and a lot of no-accounts settin' up to be bad men and interferin' with life and property and peaceful settlement."

LaFrance shook a horny finger at Tana. "What did the western man do? Do? Why, he fought them Indians, and he chased the outlaws out of the country or buried 'em in Boot Hill. He saw a job had to be done, and he done it. Direct action, that's what he was, and no waiting around for some bolder, stronger, saltier man to come along and tend to his knittin' for him. He was the man, that genu-ine western man, who made things safe for women and children. Yes, and for weaklin's, too. He was the man that settled the country."

The old voice paused, panting a little with its vehemence. When it went on, it was gentle with significance: "Tana, there's a heap of the old west in West Cawinne."

The girl persisted obdurately: "But it's so terrible! He acts so ready to fight. He goes to meet trouble."

"It's his reputation," the Judge explained.

"That's what he said!" the girl flared. "A pity about keeping up a reputation as a killer!"

"It ain't that, Tana," Judge LaFrance answered patiently. "It's just that if a man with a reputation ever looks like he's going soft, every lousy rascal in the country will be itching to take a crack at him, just for the honor of bein' able to say he was the tough gent that put an end to him. And especially where there are men settin' up to be bad ones, a man known to be quick on the draw can't let up. It would be the signal for some needless killin', includin' maybe himself. Why, I bet West has saved the lives off a lot of no-goods by showin' he won't take too much. He's discouraged 'em from tryin' to fight it out with him."

"Just the same, don't you think he's—he's touchy?"

The Judge shook his head. "Hump-uh," he denied emphatically. "Fact is, he's been so slow at getting riled some are sayin' he don't have much stomach for his work."

Wistfully, the girl said after a pause, "He's such a hard man!"

"The west never would have been settled by softies."

They both fell silent then, until the Judge leaned over and took her smooth hand in his withered fingers.

"Tana," he said earnestly, "did you ever see West exactly celebratin' because he had to shoot a man down? Does he seem to get any fun out of it?"

Her troubled gaze went to the floor. "Except once I never saw him shoot a man, or celebrate any time," she answered huskily, "but I know what you mean. Sometimes he seems awfully sad."

Judge LaFrance continued for her: "Sad and tired and old before his time. This gun business does that to you if you got any feelings."

He nodded thoughtfuly in his chair, then straightened slowly as if to rid himself of a weakness.

"But whatever his feelings," he added stoutly, "a man's got to answer if the case calls for a man."

The girl sighed. "I see, I guess," she answered, doubt and sadness in her voice, as she arose and started for the door. "Thank you, Judge."

"Listen, Girl!" he called, and when she stopped he squirmed rheumatically in his chair. "I ain't much on this kind of advice," he said then, his eyes downcast, "and I don't feel right sayin' it, but I'm old and it don't matter. Don't be afraid to like West Cawinne, case you're a mind to. No one would need to be ashamed of that, or sorry for it later, either."

Tana had put her hand on the knob of the door, but impulsively she let it drop and came over to him quickly to ask:

"Does he have to go on from here, Judge LaFrance? Does he have to go on?"

From their drooping pockets, the Judge's eyes studied her, and in his gaze now were not only the fortitude and the valor that life had taught him, but the sympathy learned in years of experience and the remembrance of his head-long youth as well.

His gaze dropped before he answered, and in his reply there was stony acceptance.

"I know what you mean, Tana," he said, gentle but unyielding. "But Robideau or anybody else, West will go where he thinks he ought to. A man's got to answer, if the case calls for a man."

A quick shimmer of tears shone in her eyes. Against the sudden pallor of her face the clear blue of her eyes and the red of her lips appeared pathetically overdone, as if a painter had attempted to put the glow of life in a dead face.

Wordless, she arose and made again for the door, but before she reached it, it burst open and Johnny Fee came running in.

He looked about for a bewildered moment, dismissing from his search the old man and the girl. His lips worked soundlessly as if practicing for the tardy impulse of his brain. Then he blurted, "Where Cawinne?"

Some inner excitement in him communicated itself to the other two. The Judge struggled stiffly out of his chair, his horn pointed imperatively at the visitor. "What say?" he boomed.

Fee stepped back, and again his mouth practised with words before uttering them. "Where Cawinne?"

"Where's Cawinne?" the girl cried at Judge LaFrance as he stared at Fee, uncomprehending.

"I don't know. He ain't been in this morning."

Johnny Fee turned nervously.

"Wait!" commanded Judge LaFrance. "Any word for him? Anything we tellum? What the hell, John?"

The breed hesitated, at a loss. His mouth moved

silently. In uneasy decision he put his hand on the door and swung it wide.

"Must findum," he announced, and as he disappeared he cast back over his shoulder one halting, portentous word, "Robideau."

"Robideau," Tana cried into the inquiring mouth of LaFrance's horn. "He just said 'Robideau'."

"So," answered LaFrance cryptically.

"Something's happening," she whispered, forgetful of the Judge's deafness.

The latter was silent, standing stooped and worried.

"I'm going," she cried suddenly.

Judge LaFrance raised a hand. His request was half command. "You stay here, Girl."

She faltered and glanced back at him, her eyes full of inquiry and alarm.

"Stay here," he asked again. "Ain't any place for you outside. We'll know, soon as anybody, and if anything's afoot you can't stop it."

The girl sank into a chair and for a long moment looked into the old face that gazed savagely out the front window of the harness shop into the sunny Main Street of Moon Dance.

CHAPTER TWENTY-THREE

RIDING A TOUGH AND RANGY BUCKSKIN, Robideau
reached Moon Dance at ten o'clock of the morning
Tana Deck was having her talk with Judge LaFrance.
The Horse and Cow Saloon, hang-out of the Indian and
the part-blood, is located at the straggling southern end
of Main Street. He tied his horse to the hitching rack
at its side and clumped in.

Louis Swan, proprietor, swart product of the teepee,
who had shown an astonishing ability to get ahead according to the white man's rules, pushed himself away
from the bar against which he had been lounging.

Robideau's quick eyes swept the empty room.

"*Comment allez-vous?*" greeted Swan, and added
complainingly in broken English, "Business, he's bad."

Robideau snorted disgustedly. "It smells like the
coyote den here," he said. "Straight."

The saloon keeper put a glass and bottle on the bar.

Before he drank, Robideau brought a derringer from
his waist and slid it across the bar. "The papoose pistol,"
he explained, "I need no more." Significantly, he patted
his holstered thighs.

Swan nodded in approval. "This town, he's calmed
down," he answered reassuringly.

Robideau poured his glass but half full and drained it
slowly, disdaining the chaser of beer that the saloon man
set out. He motioned for Swan to remove the bottle and
spun a silver dollar on the counter.

"A little is always plenty much for you, eh, Robideau?"
the barkeeper observed as a pleasantry.

The gunman grunted. "A little of whisky. Of other things, no." His thick-lidded eyes glittered like gems, as if the implication of the words hung visible before him.

Making change, Swan chuckled knowingly. "Of shootings and women, never, eh?"

Robideau looked at him, and the man's mirth trailed off nervously.

"You see anyone around?"

Swan gestured with his hands like a Latin. "Fee Simple, he was here already, and St. John, and maybe one-two others."

"All?"

The bartender studied the dark, rough-chiseled face for his answer.

"Fee and West Cawinne," he ventured tentatively, like a man testing a quicksand, "they together early, I hear. No one see Bally Buck."

"What goes on?"

Swan dared to laugh, a little uneasily. "Buck, he's sore at Cawinne because he tell him nothing. Rest of town say everything over anyhow. What the hell?"

"On the Crazy Cree we know that already. This Cawinne, he's said any more, no?"

Swan shook his head positively. "Not him," he said. "He's quiet like the hunting cat."

The man's eyes dilated suddenly as his roving glance caught the other's slitted stare.

"*Mon Dieu*, Robideau, no killing here!" he prayed.

Robideau looked at him, and his eyes faded slowly, like cooling embers.

"Already they say they close me out."

A feral grin pulled at Robideau's wide slash of mouth.

"Keep hold on the horses," he advised with amused contempt. "Nothing happens unless he starts it."

"Keep away! Keep away!" Swan entreated. "This town it is not friendly to me since that sheep herder's rolled in the alley behind."

"You scare very easy," Robideau answered indifferently, and made himself a cigarette.

When he had it going he gestured an abrupt good-bye and turned toward the door. "I go to Adlam's," he said over his shoulder. "Soon I be back." He pulled at his sagging belts with their heavy twin revolvers as he went out.

He walked leisurely up the street, his eyes alive and quick in his unturning head, and let himself in the other saloon.

A hush fell on the place as he bellied up to the bar. Spying him, Jake Schwartz came from the lower end of the counter and inquired briskly, "What'll it be?"

"Straight," answered Robideau.

A half-dozen men were at the bar, and four or five lounged at the tables. It was early yet for a poker game. At the table farthest in the rear, in company with three other part-bloods, sat Johnny Fee, the defective. An expression of dumb terror had come into his eyes as Robideau entered the saloon.

George I. Smith and Maxie Roser, drinking beer, nodded shortly to the newcomer, then resumed their conversation as others adjourned their scrutiny and began to pick up the broken threads of talk.

Outwardly indifferent to the effect his entrance had produced, Robideau sipped his whisky.

Like an abused dog, Johnny Fee got out of his chair and came sidling to the Breedtown gunman. He touched him fearfully on the shoulder.

Robideau turned. "What you want?" he asked in a voice that carried throughout the room. "A drink?"

He motioned to Schwartz. "Give him whisky."

Fee slobbered at his liquor. Stuttering something that the others could not hear, he reached into the pocket of his ragged vest and brought out a folded slip of paper.

Robideau looked at him and at the paper. Fee thrust it on him, trembling, and the gunman took it, his eyes coldly inquiring, and spread it on the bar. His lips worked soundlessly over the words.

He stepped back then, his face dark. When he spoke, his voice was not loud, but flat and penetrating, and it brought the patrons of the place to attention like the rattle of a snake.

"Who gave you for me the note?"

Fee threw up his hands as if to fend off the furies. He flicked his lips with the thin point of his tongue.

Robideau's left hand shot out and caught him by the throat.

"Speak with the straight tongue, Fee!"

Fee stared wildly about him. His face was contorted. His mouth struggled with words. "I tellum," he blurted frantically. "It's truth."

"Who?"

"West Cawinne."

"For me?"

The miserable half-breed bobbed his head up and down above the fist at his throat.

"When?"

"Me seeum today."

The gunman's finger sank deep into the other's neck. He shook him until Fee's eyes turned inward like an epileptic's.

"Still truth?"

"Just go ahead and kill him!" Jake Schwartz advised. His fat face was swollen with blood.

Fee began to struggle against the hold like a rabbit in a snare. Robideau let up a little.

"The truth?"

Fee nodded dumbly, his mouth spread wide for air.

The gunman dropped his hand. Deliberately he turned toward the others and looked them over. "Fee Simple and West Cawinne, they together today? Anyone see?"

George I. Smith, his gray countenance vitalized by curiosity, answered: "If that's what he's telling you, you don't have to hop him any more. He's giving it to you straight. I see 'em having breakfast together at the Deck place."

"About seven o'clock," Maxie Roser added.

"This, he gave me," Robideau said, and handed the note to Roser. "Read!"

Tight with excitement, Roser's voice repeated the note:

" 'Save yourself trouble and keep out of Moon Dance. Weston Cawinne.' "

Stud Manker eased into the silent room and came to Robideau's side. Wordless, the other men watched him, their faces still and distant with questions.

It was Robideau who broke the pause. "I come to town not looking for the trouble," he said. "I do not look for the trouble now. I have enough in my time."

His bold glance, half conciliatory, half challenging, took each of them in his turn.

Manker interrupted in snarling complaint: "It ain't enough for Cawinne to burn us out. He's gotta tie a can to us."

"Shut up!" commanded Robideau, and Manker fell into uneasy silence, but the words he had spoken set the breeds to muttering.

Robideau's face with its high, curving nose suddenly was as savage as a hawk's.

"But I do not run, either," he announced.

"Whyn't you just leave on your own hook?" Schwartz ventured in his shrill voice.

Robideau's veiled gaze swam to him. "Not for you to say I run," he answered. "I give to Cawinne his chance for the trouble."

He turned to Roser. "Write for me," he asked, and with bulging-eyed alacrity the publisher got out pencil and paper and bustled to the bar.

The gunman stood with his back to him, facing the silent faces of the others.

"Write for me to West Cawinne," he said after a pause, " 'I stay here. If you want the fight, come on'."

When he had finished, there was a slow intake of breath in the crowd, in which Jake Schwartz's muttered "Here she comes!" fell like a definition of all their thoughts.

Robideau moved up to the bar and laboriously signed his name. He turned then and called Fee, who came mincing toward him unwillingly. "Take the paper to Cawinne, see? Cawinne, no one else. Go! Vamoose!"

As the messenger left Robideau said, "I go to the Horse and Cow, if anyone looks for me."

After him, the other breeds went from the saloon in a company and turned, as he had, toward the Horse and Cow.

Roser pumped his short legs after them, calling back as he took leave, "Anything happens, I got to be where I can see it."

A block down the street, he looked across at the Moon Dance House and spied Scott Hardy standing moody-eyed at the window of the lobby. He turned and crossed the street and pushed in.

"Thought you were following a delegation getting ready to call on the great white father or something,"

Hardy greeted without taking his gaze from the street. "What's up, anyhow?"

"Wait'll I tell you!" Roser broke out. "It looks like something might happen now!"

He informed the hotel man then about the developments in Adlam's Saloon, panting a little with weight and excitement as he proceeded from point to point.

Hardy whistled when he had finished.

"And you think," he asked sarcastically, "that it looks like something might happen now?"

"Doesn't it?"

"How long you lived here, Maxie?"

"Fifteen years."

"That ought to be long enough for you to learn to savvy, but it isn't, else you'd know good and well something was sure as hell going to happen."

"Yes," breathed Roser, waiting.

"It's West or Robideau now. Ain't either of them going to back down."

"West could put it off, couldn't he? One way or another?"

"He couldn't and he won't. He's got to face it out. Let him give an inch, and they'll say he's yellow—everybody'll say that—and a dozen Breedtowners will be trying to perforate his hide."

"You mean it's now? Today?"

"Now or never."

"Well, look!" the publisher persisted. "I can't understand Cawinne, sending a message like that. Looks to me like he's out of line, unless he's got something on Robideau, and if he has he ought to try to arrest him, not shoo him out of town. What did he want to do it for?"

Hardy shook his head doubtfully and paused before

he spoke. "I wouldn't know, but it looks like a dumb play, all right. People ain't going to like this get-out-of-town-or-else business. It's too much like old-time bull-dozin'. West'll lose a lot by this."

"And it'll be today! Great Lord, what a story! And here it is press day, and no time to dress it up!"

The publisher gulped with agitation and shifted impatiently on his stubby legs. "Anyhow, I'll go get some background. I'm going down to the Horse and Cow."

"And get scalped, likely," Hardy called after him.

Though it had not been an hour since the challenge had been offered and accepted, the Horse and Cow was filling with excited Indians and part-bloods when Roser arrived. Eight or ten from the upper Crazy Cree had come in early, intending to idle away the day. They formed the nucleus of a crowd that kept increasing as squatters on the outskirts of town got word of developments. A further addition was old Chief Heavy Runner, down from the reservation, who was already half drunk.

The place was a din of voices, each rushing on, undistinguishable in the swollen chorus. It throbbed to sentiment pitched higher and higher as whisky fed it. It stank of liquor and horse and campfire and unwashed bodies.

Louis Swan, busy as a beaver behind the bar, spied Roser as he entered. He jerked up straight and forbade him entrance with an overhead sweep of his hand. Mistaking the gesture, Roser waved cheerfully and came on in. "Out! Out, white man!" Swan's silent lips shouted.

Others in the room began to see the newcomer now, and the rushing tide of conversation ebbed away into a silence waiting and ominous. The old chief broke it. Sitting at a table, wearing a grimy and tattered coat made of a blanket, he lifted his rusty voice in the ancient war song of his braves. The dark faces tightened at the hoarse and creaking summons. A voice cried punctuation for it, like a wild goose honking. Feet began to thump a drum-beat.

Out of the crowd the scar-faced breed named St. John came creeping like a stalking wolf. "White man burn us out, now tie can to us," he said out of his bitter mouth.

The old chief rose, clumsy with age and alcohol, wavered over to Roser, pulled himself up stiff and straight as a stick, and after a moment of stony scrutiny spat in his face. Slowly, almost imperceptibly, the group began to move on the publisher. A rising murmur arose, like the purl of a busy creek.

The voice of Robideau boomed from deep in the rear of the room.

"Back, you fools! Back!"

Whatever effect the words had was not for Roser to observe. He had wheeled and burst out the door.

"Holy mackerel!" he breathed with his panting breath while his legs pumped under him. "A riot! A race riot! Oh, my holy mackerel!"

He ran to the corner before he looked back. Behind him he saw, not a pack of murderous pursuers, but Bally Buck, pacing placidly up the street on a bay horse.

CHAPTER TWENTY-FOUR

TANA DECK and Judge LaFrance had passed a dismal and uneasy hour in the latter's shop before Bally Buck swung in. Several times the girl had vowed to leave, but on each occasion the Judge emerged from his dark preoccupation long enough to dissuade her. "Stay here now, Tana!" he kept saying with a sharp edge of impatience in his voice. "I tell you, we'll find out quicker and better right where we are. Bally's bound to come in, if he's in town, and West, too." Finally, in the gloom of his rear room, she sat on the edge of a chair, like a bird about to fly. She laced her fingers together nervously as she fixed her gaze on the floor.

Out of sight of the entrance, she jumped to her feet as the door whined open.

Buck, seeing only LaFrance through the aperture in the partition, yelled, "It's a show-down. Where's West?"

LaFrance jerked his head in the direction of Tana half in a gesture of negation.

"No!" she remonstrated, rushing out to face Buck. "No! What is it? I need to know, too."

Buck regarded them uncertainly. The Judge let his hands fall in a motion of resignation. "Spill it, Bally," he said. "Tana here's got as much right as anyone to hear it, I guess."

The rancher put his hand on the girl's shoulder and then, in a gesture respectful and gentle, on her smooth cheek.

"It'll be all right, Kid," he promised.

"What is it?" the Judge demanded, pressing his trumpet closer to his ear.

"Near as I can get it, Cawinne sent word to Robideau to clear out, and Robideau said he wouldn't."

"Naw!" contradicted the Judge. "You must not have it right."

"That's what I hear."

Puzzled, LaFrance shook his head bleakly. "I don't follow that play," he said questioningly.

The girl's gaze went from one to the other, as if not enough had been said to explain an issue.

"And they're going to fight over that!" she exclaimed at last.

The two men glanced at each other in unspoken understanding.

"Take it easy, Tana," Buck advised. Turning to the Judge, he asked, "Where's West?"

"Ain't seen him all day."

"Maybe he sees how silly this is," Tana cried. "Maybe he won't come."

Their silence spoke louder than a spoken denial.

Buck observed, "The breeds are sure raisin' sand. They're takin' it personal. First we burn 'em out, then we try to run 'em out. Stud Manker put that idea in their head, I hear."

"But you didn't burn them out!" the girl protested. "You know you didn't. It was the other crowd."

"It don't add up, Tana," Buck agreed gently, "but when it gets to be Injun against white man there ain't any room for exceptions." He paused, then added, "You can't argue much with a man that has a six-shooter and a gizzard full of whisky, 'specially if you're a different color from him."

To the Judge the rancher announced, "There must be fifty-sixty crazy Ikes down at the Horse and Cow, all makin' powerful medicine."

" 'Bout time you were coming in," grumbled La-France, turning toward the entrance.

West Cawinne slowly pushed the door to.

"Tana and Buck and me been waiting for you," said LaFrance.

At mention of the girl's name, Cawinne halted, but the Judge ordered, "Come on back. She knows all about it."

Cawinne took off his big Stetson and walked through the door to the rear room. "Hello, Tana."

Wordless, she regarded him with a sort of indrawn and desperate disbelief. Her eyes entreated him for an answer.

"I'll want a couple of strings, Judge," he said.

Judge LaFrance turned and began to fumble among odds and ends of leather on his work bench.

"Hurry about it?" he asked, bringing his gaze around over his shrunken shoulder.

"Half an hour, little less. I told Johnny Fee to say I'd start down the street then."

"I always said you two couldn't graze on the same range," Buck said in indirect inquiry, "but I didn't hardly figure you'd be the one pushin' on the reins, sendin' that note."

"Yeah."

Cawinne moved over to a chair and sat on the edge of it and began to tie down the ends of his holsters.

The girl took two slow steps toward him.

"You are going ahead?" she asked in a voice thin with accusation and entreaty.

His head, bent over his work, nodded.

"Nothing can change that?"

He glanced at her fleetingly, and down at his holsters again.

Her air of tight restraint deserted her suddenly. She protested, fierce and breathless. "Oh, why do you have to shoot him, or be shot? What have you against Robideau that calls for this? What has he against you?"

She bent over and put out her hand, as if under the impulse to touch his black hair. "Don't do it, West!" she implored. "Please don't do it."

His gaze, grave and unyielding, lifted to her face again. Her eyes were big and bright as glass in her pale face.

For a long minute, silence held them, but as he looked down he said inflexibly, "I must."

Unobserved by him, she turned away, a picture of such helplessness and despair before forces she could not direct or comprehend that the old Judge hobbled to her and sat her tenderly in a chair.

"It'll be all right," he pledged hoarsely. "It'll be all right, Girl."

Fretful as a brooding hen, he limped back toward Cawinne. "Sure about your artillery, Kid?"

Cawinne assured him.

" 'Member to keep 'em low," LaFrance advised, and then snorted at himself. "Excuse me! I keep forgettin' you ain't green."

Buck brought his forty-five out of its holster and examined it. "Chance I might need this myself," he said.

"It would be better if you left that here, Bally," Cawinne told the rancher.

"Good Lord! Have you gone loco, West?"

"Be better."

"Listen, there's fifty-odd breeds down there, all armed and all hungry to put a hole in you. I aim to see that Robideau's the only one shootin' at you."

"You go down there with a six-gun and they'll all be shooting at both of us."

"West's right, Bally," Judge LaFrance put in. "And something he ain't sayin' to you, bein' too polite, is that you'd sure rile 'em up, with the temper you got. You'd blaze away because a man made a face."

"This could easy enough be a free-for-all," Cawinne urged.

"Put it up, Bally!" the Judge commanded. "West's right. Be a lot of blood spilled around here if we ain't careful."

Buck's breath rushed out in a disgusted wheeze. "Looks like West is the only one around here growed up enough to carry firearms," he objected, but he slid his pistol onto the bench.

Cawinne consulted the dirty-faced clock in the window, and, as if reminded suddenly that time had passed, the others looked at it, too.

"Smoke, and then I'll have to go," Cawinne said.

As if under a spell, Tana watched his hands, sure and steady as he sprinkled tobacco into paper, rolled it into a neat cylinder, and sealed the edge with his tongue.

She arose and stood stiffly, her mouth tight with strain. Her eyes were fixed on his face as if studying a mystery too dark for comprehension, too brutal for sympathy.

"I'll be goin' down the street a ways with you, anyhow, West," Buck said, and hitched his trousers up on his thick middle.

The Judge said, "We'll wait."

Cawinne ground his cigarette out on the floor, set his hat on his head, felt experimentally of his weapons, said "So long," and started for the front door.

The Judge's voice creaked after him, "Good luck, Kid!"

Tana took a quick step forward, whispered "Good luck," and, as the door banged shut, let herself down into a chair, where she sat stiff and still, as if in the house of an enemy.

Main Street appeared sleepy and half forsaken as Cawinne and Buck swung out on the sidewalk. Not an animal stood at the hitch-racks. No rider traveled the street. No rig rolled along it. But knots of men, falling silent as the two appeared, clustered about doorways. A brassy sun beat from straight overhead on the slaty dust of the road, which caught the glare and flung it back.

Buck halted Cawinne for a minute. "Listen, Son," he said, his face red, "I got you into this, and by Joe I'll help out. Just say the word."

"Even from an old friend, Bally, that's hard to take."

Buck made a violent gesture of agreement and futile rebellion.

"Hell, I know!" he burst out. "It's your fight. Go on and get him!"

"You stick to the sidewalk," Cawinne asked, and quartered out into the street.

At a dozen doorways, clusters of men deployed to get a view of him. A few of them called out, their voices high pitched. Others made small gestures of salute. At the windows, eager faces were flattened. As buildings fell behind him, the groups deserted the doorways and came scurrying after him to other entrances closer to the scene of combat. Earlier, the saloons had been full, and betting men had engaged in eager traffic. At Adlam's and the Family Liquor Store, where sentiment favored Cawinne if judgment did not, the betting was six to five against him. At the Horse and Cow, there was money at two to one, with few takers. But the offering and the covering were over now, and backers of both men crowded the limits of safety to see the fight.

Heedless of greeting and salute, Cawinne walked slowly down the street, his shoulders and arms giving loosely to his stride. Outwardly, he was as impassive as any poker player. A little eddy of air, playing in the dirt, tugged at the back of his gray shirt. Low on his flat hips his holsters hung, and out of them, big and black, arched the butts of his guns. Save for them and save for his ranging vigilance of eye, he might have been an idle cowpuncher decked for town.

Seeing him from the doorway of the Moon Dance House, Scott Hardy called out, "Easy does it."

As Buck clumped up in the lee of Cawinne the hotel man turned on him his protuberant brown eyes, agleam now with a fierce admiration. "See him?" he hissed exultantly. "See him? Loose as a goose!"

"Watch for Robideau," the rancher said out of the corner of his mouth. "Ought to be out." He went on by, disdainful of the cover that the crowd behind him had begun to seek. Hardy closed the door and followed.

Cawinne passed the Stockmen's Bank, and it was a block to the Horse and Cow.

"Here he comes!" Buck grunted as a warning.

The door to the Horse and Cow had swung out, and Robideau came onto the walk.

He glanced quickly about, his eyes narrowed against the dazzle of the sun, and after an instant of adjustment to the light, slanted out into the street. Behind him, the dark, avid faces of his supporters crowded the doorway. Three of the breeds pushed out and sidled watchfully along the front of the building.

Between Heizer's Meat Shop, which corners the block, and the Horse and Cow Saloon, there are Mrs. Smith's Millinery Store and Ice Cream Parlor, the Powder County Implement Company and the DeLuxe Barber

Shop. A space of ten or twelve feet separates the two places last named. Years ago, in a burst of civic pride, the town boarded up this divisional space and painted the screen white. Succeeding years, however, found the passion for beauty somewhat diminished. The boards had gone unpainted for many seasons, and one of them had splintered, so that a two-inch crack provided a glimpse of the back alley disorder that the town once had sought to conceal, or of Main Street itself if the observer happened to be on the other side.

As Cawinne came in line with the screen, Buck stopped dead.

At his elbow Hardy squeaked, "Look! It's a gun, maybe! See? See the flash? Behind the boards?"

Buck's hand, feeling at his hip, froze there. He grated, "Damn! Gun's at the shop."

"Yell to West!"

Buck silenced him fiercely with a backward sweep of his hand. "And throw him off!" Suddenly subdued, he said as a man might say a prayer, "Maybe he seen it. Maybe he seen it."

In a deadly saunter, the two fighters closed in. The dust of the street jetted out in little puffs from under their advancing feet.

With no more than ten yards between them, they halted as by a common impulse. Legs apart, Robideau settled back on his heels in a half slouch, his body melting and relaxed as a waiting beast's. His short, beaded buckskin vest hung open on his thick chest. The brass adornments on his broad-brimmed hat glittered in the sun. One foot in advance of the other, Cawinne was bent forward slightly at the hips. His arms hung loose at his sides. He was without coat or vest, and the curving butts of his guns shone dark against the gray of his shirt.

"Go for it!" he said.

Robideau waited, wordless and motionless, a squint on his swarthy face as their eyes locked. He waited while the other waited, and all at once he had had enough, and his hand came to life like a striking snake.

Cawinne's arm was a blur. From hip to horizontal it leaped like a trick on the eyes, jerking at the end as the gun roared in his hand.

Into the almost simultaneous explosions there merged a third report, and smoke streamed from the crack in the screen.

Cawinne's hat jumped to the side of his head and slid over his ear to the ground, but, quick as the thrust of a cat, his arm had come across. His slug knocked a splinter from the splintered board in the screen.

Facing half to left then he waited, his lean body bent forward, as deadly in its stance as the gun in his hand. Robideau was folding in the middle, like a jack-knife closing. He fell in the dust.

Cawinne nosed his revolver into its holster.

Cursing like a freighter in rage and exultation, Buck ran by him, tore a board from the screen and broke through.

Men began to push into the street, with excited expletives breaking the tension that had held them.

Cawinne went to Robideau and turned him over. All the venom had gone from the breed's obsidian eyes. "You are ver' fast," he muttered dully. A spreading circle stained the front of his shirt above the abdomen.

Doctor Kink forged through the gathering crowd, elbowing Cawinne aside and, stooping in the dust, made a hurried examination.

Buck came hastening back. "That gentleman behind the boards," he puffed, "was Stud Manker. Your message caught him fair in the head." The rancher's voice was full of awe.

Robideau's heavy eyelids raised.

"Manker?" he asked, his voice a weak growl.

"Your friend," Buck retorted scornfully, "tryin' to save your bacon."

The fallen gunman struggled to rise. His gaze fixed itself on Cawinne, who had stooped quickly beside him as Doctor Kink got up shaking his head.

From the half-breed's right forearm, Cawinne ripped back the sleeve. A furrow ran red along the skin above the wrist, sank into the bulge of muscle, and reappeared just below the elbow joint.

"I've been wanting to see that arm, Robideau," he said stonily. "I figured Miles Larion had left his mark on you."

Weakly, the part-blood raised his hand, as if to seize Cawinne for emphasis. "I am not knowing about Manker." The hooded glitter of his eyes had been replaced by a look as beseeching as a hurt dog's. "Me, I do everything, rustle and kill. But everyone the chance. I do not plant Manker."

His breath was fast in his throat, and his clipped speech quickened weakly with it. "Manker, he fire at you from behind, that night, and I should killum, but I whip him bad, anyway, for that."

The face, with its lusterless, imploring eyes, was no longer the face of Robideau the gunman but the tragic face of universal man before man's inevitable fate, and Buck looked away and wiped his forehead and cursed under his breath, as if to restore himself to old convictions.

"You got Larion," Cawinne prompted remorselessly.

"He had the chance, too." The breed's eyes closed. "I beatum" came out of the slack mouth.

"Where's Salter?"

With visible effort, the wounded man gathered his strength for an answer. "He die—from bullet you shoot at Indian Pete's."

The lids fluttered up again, and the wish for belief was so strong in his sagging face that it seemed to shut him off from pain and death itself. His eyes ran liquid with entreaty.

"You listen!" he strained. "I do not plant Manker."

"All right," agreed Cawinne.

A look of weary peace came over the gunman's countenance. "Robideau give the chance, all time," he sighed.

Secure in the reputation he coveted most, Robideau, rustler, gunman, killer, let himself die, on his lips an expression of loyalty to the only morality he had ever honored.

Cawinne raised himself slowly, looking worn and old. He brought his sleeve across his brow. A light breeze fanned the hair on his bare head. Heedless of the hands extended to congratulate him, he walked through the watching crowd.

CHAPTER TWENTY-FIVE

LaFrance's harness shop was full and overflowing. He had pushed his battered work table out, to serve as Judge's bench, and sat behind it, facing the crowd that had packed into the back room. In the doorway giving to it from the front office, men were pushing for space. Beyond it into the office itself and about the entrance outside the curious were crammed.

Hemmed about by a sweaty, shuffling humanity, Jim Northcutt, the lawyer, stood at one end of the table, his thick thatch gleaming white above his ruddy face. At the other end, with the faces of the congregation ranked above him, West Cawinne sat in what had been designated as witness chair.

The Judge rapped on the table with the handle of an awl.

"Court will come to order."

Slowly, like a receding wave, the noise of restless feet and questioning voices died, save now and then for the impatient voices of outsiders still ignorant of proceedings.

The Judge boomed on: "The Court ain't exactly sure how wide a swathe it can cut, since these matters mostly are taken care of down at Cottonwood, but Jim Northcutt says the Court has jurisdiction, and being as everyone is anxious to hear it anyway, the Court will go ahead and hold a hearin' on West Cawinne, who owns up to killin' four men in the performance of his duties, and has to be put in the clear about it even if they needed killin'."

LaFrance paused to survey the crowd authoritatively,

and then, obviously relishing his place as presiding officer, went on:

"The Court has appointed Northcutt as the State's attorney, but don't make it too stiff and proper, hear, Jim? And if the story ain't plain to any of you as it goes along, why, speak out! We want everyone to be satisfied in his own mind, and so we won't go too strong on dignity."

The Judge studied his audience severely over the rim of his glasses, as if on watch for a challenge, knocked on the table again, and motioned to Northcutt to proceed.

The lawyer moved over toward Cawinne. Facing the bench he said, "Perhaps it might be well to set forth that the case to be heard involves the shooting to death of Seldom Wright, Whitey Salter, Stud Manker and Robideau. The Court is aware," he suggested, "that the defendant has the right to demand counsel?"

"He don't want it," LaFrance retorted for Cawinne.

"Mr. Cawinne also knows, I presume, that he is not obliged to testify."

"Go ahead!" ordered the Judge. "He wants to."

The suggestion of a smile worked at the lawyer's lips as he addressed the Court again. "Under the circumstances, your honor," he said, "if it please the Court we shall dispense with the customary questioning as to qualification, as well as of the preliminary incidents leading up to the crimes of which the defendant is accused. We all know that he is Weston Cawinne, a duly authorized officer of the law, who was retained by the Stockmen's Association to look into the matter of rustling and murder."

LaFrance rapped lightly on his bench. "That's right. Skip it and get down to business."

Northcutt turned to Cawinne. "Now West, suppose

you tell us, in your own words, who killed Marty Mc-
Lean and why, who killed Miles Larion and why, and
who killed Often Wright and why. Then go on and
tell us how you found out all you know about it, and
then, finally, why you had to shoot and destroy Seldom
Wright, Whitey Salter, Stud Manker and Robideau.
Go ahead!"

Before the crowd that stood above him, Cawinne
crossed and recrossed his legs uneasily and rubbed the
back of one hand with the ball of his thumb. It was the
first sign of nervousness that any of them ever had seen
in him.

When he spoke it was in the low tones and spare
language of a man unaccustomed to crowds, for whom
few words ordinarily sufficed.

He shifted in his chair. "Seldom Wright shot Marty
McLean."

LaFrance pushed the mouth of his trumpet far over on
the table toward the witness. "Speak up, West!" he
ordered. "There ain't any purpose in holdin' Court if the
Court can't hear."

The crowd in the front office began to yell "Louder!"
and there was the sound of struggle as its members shoved
for better position.

The Judge banged on the table with his make-shift
gavel. "Order! Order!" he bawled. "You fellows just
hold your horses a minute and you'll get to hear all
right."

Northcutt prompted the defendant: "Tell the Court
how you know Wright killed McLean."

"Old Marty didn't have any enemies, so the one that
shot him did it for what he could get out of it."

"And Seldom got something out of it?"

"He got Marty's spread, which he would have lost if

Marty really had the secret of the Early Day, and maybe he thought he was getting a map to the mine, too." He paused and looked enquiringly at the lawyer.

Northcutt nodded to him, and when Cawinne resumed, it was with more confidence. "McLean was shot from behind. That made it look like it might be the work of an outsider. Usually, western men give a man a chance."

"How did it make it look like Seldom Wright's work, particularly?"

"In the Kentucky hill country where he came from there's considerable dry-gulching." Cawinne looked toward Judge LaFrance. "The Judge himself has got a paper telling about one case."

"Had you any tangible clues as to the identity of the killer?"

Cawinne reached into his pocket, drew out a worn nut, and handed it to Northcutt, who turned it enquiringly in his fingers and then held it out for the spectators to see. A buzz rose among them as they turned questioningly to one another.

"For everybody's benefit," the lawyer said, "perhaps I should explain that this nut is what is known back East as a buckeye, the fruit of a tree that grows in the midwest and south, but not here in the northwest. Mr. Cawinne, will you tell us what a buckeye has to do with Seldom Wright or McLean?

"Well, where they grow, people sometimes carry them as pocketpieces. In Kentucky, for instance."

"Exactly. And where did you find this one?"

"In the bushes along the Smoky Water ford, where the man was hunkered who shot Marty McLean."

"I suppose it's unlikely that a native-born westerner would carry such a token?"

"That's what I thought."

"And you have already said that Seldom Wright was originally from Kentucky."

Mike Looney, the barber, wedged into the front row beside Blackie Cox, interrupted: "I swear I believe I saw Seldom playin' with that nut, one time when I was trimmin' his beard."

Northcutt ran his fingers through his thick roach of hair. "The buckeye is suggestive," he told Cawinne in friendly tones, "but it is hardly enough to make a case against Wright."

"No," agreed Cawinne. "I wouldn't have gone after him on that case without more proof. But before I could pin him down he got into another jam that panned out quicker."

Nodding judicially in his chair, Judge LaFrance smiled encouragingly at Cawinne, and murmured, "Go right on, Son!"

"Well, Wright got the McLean place, all right, but there was a hitch in his plans. Robideau, or one of his men—I don't know which—saw him take that pot shot at Marty, and so Robideau set out to blackmail him out of the map to the Early Day. As a matter-of-fact, my guess is that Robideau himself was figuring on doing away with Marty that night, in order to get hold of the map, and so he followed along after him, too, but when Seldom beat him to it, he saw a lot easier and safer way of getting the map than by spilling blood."

"You think Robideau believed in the existence of the mine?" queried Northcutt.

"Yes, sir!" the witness answered emphatically. "All the Indians do. The story of it has come down through the tribe. Robideau was crazy to get that map."

"Wright and Robideau were both at Adlam's on the

day Marty boasted of being in possession of the secret of the mine?"

"Both, and some others."

"Is there a possibility that one of these others might have killed Marty?"

"Everyone who was in the saloon that night came under suspicion, of course, but it turned out they didn't figure in the killing."

"All right," pursued Northcutt. "Now how do you know that Robideau tried to blackmail Wright?"

"The first day I was back in town, just after the Stockmen's Committee had talked to me about being detective for them, I met Miles Larion. He knew about the job they wanted me to take, and I could tell he knew something about the McLean murder. He was in a hurry, and he said he had news for me if I came out to see him. He was shot before I got there."

"He was killed," Northcutt said, "and then what?"

Cawinne fished in his pocket and brought forth a folded slip of paper. "I found this note on him."

"Read it out, please."

Cawinne read aloud: "We see you at the Smoky Water. You be at Hangman's Tree tomorrow at 3, with map, or we talk. Friends, maybe."

The men within the room stood silent, their curious eyes on Cawinne. At the doorway there was again the sound of repressed struggle as men in the front room of the shop strove to push through.

LaFrance tapped hard with his gavel to call for silence.

Northcutt asked, "What makes you think the note wasn't addressed to Larion originally?"

"First of all, because I knew Miles. Then on that same day I talked to the committee, it came out that Seldom

Wright's shack had been broken into. Seldom said everything was messed up, but nothing was missing."

"I see," said the lawyer. "You mean that this was the note Robideau wrote to Wright, and that Larion found it in Wright's shack?"

"Sure I do. Miles wanted to get something on Seldom, and when he found this note, he knew that he had him cold. With that he'd have turned him up himself if he'd lived."

"Do you think that Robideau got the map?"

"There wasn't any map. Marty McLean was just bragging when he said he had it. Trying to draw it when he was drunk, Sven Svenson just scrawled a couple of lines that didn't mean anything."

"You have the piece of paper?"

"No, but if you want more evidence, I can bring a witness who saw it."

"We don't need the witness," Judge LaFrance interjected. "The Court himself has talked to Tana Deck, and he knows it wasn't a real map."

"So?" Northcutt asked of Cawinne.

"Not having any map, Wright of course couldn't produce one, and he knew Robideau would never believe that that scribbled paper was all he got off Marty, so his next move was to turn the heat on Robideau. He had the stockmen ready to string up Robideau, telling them there wasn't any doubt who killed Marty McLean."

"Yes, it would seem logical enough," the attorney commented, "in view of the half-breed's reputation and the fact he had heard Marty tell about the map."

"Oh, it sounded reasonable all right."

"But what did Robideau do after Seldom turned on the heat?"

"When Seldom didn't come across, and, instead, tried

to get the ranchers to string him up, Robideau was keen
to balance the score. He got his chance when Seldom
Wright and Miles Larion had their run-in on the street.
Robideau was in town that day. You remember, when
Miles chose Seldom, Seldom wouldn't fight. He said,
instead, that there were other ways and other times to
settle trouble. When Robideau heard that, he streaked
it out to the Smoky Water crossing and shot Larion
down when he came along on the way home. Robideau
knew Seldom would get credit for it, you see, and he
knew, too, that people would think it was dirty work,
since Wright had refused the issue, out in the open, just
a little while before."

Maxie Roser, trying to take notes in a crowd that
locked his arms at his side, gasped "Great day!" as the
witness paused, and a rising chorus of astonishment came
from the audience.

"Order!" rapped the Judge.

"You mean," the surprised Northcutt queried, "that
Robideau deliberately murdered Miles Larion, against
whom he had nothing, just to even the score with Seldom
Wright?"

"That was the Indian in him."

"But what made you think Wright himself didn't kill
Larion? I know that Robideau when he was dying owned
up to it, but why had you already decided that Wright
wasn't guilty?"

"I figured, for one thing, that Seldom was too smart.
Only a crazy man, after that run-in with Larion, would
have killed him where there was no one to see it was
a fair fight."

"Any other reason?"

"Yes. Larion was shot from in front. He had had time
to fire once. If Seldom was afraid to shoot it out with

old Marty, who was potted from behind, it didn't seem to me to stand to reason he'd go up against Larion, or that he could beat him to the draw if he did."

"That's perfectly reasonable," agreed Northcutt, "but surely it might have been almost anybody except Wright, then, who shot Larion. Wasn't Larion carrying quite an amount of money, and wasn't it taken from his body?"

"Sure. It might have been anyone at all," Cawinne conceded, "but it didn't work out that way, and there was one thing that definitely proved Seldom didn't do it. Bally Buck and I knew the boys would want to string Seldom up, as any man would, believing he'd pot-shot Larion, and Bally hurried over to the Box-O to warn him. He found Seldom fooling around the place. Now if Seldom had shot Larion, he wouldn't have been waiting around there to welcome a necktie party."

Buck's voice suddenly broke in, loud and assured in the smoke-filled room: "I found him all right, and he wasn't expectin' no caller, either, and he didn't know Larion had been shot. Soon as I told him, he lit out, scared as a rabbit."

"So?" asked Northcutt.

Cawinne resumed: "Seldom headed for the mountains, expecting, I guess, to catch a train at Crazy Cree Pass. On the way, though, he happened to spot Often, who was out riding the back stretch of his range. That gave Seldom an idea—a crazy one and a mean one, but it's the only possible explanation.

"What idea was that?"

"Well, first of all, you have to keep in mind that Seldom and Often, though brothers, were much more enemies than friends, and that Seldom was willing to do anything to save his skin and his stake. They were twins, too, and they looked alike, though nobody knew it around here but them, since Seldom's face always was covered with a beard."

The witness hesitated, and Northcutt suggested: "All right. Seldom spotted Often, and then what?"

"He shot him."

"Shot his own brother?"

"Shot him, and swapped horses, and put Often's saddle on his own horse. It had a bullet hole in it, you know. Then he got on Often's horse and started his own toward home. Of course, when it got to the Box-O without a rider and with that hole in the saddle, it made it look like Seldom had been shot."

"Slick old bird," commented Buck out of the corner of his mouth, as Northcutt let the witness pause to give the audience time to digest his extraordinary testimony.

"Yes?" he prompted finally.

"Seldom had to do something about Often's face, if people were to believe Seldom himself had been killed, because Often's face was smooth and his own was bearded. So he cut off the head. While he was doing it, or maybe before, it must have struck him that the mutilation of the body would look like Indian work, and that Robideau would get blamed."

"Get blamed for killing Seldom Wright and mutilating his body?" the attorney asked by way of explanation.

"Yes, it fitted in all right, since Seldom himself had predicted more than once that the Breedtown gang would get him. Anyhow, after Seldom got the head off, he butchered the body some more, to make it look still more like Indian's work. Then he took the loose parts, including the head, to Often's place and buried them in the barn. His next move, of course, was to shave off his own beard. With it gone, you couldn't tell him from

Often. So all he had to do was to set himself up as his own brother."

Northcutt filled in a pause: "This explanation of what occurred seems somewhat speculative, but I suppose that you have proof of the fundamental facts? Were the missing parts of Often's body unearthed and identified before being reburied?"

Judge LaFrance answered: "All taken care of proper. The Court seen the parts himself."

"Will you tell us," Northcutt went on, "how you suspected that the man who posed as Often was really Seldom?"

"Yeah," endorsed the Judge. "Tell us all about how you happened to get on this trail. It's hard enough to follow, even when you blaze it for us."

"Well, the burglary at Seldom Wright's and the note in Larion's pocket—they kind of ran together in my mind. Then that buckeye in the bushes made it look all the worse for Seldom."

"So far only as McLean's death was concerned," the lawyer pointed out.

"Yes. Then after Larion was killed, I called on Robideau, and when he came to the door he had on a sheepskin coat, but no boots, which seemed a little queer, and he wore that coat in the cabin even after the stove got hot and the sweat was pouring down his face. What's more, every move he made, he made with his left hand."

"Go on."

"I didn't realize it at the time, but I figured it out later. The reason he had pulled on the coat and the reason he used his left hand must be that his right arm was bandaged, where Larion's bullet had hit it."

"I believe your honor has seen that the body still bears the mark of the bullet," said Northcutt to the court.

"Yup. Go ahead."

"Now," Northcutt directed, "Let us consider another angle of the case. We have so far had no mention of Whitey Salter's involvement in the case, or of the abduction of Miss Deck. In view of what happened later, there appears to be no doubt that Salter kidnaped Miss Deck on order of Robideau, who hoped to learn from her the secret of the Early Day, but we should, nonetheless, like you to tell us whether you were guided in that instance, too, by some essential clue."

"Everything joined together, once you got a right start. I spent one night with Sven Svenson, and he kept talking about ghosts, and he was afraid, too. I might have thought it was just sheep herder's talk, but someone had beat him up. His face was black and swollen where he had been hit. I couldn't figure it out."

"No," commented Northcutt, "a ghost couldn't assault a man."

"But an albino could."

"Yes," the attorney amplified, "an albino, say, like Whitey Salter, who looked like a ghost. An albino who was bent on extorting information about the mine for a man like Robideau."

"Uh-huh, but all that didn't occur to me until later."

"It never would of occurred to me a-tall," Buck volunteered admiringly.

"Now about Salter and the kidnaping," the prosecutor prompted.

"The man I shot at Indian Pete's could see in the dark. He came into that black cellar, and he saw me right away, even though I was over at the side in the deeper shadow."

"You are suggesting," said Northcutt, "that a man with

ordinary eyesight would have had to wait for a minute for his eyes to accustom themselves to the dark?"

"An ordinary man would have to wait, but maybe an albino wouldn't."

"Maybe not," agreed Northcutt, "though I'm not sure what the medical profession would say on that point. It seems reasonable to suppose, however, that since Salter had to squint to keep out the light, he could see in the dark more readily than a normal man. No matter," he said, dismissing that question, "Robideau himself has confirmed the belief that the kidnaper was Salter, so your reasoning seems to have been sound."

"What I want to know," insisted Judge LaFrance, "is how you ever suspected that the man settin' up to be Often Wright was really Seldom."

"That occurred to me all at once, along with the rest. I was sure Seldom had killed McLean. I was playing around with the idea that Robideau killed Larion to set a mob on Seldom. It didn't make sense, then, to figure Robideau butchered Seldom, too. Why should he? He already had him where he wanted him, on the run from a mob. I kept hanging up right there."

"What finally put you on the track?" questioned Northcutt.

"Buck and I called on Wright one afternoon, and he had a pup there that was playing with a ball of hair. Wright said the dog had pulled the hair out of a mare's tail, but for some reason or other he didn't want the pup playing around us with it. It was plain to see it aggravated him, more than seemed reasonable, and he batted the pup across the nose and sent him yipping away."

As Cawinne hesitated, Northcutt encouraged him with "A ball of hair?"

"Yes. It didn't seem natural, him getting so upset at

that pup. And then I remembered Buck had told me Seldom and Often were twins, and I thought, if that ball of hair was Seldom's beard, maybe Seldom would look like Often."

Buck interrupted, "For a careful man, Seldom was sure careless with those whiskers."

There was a whispering of admiration in the crowd which Northcutt broke into. "With that suspicion in mind, how did you go about determining whether Seldom was, in fact, impersonating his dead brother?"

"That first day I was back in town, while Seldom and Larion seemed about to mix it, a man drove up with a live rattlesnake hanging onto the side of his car, and I noticed that while Seldom was deathly afraid of it, Often wasn't. So when I went again to call on Often, or Seldom, I carried a little garter snake I'd got purposely down along the creek. By and by I took it out of my pocket, and he fell over himself getting away from it."

"And you had to shoot him then?"

"It was shoot or be shot, after I called him Seldom."

"Did he confess?"

"He told me where to find Often's head."

Northcutt held up a finger.

"All that you've said pieces together logically," he said. "The State feels sure the Court will admit the identity of Seldom Wright, as well as Robideau's dying admission to the murder of Larion. But in advance of that admission, you had nothing on Robideau except some inconclusive circumstantial evidence and a joining of plausibilities in your own mind. There was nothing at all to implicate him, not even the kidnaping, for you couldn't prove then that one of his agents was the kidnaper."

"That's right."

"Was your gun fight, then, accidental and unrelated to the crimes you were attempting to solve?"

"No. It was connected with them."

"Why did you warn Robideau to stay out of town?"

"I didn't."

"Didn't! Roser read your note to Robideau in the presence of witnesses at Adlam's Saloon."

"That was just an act."

"Explain, please."

"Robideau had shot Larion, I was sure, and no one had seen him do it, and he hadn't left any evidence. If I was to get him, I had to lead him into a trap."

"A trap?"

"If I could make him think I suspected him, and that I was the only one who did suspect him, he might want to shoot it out, provided there was no danger afterward of the law or a mob."

Northcutt nodded. "As a matter of fact," he supplemented, "Robideau's position in the public regard had improved a great deal after the sack of Breedtown, when it developed that there was nothing to indicate he had had a hand in the kidnaping."

"That's so; and people felt a little guilty about burning him out."

"In other words, he had not so much to fear from the public in case of a fight with you?"

"Not as much as he had had."

"And so you set the trap?"

"I got Buck to act drunk."

"Didn't have to act so much, either," the rancher interjected with a sheepish grin.

"What was the purpose in that?"

"By that time, a good many people knew I liked to work by myself." Cawinne looked at Buck and gave him a small grin. "And I guess everyone in town knew that Buck got pretty sore, now and then, thinking I was dealing him out. He talked about it some."

"You oughtn't to jump on a man when he's down," Buck protested plaintively.

The lawyer resumed: "And you set the trap on the fact that Buck wasn't altogether pleased with you?"

"Buck went into Adlam's, acting drunk and sore and talkative, and made it seem like he'd reached the end of the trail with me."

"Yes?"

"He also let it out that I wasn't through with the case with the death of Seldom. He said everybody knew everything was cleared up, but that I suspected another man just the same, but wouldn't give a hint to anyone until I had the case sewed up. It was because I wouldn't tell him anything that he was supposed to be fed up with me."

"I see," said Northcutt. "You were playing on Robideau's sense of guilt. You meant to put the thought in his mind that he was under a suspicion that he might dispel entirely if only he could remove you from the scene."

"Yes," answered Cawinne. "I knew someone, hearing Buck, would get the word to Robideau."

Blackie Cox's face was red. "Buck didn't fool me none," he said through his long lips.

"Two things helped me," the witness went on after a slow, sidelong glance at Cox. "One was that Robideau's standing had improved, so he could get into a fight without much danger of being strung up just on general principles. The other was that he just naturally wanted to put lead into me."

"Because you had a reputation as a gunfighter."

The lawyer's statement was not put as a question, and Cawinne made no response to it.

"Now about the act," the prosecutor directed.

"Robideau had been afraid of a mob ever since one ran him out of Arizona. He didn't like much the idea of coming up against the law, either. So he put the load on me, and trained Johnny Fee to help. That note telling him to get out of town, he wrote himself, putting my name on it. Then he had Johnny Fee deliver it to him. Just to make things look plausible, he made sure that Fee would be seen with me earlier in the day. Fee was scared to death of him and would do anything he ordered."

"It put you in a bad light, that note," the attorney asserted.

"He wanted it to. If he did for me after that, people would say it was no more than I deserved, trying to run out of town a man there weren't any charges against. He wouldn't have had to answer for the killing."

Shaking his head, Buck interrupted: "By Joe, West! You never denied sendin' that note. You should of told us."

"Why?" asked Cawinne. "If he got me you wouldn't have had any proof against him. There wouldn't have been anything you could do, unless you wanted to shoot it out with him."

Judge LaFrance, who had been following the exchange by swinging the mouth of his trumpet, rapped on the bench. "What he's tryin' to tell you, Bally, is that he wanted you to keep a whole hide."

Cawinne continued, "Besides, who would have believed me if I had denied the letter?"

Northcutt moved his head up and down thoughtfully. "It would have looked like a case of cold feet."

The Judge broke in again. "Everyone except me and Bally, maybe, would of said you was afraid to back up your play."

A little murmur of understanding agreement eddied in the gathering.

"He sure did it slick," said Buck, of Robideau.

Northcutt spoke reflectively. "So Robideau wrote the note, thus falling into your trap, and knowing what you did, you knew he was guilty when he set up the fight?"

"Yes."

"But though you knew it, there was no way you could prove it?"

"Not to anybody else's satisfaction."

The attorney stepped closer to Judge LaFrance and spoke into his horn. "Unless the Court wishes to hear evidence in the death of Stud Manker," he said, "the State is ready to close the case."

Over his glasses LaFrance looked about the court room. "No need of that," he answered. "Everyone knows Manker tried to pot West and got what he deserved."

As the attorney started again to speak, the Judge broke in. "Wait a minute now, Jim. Wait a minute. We got everything cleared up except the gold mine. I ain't going to adjourn Court without tryin' to get to the bottom of that, too. How about it, West? Any developments?"

Cawinne went in his pocket for a paper. "I have the assayer's report, Judge," he responded. "Those nuggets that Sven and Marty were showing around were pyrites."

"Fool's gold!" snorted the Judge. "I thought so. Ain't any real gold this side of the mountains." He beat the bench with his awl. "Go ahead, Jim."

"It appears to the State," the latter announced, "that Weston Cawinne was acting solely in the line of duty when he shot the four men for whose deaths he is responsible, and that he displayed both a most unusual gift of logic and acute observation in the unraveling of crimes that would not have been solved except for him. More than that, in the public good he courageously risked his life against the fastest gun, saving only his, that this community has ever seen. If it please the Court, the State rests."

LaFrance hammered the bench again. "The Court has heard enough, if you men have," he announced in his toneless bellow.

A sullen satisfaction had settled on the face of Blackie Cox. He sneered: "Of course West Cawinne's story's bound to stand up. He killed all the witnesses."

"Not quite," contradicted Cawinne. His eyes narrowed as they rested on Cox.

"Blackie," he said, his words slow and measured, "you're half killer, half thief and all fool, and you're under arrest for stealing fifteen hundred dollars from the dead body of Miles Larion."

Cox lurched out from the front rank of the crowd.

The hoarse roar of Bally Buck, stationed behind him, filled the room. "Whoa, damn you!" A revolver shone in the rancher's fist. "Don't make a move, Cox. I'm hungerin' to put daylight through you."

The Judge's voice boomed for order. His awl rapped on the table.

Northcutt was smooth as oil. "Perhaps," he said, "the Court would care to hear the case of Blackie Cox."

"The Court would."

"What can you tell us?" Northcutt purred at Cawinne.

"Larion was carrying a roll of bills he'd won in a game. I know, because I saw them. They were gone when I got to the body. I knew Robideau didn't take them. If he had, he'd have seen in the wallet the black-mail note he wrote to Seldom Wright. He would have taken it."

"Why?"

"In the first place, there was the chance it would incriminate him, being in his handwriting. In the second, he wanted the crowd to be set against Wright for killing Larion, and this note, by putting Larion in a bad light, too, mixed up the case. That is, it would have confused it if the crowd had found it. It might have meant that there wouldn't have been any party setting out to get Seldom."

Cox's expostulation was so violent that saliva sprayed from his sputtering lips and hung like dust particles in the close air of the room. "You ain't fools enough to take that serious!" he cried.

"Have you anything more definite?" Northcutt asked softly.

"Cox was first to Larion's body, by his own admission."

"Yes."

"And last week he deposited fifteen hundred dollars in the Cottonwood State Bank."

"Perhaps," said Northcutt smoothly, turning half about, "Mr. Cox can explain the circumstances of that deposit."

Cox's surly countenance was livid. In a string of curses he inserted: "Since when does a man have to account for his money?"

Judge LaFrance's bellow shook the timbers of the shop. Judicial dignity, personal impulse and frontier informality were strangely mixed in his pronouncement.

"The Court finds," he ruled, "that West Cawinne was forced to shoot Seldom Wright, Whitey Salter,

Robideau and Stud Manker, for reasons good and proper and in the line of duty, and the Court absolves him from all blame and hereby tenders him its thanks. As for Blackie Cox, the Court is right glad to order him held for further action."

He leaned forward, his old eyes hard and exultant, his mouth tight with outrage and satisfaction. "The bond," he said, "will be that fifteen hundred dollars."

CHAPTER TWENTY-SIX

"F ROM THE TOP of the bench, you get your first glimpse of the Bar-G-Bar," Cawinne told Tana Deck.

"In two years in Moon Dance, I've never seen it," she answered.

Side by side, they rode leisurely in the warm morning. It was late June, the Indians' Moon of the Wild Rose, and earth and air stirred with growth and the small concerns of furred and feathered things. Before them, blue as paint, so clear they seemed within reach, the distant mountains lifted, their dizzy heads patched still with snow. About them, the plain spread green and rich. Blue joint and buffalo grass, just coming into head, grew thick and straight and rippled to the moving air like water to a flung stone. The first bold gaillardia turned to the slanting sun. Where the soil was damp, tiger lilies raised their flaming cups, and where it was clumped and rocky the wild rose flung its wanton bloom.

With a great drumming, a prairie chicken rose heavily from under the horses' feet, fell back to earth, and tried piteously to flee, dragging a ruffled wing.

Cawinne dropped from his horse and searched minutely in the grass while the bird crippled close, tempting him to pursuit. When he arose he held cupped in his hand a small fluff of feathers animated by two sharp, unblinking eyes.

"Sometimes you can find them, but oftener you can't," he said, offering it for Tana's inspection.

She exclaimed as she held it in her hands and felt its wild heart beat against her fingers, and he returned it gently to the grass then, and it scurried away on its thin legs. For yards, the hen followed them, using the ruse of the broken wing to decoy them from her brood.

"Nearly always there has been a covey around here," Cawinne said reminiscently. "Riding home from school and seeing them nearly every day, I used to feel that they were friends, and I hated to see the hunting season open and have them scattered and broken and made wild by the hunters."

Silent, she looked at him strangely. Back with his memories, he continued in a quiet confidence that time and place and person inspire even in reserved men.

"I liked to top the bench here, too, after a day in town, and see home lying in the mouth of the coulee, and to know that in a half hour I'd be where my mother was and my dad was, and that there would be food cooking in the stove for supper and maybe a colt out in the corral that Dad would be breaking. And afterward there would be an hour around the fire, with an apple or maybe popcorn to eat and a book to read, or, better yet, just talk, when Dad was in the mood, about cows and horses and coyotes and haying and branding and homesteaders and, once in a long while, the bad men that had to be put down. Home was the finest place in all the world to me."

He fell silent, this hard man, occupied with his thoughts, and she was wordless, too, as if fearful of fracturing the magic of the moment. A curlew circled about them, piping its shrill rising cry as their horses buckled into the slope that lifts to the benchland. Far behind and below them, like a bright ribbon, the fresh green of cottonwood and willow and birch marked the winding journey of the Crazy Cree. Nearer, cattle dotted the grassland.

"Now you can see home," Cawinne announced, pointing.

They stopped their horses.

"Where the grove is?"

"Yes. The trees and bushes haven't been tended much, or we could see more of the house. You can see the corner of it, though, white through the trees to the right."

They rode on again, while the saddles creaked occasionally to the swing of their steeds and the hoofs of the horses fell muffled in the soft earth.

Cawinne looked over at her, and their eyes met, and they both smiled, the hesitant, restrained, revealing smile of youth before mystery.

The air had flushed the girl's face, and the breeze had ruffled her hair. She looked young and eager, and boyish except for a tenderness that lay about her lips and an understanding that her eyes spoke.

"The Judge was right, ordering you to take a ride," Cawinne remarked after a while.

The girl objected: "He said I looked peaked."

"He couldn't say that now."

"Maybe he was right about you, too." She mimicked the words of Judge LaFrance: "It's a cryin' shame you ain't been out to the old place but once, West. Go out there and see what she needs. You ought to be conservin' your interests."

He smiled, but there was gravity and sadness in his tone when he spoke again.

"I want to fix it up," he said. "I want to live there. I want cattle on the range and hands in the bunk house and a string of good horses to pick from, like there used to be." He paused. "I want it to seem like old times, if it can ever seem that way again."

"I know. I know," the girl whispered with quick

sympathy. Her eyes shone with a film of tears. "People go—and things never are the same, ever again."

On the rim-rock to the west, an antelope limned itself against the sky, and another joined it, and they stood in survey of the world.

Without command, their horses stopped and fell to browsing in the fresh grass.

"It will be lonely," he said, his eyes on the ranch house.

"Yes," she said.

A certain agitation in his manner communicated itself to her. The blood climbed into her throat and face. Her glance went to the ground.

"You are so young," he said wistfully.

"I'm past nineteen."

They looked in each other's eyes then, and his face was grave and stern as she had often seen it. He said simply, "You must know I love you, Tana."

Her gaze stayed bravely on his face. "I'm past nineteen, West, and I've been waiting."

His breath drew in sharply. He reined his horse closer to hers and gently, wonderingly, put his hand on her shoulder.

"You might kiss me," she whispered, and raised her tender mouth to his.

Afterward they rode on, hand in hand.

"We will have the best place," he exulted, "and all the past will be past, and all the things you hate. The guns go on the shelf for good."

She looked at him with shining eyes, and there came into her gaze fear and courage and regret and understanding and a great pride.

"Until the case calls for a man," she said.

(The End)